CRAZY LOVE

MICHELLE PACE

Crazy Love
Copyright © 2014 Michelle Pace

This is a work of fiction. Names, characters, places, brands, media, and incidents are either the products of the author's imagination or are used fictitiously. The author acknowledges the trademarked status and trademark owners of various products referenced in this work of fiction, which have been used without permission. The publication/use of these trademarks is not authorized, associated with, or sponsored by the trademark owners.

Robin Harper, Wicked by Design-cover artist
Carmen Comeaux-editor
Self Publishing Editing Service-formatting

ISBN-13: 978-1495431166

For two of my dearest friends-
Heather Halloran and Jay McAtee,
Founding members of The Little Black Hearts
Club...
<3
xoxo
-M

PROLOGUE
Annie, 2004

"Annie, I'm hungry." Becca whined, twirling her wispy hair around one chubby little finger. My little sister tugged absently on my t-shirt, something which normally would have infuriated me, but then she stuffed her thumb into her mouth. She hadn't done that in over a year. She was terrified. So was I.

I stroked her honey hair. "Me too, Becca. Go on and play, and I'll see what I can find."

As she retreated down the stairs dragging her doll behind her by one arm, I cracked my knuckles anxiously. I already knew the cupboard was pretty damn bare. Mom went out on Friday night and hadn't come home. Not last Friday, but the Friday before that. Eleven days ago to be precise.

I staunchly ignored the unopened mail piling up on the dining room table as I wandered into the kitchen. She'd left us alone several times in the past year after breaking up with "The Monster," but never for this long. Anxiety began to peck at me, and I considered calling my grandparents. I knew Mom would kill me if I did. Even though her disappearance wasn't uncommon, I was beginning to question how long she had to be gone before it would be acceptable to worry. I wondered if she was dead in a dumpster somewhere. Maybe she'd had a one-nighter with the wrong dude or something.

She probably borrowed money from the wrong people.

Maybe we'd be better off if she never came back.

I pulled a chair up to the highest cupboards to see what was buried in the back. We'd already cleared out what little was in the freezer and had eaten every last Cheerio in the pantry. Condiments were all that remained in the fridge. Butter, ketchup, mustard, and some ancient olives. The mayo was gone; I'd used it, along with the last of the bread the night before making BLT's (minus the B and the L) with tomatoes stolen from the Johnson's garden across the street.

My cupboard search revealed a half empty container of flour, a bag of sugar, a partial bag of brown sugar and some baking powder. As I continued to dig, I found a package of food coloring that I'd bought for my brother's birthday six months earlier. Not an incredibly useful or tasty discovery. I was about to close the cupboard, when I spotted the corner of some kind of package. I climbed up onto the counter and reached back as far as my hand could reach. When I pulled it back out, I had not one but two forgotten packets of Ramen noodles.

Jackpot.

A heavy weight lifted from me. I had something to give the kids for dinner. And it was something they actually liked to eat.

We'd be alright for a little while longer.

As I boiled water, I caught a glimpse of myself in the reflective surface of the microwave. I squinted at the pale blonde roots peeking out from my jet black hair. I really needed to dye it again. Mom promised to pay me for babysitting when she got back from the riverboats. That seemed fair considering it was Dylan's and my child support she was using for her casino fund. I frowned, knowing if she hadn't come home yet, she'd probably blown it all and I'd have to steal some hair color from the pharmacy near the school. I really wasn't a delinquent by nature, but it seemed like nurture had something more to say about the matter. I sighed wearily and flipped open the cookbook to figure out what I could make the next day with the rest of the pathetic rations.

The phone rang, and I rushed to see who it was. Maybe it was Mom or possibly my boyfriend, Nick, calling to ask what I was wearing in that deep sexy voice of his. When I saw my friend Ashley's number on the display, I rolled my eyes and let it go to voicemail. Knowing Ashley, she just wanted to bitch some more about how she and Robin were going to be stuck in the balcony at the Blink 182 concert.

I scoffed to myself as I added salt to the warm water. That should be me. Those two hadn't even known who Blink 182 was until *I* forced them on their Kelly Clarkson-listening asses. I shook my head. I really hated feeling angry and bitter all the time. At 15 years old, my biggest concern should have been having crappy seats to see my favorite band. But I was from a way different world than my friends. A trashy third world, where scrambling to keep my little brother and sister from starving to death was business as usual. There I was on a Thursday night, trying to figure out which one of my neighbors had a fruit tree in their back yard and didn't have a big barking dog.

I hate you right now, Mom. I just really fucking hate you. Where the hell are you?

I heard the low rumbling of a truck coming down our street and felt the hair on the back of my neck leap to attention. After Mom finally left him, "The Monster" got an apartment down the street to be near "his kid." Every time I heard him drive by on his way to and from work, I could practically *feel* his sweaty hand slipping underneath my night-gown. The distinct sound of his truck sometimes woke me from a sound sleep, and I'd lay awake until the sun came up. Even in broad daylight, that obnoxious sound made me want to push my dresser in front of my bedroom door.

That particular night, I could feel the distinct reverberation of his truck's dual exhaust in the floorboards beneath my feet. Wow, that sounded close. Too close. As in *right in our driveway.*

My mouth went dry, and my pulse revved full throttle. I flipped off the overhead lights so he couldn't see me inside. Rushing down the stairs of our split foyer rental, I made sure the door was locked. Peering through the gap in the curtain, I could see that he was already on his way up the walk. No time to warn the kids to act like we weren't home. I slid the chain across the door with a trembling hand and took a huge breath, trying to move air past the super-sized lump in my throat.

When the doorbell rang, I jumped, stifling a shriek. I found myself unable to move as I stared wide-eyed at the curtain. Somehow I knew he wouldn't go away, so answering it was inevitable. Still, I was frozen in place, my brain reeling with my potential futures if I opened the door.

"I know you're home, Mutt. I saw you when I pulled up. Open the damn door."

Shit.

My cheeks burned, and I clenched my teeth with such force that my jaw ached. He always called me "Ugly Mutt." Up until a year ago, Becca called me "Ugwy Mutt" as well. It wasn't her fault; when she was learning to talk, he would punish her any time she tried to call me by my real name. And all the while, my mom ignored it, something which made me loathe her.

I saw my hand reach out toward the knob and felt like I was outside of myself, watching a slasher film and shouting "no" at the screen with paralyzed vocal chords. With a slight tug, I cracked the door. The flimsy chain seemed to cut The Monster's face in half, but I could still see his muddy eyes peering through the crack. A small voice in my head whispered that if he really wanted in, he could easily kick the door and break the cheaply made chain. My stomach clenched at the thought. He wasn't really that big of a man, but he was *mean*. And I knew all too well he was far stronger than he looked.

In order to rally an ounce of bravery, I immediately focused my gaze on his chin.

"What do you want?" My voice sounded cold and much stronger than I felt.

He paused, and I felt his eyes on me like spiders skittering across a tiled floor. "I know your mom's not here. Where is she?"

I honestly had no idea where she was. I'd been wracking my brain for days trying to remember what she'd blathered on about before leaving. She'd told me she had a new man. He lived in Illinois, and his name was John. She didn't tell me his last name, and I figured she wouldn't be with him long enough to bother asking for it. I'd never met him and didn't have a phone number or even know what city he lived in. I assumed she was with him, but even that was a dangerous assumption.

He sighed at my continued silence. "How long has she been gone?"

"A couple of days. No big deal." I lied.

"Bullshit."

"We're fine, Travis."

"I know *you* are. I'm concerned about Becca." I couldn't blame him for that. She was only four, just starting pre-K, and she actually *was* his biological daughter. If I were totally honest with myself, I was pretty concerned about her too. "Do you have enough to eat?"

I said nothing. This man had been my own personal Satan for years. But it had been days since we'd had meat or peanut butter, and the kids needed food.

Out of the corner of my eye, I saw him nod, as if my lack of response told the story. He had lived with my mom for three years, so I guess it probably did. "I'm calling the police."

"No, don't!" I blurted. I didn't want the kids to end up in foster care. My grandparents would probably feel obligated to take us in, and I sure as hell didn't want to change schools. I couldn't lose Nick.

He was my everything, and I couldn't imagine being an hour away from him. "We're out of food."

"That's all you had to say, Mutt. If she isn't back in 48 hours, you call me – you hear?" As quickly as he appeared, he was gone. I shut the door and flipped the deadbolt so hard that my thumb felt sprained for the rest of the night.

A hissing sound alerted me that water was boiling over on the stovetop. I dashed up the stairs and slid the water off the crackling electric burner and added the noodles. My lip quivered and I shook my head, forcefully digging my fingernails into my palms.

"No. I'm not gonna cry." I rapidly blinked my stinging eyes. Travis could go straight to hell. If Mom wasn't back the day after next when we got off the bus, I'd take the kids to my friend Robin's house. She had the whole basement to herself. Her parents never came down there, so they'd never know we were squatting there.

Thirty minutes later, while the kids slurped the last of their noodles, I heard his truck pull up again. He revved that obnoxious engine of his twice and blared on the horn, holding it down just long enough to piss off the neighbors. I trudged down the stairs and cautiously watched through the curtain as he pulled away a second time. Releasing a long shaky exhale, I opened the door; and when I saw two bags of groceries sitting on the stoop, my legs gave out, and I fell to my knees.

That's when I actually did break down. I choked out sobs in the entryway until my brother Dylan crept down to ask me what was wrong. I couldn't answer him; I wouldn't have known where to begin. I wasn't crying because I was grateful for the food, though I obviously was. I wept because I despised myself for being grateful.

To a fucking monster.

But a monster that—for one night at least – was a much better parent than either of my own.

CHAPTER ONE
Sam, 2013

Damn, this place is hot as hell. It was only 80 degrees, but humidity hovered like an ex-lover trying to get a glimpse at the new lady in your life. Though it was officially the first day of autumn, the sweltering weather wore me down as I slogged along as if wearing ankle chains. On mornings such as this, a Savannahian could step outside into the sultry air and feel like he'd just taken a second shower. There was nothing for it; waiting for some sort of improvement before my daily stroll would have kept me at home, and I couldn't imagine a more dreadful fate.

I wiped the sweat from my brow as I crossed Victory Drive, happily leaving Ardsley Park behind me. Weeks had slipped by since I'd returned home after dropping out of law school. I'd spent the last year north of the Mason Dixon line and needed to re-acclimatize to the sub tropic heat of my hometown. I chose to forgo driving my father's

Mercedes (since there's no better way to adapt than immersion), proceeding on foot toward the river. Watching the water helped me to think, and having scrapped my plans to practice law, some inner reflection seemed in order.

Squatting in the carriage house of Mama's mansion was distressingly Beaumont of me. Since I no longer took pride in the Beaumont legacy, self-loathing won out over my typical apathy. While I coasted through the last of my pre-inheritance purgatory, I felt it best to be back in Savannah. Unfortunately, serving my sentence in the family home had ignited my legendary negativity. My mother seemed to pick up on this when she rang to wake me earlier that morning.

"Samson." That's Mama. No 'hello,' no 'good morning.' "Come have Eggs Florentine with me."

"Sam, Mama. I've asked you to call me Sam."

"I don't like it. I think it sounds vulgar."

No, Mama. Naming me Samson was vulgar.

I chewed bitterly on her refusal to respect my wishes as I descended the stairs into the stifling heat. Crossing the courtyard to "the big house," I reminded myself that Mama's twisted logic never made much sense to us commoners. She *never* referred to my older brother, Trip, by his given name. In her defense, Reginald Jefferson Beaumont III was a mouthful, and few had ever lived up to a nickname like Trip had.

I made my way through the house, intentionally taking the long, scenic route to avoid my father's study. Pausing in the foyer, I cocked an eyebrow at the conspicuous new wall furnishings. Gone were the two antique portraits that had hung there since my grandfather was a boy, and in their place were two darkly disturbing paintings I assumed were my brother's handiwork. No doubt Mama gushed with motherly pride as she paraded her bridge club past them. I wondered if her friends harbored the same suspicions as I did.

Money troubles.

Eventually I entered the sunroom where she always took her morning meal. Struck blind by the easterly sunlight, I blinked rapidly to combat the assault on my eyes. When my vision returned, I spotted my mother enthroned at the head of the table. With her silver reading glasses perched near the tip of her nose, she haughtily skimmed The New York Times. My brother Trip and I had nicknamed her "Cosmo" when we were kids, but never dared to call her that to her face. My mother was pretention incarnate. Though she simply considered herself "worldly," she talked down to anyone unconcerned with the outside world, smug in their Savannah insularity. Since this included the majority of Savannah, I failed to understand her popularity. Knowing the societal folks she rubbed elbows with, I think it had to be fear-based. This morning Mama appeared particularly cosmopolitan, her butterscotch hair styled to perfection.

"There you are, Dahlin'." She barely lifted her gaze from the paper as I obediently pecked her leathery cheek. "Are you going to the gallery today?"

One of Mama's pet projects is a gallery on River Street. She'd named it Imogene's, after herself. Two nights before, she had announced that she'd arranged for me to work there while I decided what I want to be when I grow up. Or more likely while I continued to decide what I don't want to be.

"Yes, Ma'am." I planned to do nothing of the sort, and she probably suspected as much. And so we continued our age-old dance. She and I were bizarre tango partners, but we were well rehearsed. "I'll hit the gym after."

"You really need to go and visit your brother. He must think you're avoiding him." She sipped her chicory-laden coffee and fixed her steely eyes on mine. I'm not sure what she was looking for as she searched me for a reaction, but I'd be damned if I were going to flash any tells.

I am avoiding him. I want to see him about as much as I want to scratch my back with a cheese grater.

"Fine. I'll go see him. Is he still living down the street from Vi?" Trip's wife, Violet, had kicked him out about two years ago. I had to give her credit; she'd stayed with him a hell of a lot longer than I'd wagered she would. To Vi's misfortune they had a child, so the divorce wasn't exactly a clean break. Stalking her was one of Trip's favorite pastimes. It was bizarre how committed he could be when he made up his mind to persevere. Too bad he couldn't just make up his mind to stay sane and sober.

"No. That landlord had unreasonable expectations." Mama drawled. "He's living in the Victorian District. I'll text you the address."

As she picked up her cell phone, her peach painted lips twisted as if she'd just sucked on a lemon. Undoubtedly, the former landlord's "expectations" included tenants who were neither drunk nor disorderly. These *were* terribly unrealistic expectations where Trip was concerned.

"Honestly, I don't know why he doesn't just live here." She set down her phone, then folded her paper and tossed it aside.

"I imagine it's not very bohemian to be thirty years old and live with your mother." I offered, taking a bite of superb Eggs Florentine. Money problems or not, Cosmo found a way to retain both her chef and housekeeper. I looked up in time to see her roll her sapphire eyes at my reply.

"The house belongs to the two of *you*." She set her cup down with flourish, as if to emphasize the point. Daddy had left the house to Trip and me when he'd killed himself four years earlier. We'd each inherited fifty percent of his business interests, and Daddy's family money had been added to our existing trust funds. Naturally, Mama still had her own inheritance from her parents, but she was still bitter about the surprises in Daddy's will.

"Mama..." I gave her a 'can we not do this again' look. She regally waved her hand in response.

"It's too hot for you to walk downtown today. Take the Mercedes."

"I like to walk."

She shook her head as she refilled her coffee. "I cannot fathom why both of my sons insist on living like vagabonds. You are Beaumonts and Moores, for heaven's sake." I said nothing in response, but I doubt she expected one. Since Daddy's death, both Trip and I had an unspoken agreement against falling in line and playing the blue blood role Mama expected. Neither of us could stand to live in the family estate since Daddy had taken his own life here. Even the carriage house was a little too close for comfort, and I was counting down the days till my twenty-fifth birthday, at which time I planned to ditch the family role handed to me.

Reluctantly, my mind wandered back to the memory of my father dead in his study. I'd been home from school for spring break and had just come back from the gym when I'd been unfortunate enough to discover the body. I'd heard something amusing on the radio that I knew he'd enjoy and wandered down the hall toward his study to tell him about it. I think I immediately knew something was wrong – the hall smelled like the fireworks that Trip and I used to light in the backyard. I heard the familiar blaring tone of a phone off the hook (he could never hang up the damned phone), and I poked my head in the door. Daddy was slumped back in his chair, eyes closed. His pistol was on the floor at his feet and a half-drunk bottle of Madeira sat in front of him. To this day I can't enter that hall without smelling gunpowder, though the smell can't possibly still permeate the house. This not-so-Norman Rockwell moment is most likely why I'm as fucked up as I am. The image of his brains splattered on white plantation shutters still causes me sleepless nights.

Under the heat of the relentless Georgian sun, I shivered at the memory. With determination, I soldiered on down Savannah's perfectly manicured streets. Slamming an imaginary door on my childhood trauma, I shifted my focus to what to do with my day. I had zero intention of working at Imogene's Gallery…ever. Cosmo's hobby was a tax write-off and a place to showcase Trip's work, nothing more. For the last week, I'd been looking at properties with my cougar realtor all over town, and frankly, I was burned out on the endeavor. Besides, my nip/tucked agent had invaded my personal space in a major way at the last showing, and I needed some breathing room from her escalating advances.

After sifting through my imaginary to-do list, I came to the conclusion I would have a stiff drink with lunch while brainstorming how to spin my degree in business (with a minor in political science) and the one year of law school I'd managed to complete into some semblance of a career. Though I didn't really need a job, my social circle expected me to masquerade as a productive member of society.

At last, the river appeared on my horizon. I turned the corner and made a pass up River Street to select a lunch destination. Tourists bustled under the awnings of the historic buildings, snapping pictures with their phones and chattering about how "charming" Savannah was. Suppressing an eye roll, I waited for a streetcar to pass and then stepped off onto the cobblestones, quickly looking in either direction before crossing. I managed to stop just short of walking into a family's snapshot with the statue of *The Waving Girl.* Clearly the weather in Savannah wasn't the only thing I needed to re-acclimate myself to.

Wandering into one of the open air sheds at the River Street Market Place, I glanced casually from booth to booth, enjoying both the reprieve from the oppressive sun and the breeze from the whirling ceiling fans. I stopped to buy something cool to drink, and that's when I spotted...*her*.

A stream of sunlight fell on her long golden hair as if Mother Nature had trained a spotlight on her. Radiant was how I'd describe her, but with a girl-next-door quality. Long, and lean, she was casually dressed in faded jeans and a light pink cotton shirt. She carried herself in a proud and assertive way that set her apart from all of the pliable Savannah girls I knew.

Though it might make me sound stalker-ish, I have to admit (with a certain amount of shame) that I'd gone there hoping she'd be there. I'd noticed her here a couple of times before and had been dying to meet her. I'd had little to fill my days with since I'd been back, and it's embarrassing to admit that the thought of seeing her again that day had been the motivation I needed to get out of bed. Unfortunately, she was always swamped with customers, and I didn't want to interfere with her business. As I threw my cash down on the counter and picked up my cup of lemonade, I found my feet taking me in her direction. As I drew closer to her, the view only improved. I decided today was the day I would introduce myself.

The beautiful girl who'd captured my attention bagged a purchase for an elderly couple and with a hint of a smile, waved farewell. Those eyes, which I could now see were robin's egg blue, appeared guarded. Though I figured she was roughly my age, her eyes seemed ancient, like those of a scarred and damaged soul. Though something in the back of my cluttered mind told me to keep on walking, I found her absolutely mystifying. I've always been a people watcher, fabricating their histories in my imagination. This woman's story completely eluded me, which naturally had me curious as hell.

Her bronze skin was flawless except for a scattering of freckles across her nose and cheeks. As she lifted her hair off her shoulders and fanned herself, my eyes drifted to the glistening skin of her cleavage and I imagined nuzzling the long, slender neck that her open top buttons exposed.

Her table displayed framed art of some sort, but I'd been too distracted by her looks to take a second glance at what she was hocking. I lingered at a neighboring booth, feigning interest in their imports from Thailand. I watched as she took advantage of her lull in customers, flipping open a thick textbook. Though I couldn't make out the subject, the fact that she appeared to be a student only served to stoke my attraction. With her distracted, I was able to get a better look at the inventory she sold.

As my gaze passed over the 5X5 booth, I saw she exclusively sold framed gravestone rubbings. Now, having a brother who'd studied painting, I'd been schooled in art basics through osmosis. But cemetery art?

I shook my head. The impressions were done in

various hues of chalk, on high quality paper, and likely executed by someone who knew what they were doing. That was the entirety of my knowledge about this particular medium. Caught flatfooted, I had no idea how to begin to talk to her about her morbid product.

As I paused, puzzling over an opening line, a man crossed in front of me temporarily blocking my view. My dream girl looked up from her book and greeted him with a white, welcoming smile that froze me in place. The man stooped to kiss her cheek, and she gave him an admiring once over with those killer eyes of hers. As they chatted, he leaned on her table in a familiar way. She tossed her hair, and I realized I was grinding my teeth. My stomach dropped into the basement as I recognized the man's stance, his build, and the taken way she looked at him.

It was Trip.

CHAPTER TWO
Annie

God, I love books. The smell of them, the texture of the paper between my fingers as I prepare to turn the page, the sound the spine makes when you are the first person to crack one open. Books have been my safety net since I first needed to escape my reality. My mom used to punish me by taking the light bulbs from my room so I couldn't read at night. Of all the things that woman did to me (and allowed to be done to me), that was probably the most traumatizing. My little brother felt sorry for me and shoplifted a flashlight for me. I'd spent many nights burrowed under the blankets losing myself in alternate worlds. I remember almost everything I read. I can even tell you where something is on the page. This secret talent of mine had been a huge advantage, considering how much school I had missed over the years.

I cracked open a textbook as I wilted in the heat of the River Street Marketplace where I attempted to sell my rubbings. Rubbings. My roommate, Jayse, always giggles like a thirteen-year-old school girl when I use the term. As cultured as he likes to *think* he is, most of the time Jayse's behavior is very junior high.

After years of having my ass grabbed at Hooters while I put myself through undergrad, I'd decided to press on to pharmacy school. Thanks to my mom's complete lack of maternal instincts, I'd had a full ride for all four years at Mankato State. I still had to waitress, though; not every college student has the added responsibility of feeding two younger siblings. But then, not everyone has a mommy like mine. Thankfully, the winds of fate blew my egg donor back into our lives right before graduation, and this time she happened to be "on the wagon." Since my grandparents and aunt lived close by and could keep tabs on her, I took a chance and chose a school many states away. For the first time in forever, I was on my own. I spent year one of the program doing nothing but hitting the library and working. Now I was well into year two, and my grades rock--- if I do say so myself. Maintaining my grades for grants was still my top priority, and my study routine was non-negotiable.

But a girl has to eat. No longer flush with overly generous tips from horny Vikings fans, I picked up shifts waitressing at Black Keys, a swanky local piano bar. The tips weren't quite enough for me to buy much more than ramen noodles, so I'd recently started selling my tombstone rubbings a couple of weekends a month.

Between customers, I crammed. That particular morning I was prepping for a Pharmacokinetics test. South University Pharmacy program had been a mega bitch to get into. It was a pretty exclusive program, and I'd studied my ass off for the PCAT. I took it twice to be extra competitive. Succeeding in the accelerated program would be cake if I could keep my shit together.

Easier said than done, based on my track record.

For the first year, hanging out with my roomie and his crew had been plenty of social life for me. They were a rainbow-colored safety net; being surrounded by a gaggle of gays provided the platonic security blanket I needed to cushion me from myself and my less-than-stellar judgment. But this semester I'd been partying way too much. Year two of rooming with Jayse Monroe was starting to take a toll. A vocal music major, he and his zany Armstrong College friends were highly trained canines when it came to sniffing out "an occasion." Nightly invites to raves and drag shows certainly weren't helping me stick to my carefully crafted study schedule. Having reluctantly embraced "*the* party capital of the south," I'd been balancing my work, study, and social schedules like a circus performer juggling torches. Deep down I knew I'd end up toasty, but that's how I roll. I'm ashamed to admit I take comfort in all the chaos.

After a few hours of between-customer cramming, I felt like I'd absorbed most of what I needed from my reading assignment. I was going back over the finer points when Trip Beaumont arrived. I smelled his sexy cologne before I saw him, but the sight of him *never* failed to impress me. Ripped, swaggering, deliciously dangerous Trip. Looking into his bedroom eyes, it was easy to see how a silly girl could throw away her aspirations for some sweaty extra-curricular activities with him. Good thing I'm rarely silly.

Still, he'd been friendly as hell, and something about him really revved my sex drive. *That* made me super nervous. I could smell "bad boy" all over him as easily as I could smell that musky scent he wore. So far, I'd managed to keep things casual, but the more we hung out, the more I enjoyed his dry humor and laid-back confidence. I'd confessed as much to my sage roommate the night before, and he'd advised me to "stop being such a prude and bed that boy".

In jeans and a simple white t-shirt, Trip looked especially fine that particular Sunday. I was very tempted to take Jayse's advice. As Trip approached my booth, his dark, unruly hair fell into his eyes. He brushed it carelessly aside as he leaned in and kissed my cheek. When he lingered a second longer than appropriate for a casual greeting, I may have tingled in unmentionable places.

"Mornin', Annie." His baritone voice had a raspy quality that most likely came from smoking too many imported cigarettes. The romantic in me – as deprived of oxygen and sunlight as she was – liked to imagine Trip was born speaking this way, skipping the prepubescent stage completely. That drawl of his was something straight out of *Gone with the Wind.* Though I'd been raised by a southerner – and I use the term "raised" loosely – hearing that coastal drawl fall from his perfect lips made me want to ditch my stuff and drag him to his place…or mine.

Get a grip, Annie. Time to pull out the KYPO list.

Whenever I find myself too distracted by a boy, Jayse and I construct a "keep your panties on" list – KYPO for short. Trip's wasn't very long, but it was drama ridden and written in bold capital letters. He was 30, older than me by five whole years. This fact did little to discourage my interest, since I'd always preferred older men. He was also divorced, *and* he had a kid. Not ideal for me, by any means. I silently chanted these items from my list to myself like a mantra.

Lately, Trip had become a sweet distraction and he'd appeared in the right place at the absolute worst time. We'd first met at Bonaventure cemetery four months ago. Covered in charcoal, I was rubbing gravestones when I first caught sight of him. I sat in stunned silence as I watched this breathtaking man focus intently on the tree line. His brow furrowed, and he made large sweeping motions with his paint brush as I drooled over him. As if he sensed my eyes on him, he turned those baby blues in my direction. A crooked, approachable smile overtook his chiseled face, and I found myself grinning stupidly back.

It was obvious from early in our first conversation that we had several friends in common, not to mention chemistry! We had exchanged phone numbers that afternoon before going our separate ways. As luck would have it, I saw him again a week later at Jayse's boyfriend's art show. He'd purchased two of Dale's sculptures, one for his mother's gallery and one for himself. Trip had several women flocked around him that night, but as soon as he saw me, he walked away from them without a word. We flirted a bit more, and I'd been surprised to discover that Trip and Dale were good friends. He was so hot and so easy to talk to that lately I thought about him when I should have been thinking about drug classifications and their negative side effects.

I was starting to think this was one-sided. With the tiny exception of suggesting I pose for a private nude sitting, he'd remained a total gentleman. A kiss on the cheek and the occasional hand on the small of my back had sadly been the limit of our physical contact. Feeling like a profiler, I worried aloud that he might be gay. Jayse, Grand Wizard of Gay-dar, assured me he wasn't.

I didn't know a whole lot about him. Trip was a master of turning the conversation back on me. That first day we met, he asked me how I got into rubbings. I explained that I started doing them when I was twelve. Back then, the house we rented backed up to a graveyard, and it was my personal retreat from the yelling and ugliness with my mother and her scumbag boyfriend.

After school, I often detoured to that cemetery. I'd pull out my library books and read nestled amongst the mature trees and headstones. Soon I was sneaking there on weekend mornings to avoid the two of them altogether. One day, as I sat under a large oak, I spotted an elderly woman spraying down an ancient grave marker with a bottle of water. Curiosity tugged at me, and I earmarked the page of my book and crept closer to see what she was up to.

Using a soft brush, she gently removed bird droppings from the stone. She dabbed at the stone and paused...and I, feeling a bit spellbound, waited to see what she'd do next. After testing the stone, presumably to see if it was dry enough, she used masking tape to fix some funky type of paper tightly to the stone. I watched as she took rubbing wax and coaxed the design from the stone's surface onto the rice paper. She spotted me watching and introduced herself as Pearl. Pearl explained that time and the elements wore away the information on the old tombstones and that she was preserving historical records. For whatever reason, I found the whole thing terribly romantic and became enamored on the spot. It wasn't long before I was trying it myself.

When word got out about my ghoulish hobby, the kids at school teased me pretty badly. I'm sure if they'd had my home life, they would have preferred hanging out with the dead, too. By the time I reached high school, I'd chosen to embrace my creepy reputation and went full-on Goth. I dyed my hair jet black (huge mistake), and let my boyfriend tattoo an onyx rose on my shoulder blade. That phase (and the boyfriend) had come and gone, but good old Black Beauty was sure to be with me forever. Ya gotta love the wisdom of youth.

I wondered what Trip might think of my rose tattoo and blushed when I realized I hadn't responded to his greeting.

"Hey." I blurted and flipped shut my pharm book with an audible thump. Though my mind shrieked 'no,' my hormones screamed 'do me, do me, do me!'

"Making buckets of money, Angel?" He'd started calling me Angel when he'd come to see me

at Black Keys a month ago. It made me feel a .
princess-like. I'm usually fairly pragmatic, but ev
ry girl likes to feel special once in a while. And Angel was a hell of a lot better than Ugly Mutt.

The mere thought of that nickname pummeled
me. I shuddered, surprised by a wave of intense
memories of my mom's ex-boyfriend/my childhood
monster. The hate in his voice...the foul stench of
his whisky-laden breath...his unwelcome hands.
My rational mind knew he was far back in my rearview mirror, but certain smells, sights, or even
songs could reduce me to that awkward 'tween he
used to hurt in no time flat.

The past threatened to tackle me, but I shook it
off and forced my focus back onto Trip. Right then
and there, I decided I wanted *him* to be my new escape. His soft smile felt gently seductive, and I was
long overdue for some serious play. As he leaned on
the table, I couldn't resist a peek at his sculpted
arms.

"I'm doing alright. How's that masterpiece
coming along?" I'd run into him the week before at
Jayse's choir concert. Dale, Jayse's boyfriend, had
invited him. Apparently Trip was not only an enthusiastic supporter of the local art scene, he was also a
big live music fan. That night, he'd told me he'd
started a new project and having seen firsthand that
he was an exceptional painter, curiosity was gnaw-
ing at me.

ately in need of a blonde muse.
o might pose for me?" he drawled,
le across his bottom lip in a way
ious of the knuckle. The color of
his eyes reminded me of the water out at Tybee Island, and my dirty mind immediately imagined rolling around in the sand with him.

I swallowed hard in an attempt to suppress the filthy smile threatening to surface on my face. Trip tilted his head ever so slightly, and his eyebrow twitched, a non-verbal acknowledgement that he saw my defenses crumbling.

"Clothing optional, I assume?" I flipped my heavy hair over one shoulder as much to relieve my skyrocketing temperature as to flirt. Trip cracked a lopsided grin and pulled out a black cigarette with a gold filter. I hate smoking. *Despise it.* I silently added this to the KYPO list. I watched longingly as he placed the cigarette to his lips wondering how he made it look so hot.

"Clothing is definitely *not* an option." He smirked behind the cigarette.

"You know they don't allow smoking in here." I murmured. He shrugged and flicked open his Zippo. Fittingly, it was adorned with Edvard Munch's, *The Scream.*

He cupped the flame, touching it to the tip of his cigarette. I watched as his gaze shifted above the flame to something or someone behind me. When I looked over my shoulder, I met the eyes of a man I'd never seen before.

I immediately noticed this man's uncanny resemblance to Trip. The devil on my shoulder shook her tassels exuberantly at the idea that they might be twins. Forcing my demon alter ego back into her cage, I took a long second look at the newcomer.

Trip was slim and toned like a swimmer, but this new guy was bigger and broader through the upper body. He stood several inches taller than Trip, and had the same dark, nearly black hair. Unlike Trip, whose ivory skin gave him a vampiric quality, this man's skin had a tanned healthy glow and he sported something somewhere between a beard and five o'clock shadow. His eyes were a vivid lavender-blue, bigger and more childlike than Trip's. I would never have believed two sets of eyes that sexy could exist, but here before me stood living proof.

"Sam." A surprised smile transformed Trip, making him seem ten years younger. He strode to Sam and engaged him in one of those odd male hug/chest bump/ hand shake maneuvers that they must all teach each other in high school. Sam seemed to force a smile, but it was a gorgeous one that worked over my already fraying self-control.

"How ya been, Trip?" Though his tone was pleasant, it seemed to me that Sam looked like he'd rather have been be just about anywhere else than engaging in this spontaneous reunion. KYPO.

"Annie, this is my baby brother, Sam. Sam, this is Annabelle Clarke."

"Pleasure to meet you." I noticed his voice was deeper than Trip's, as he leaned in and offered me his hand. I reciprocated, and he gently took my hand and shook it. I spotted a tiny butterfly bandage on his eyebrow, and wondered what he'd done to injure his handsome face. Trip's brother seemed to search me, as if I was some sort of riddle and I wasn't sure whether to feel flattered or uncomfortable. My skin felt sticky and flushed, and I realized it wasn't just from the sultry weather. He held my hand and my gaze for a moment too long, and I felt my cheeks burn. Flustered, I pulled my eyes away from his as the smoke from Trip's cigarette tickled my nose, reminding me of his presence. Trip exhaled through his nostrils and appeared completely unconcerned.

"Sam's at Harvard. He's going to practice law. " Trip informed me, carelessly flicking the ash of his cigarette onto the bricks at his feet.

"Not anymore. I quit." Sam shrugged. I noticed a petulant twinkle in his eye that made him look like a mischievous little boy. Though nothing in me approved of anyone quitting school for any reason ever, I found my lips struggle against a grin. Trip choked on his smoke and hacked a raspy cough.

"What?" Trip exclaimed, clearly mortified.

Having never seen him look *anything* but cool and casual, I blinked in alarm. Trip seemed positively horrified at his brother's announcement. Sam simply appeared amused. "I thought you were just on a break."

"I suppose I am. A *very* long one."

"Well…Cosmo must be thrilled." Trip managed to have the last word just as the manager of the Market Place sternly approached him. As if on cue, he stamped out his cigarette.

"Annie's gonna be a pharmacist. Aren't ya, Angel?" Trip ignored the manager, who gave him the hairy eye and stomped away.

I must have looked like I was watching a tennis match as I listened to the exchange between the Beaumont brothers. They had a dry, comedic timing, and the rhythm of their banter reminded me of an old black and white movie. I smiled, unsure which of them I should focus on. They were like a matching set of sexy salt and pepper shakers. "That's the plan."

Sam's eyebrows shot skyward, and he seemed to give me another once over. It was as if he just found out the stripper who was giving him a lap dance was a Rhodes Scholar.

"Well, you don't have to look so surprised!" I snapped. My tone sounded sassy, and I immediately wanted to take it back. I've always had a serious impulse-control problem when it to comes to my smart mouth. There are times when I can't even speak for fear of what might slip from my lips. But I briskly shrugged off all regrets. Why the hell should this stranger's opinion mean dick to me?

To my surprise, Sam responded with a smile so broad I could see his inviting pink tongue. All sorts of dirty thoughts trampled the imaginary KYPO list I was preparing to compose. Sam's eyes narrowed at me, and the smile vanished as quickly as it had appeared.

"Sorry. It's just...I've never had a pharmacist that looked like *you*." His tone sounded completely earnest, and Trip snickered. Sam looked contrite in retrospect and turned red all the way to the tips of his ears.

"Sammy-boy. Always suave with the ladies." Trip murmured, picking up one of my framed rubbings. I noticed Sam's eyes resting on my low neckline and crossed my arms over my chest. Surprised at his blatant admiration, I shot Trip a scandalized look. True to form, Trip did a double take at my scowl and actually had the balls to wink at me.

"Wanna do lunch?" Trip seemed to direct the question to both of us.

"I was thinking Vic's sounded good," Sam responded nonchalantly as he slid his hands into his pockets. Trip shrugged, and I tried to hide my disappointment. Vic's was pretty swanky, and though I had fantasized about the view, I'd never been able to justify such a splurge.

"You two have fun with that. I have money to earn." I took my seat and reached for my textbook. Both brothers looked at me as if I'd sprouted a second head.

Trip appeared thoughtful and returned his gaze to the rubbing he was holding. After he gave it a casual once over, he asked "How many of these do I have to buy so you can close the booth down and join us? My treat."

"For lunch?" I glanced down at my jeans and sneakers, then at Sam as if for confirmation that his brother was serious. His face was as expressionless as a Vegas poker champ, but his eyes sparkled with amusement.

"You should take off the rest of the day." Trip's tone was forceful and firm. I sat back in my chair and crossed my legs, as if this sort of thing happens all the time. I skimmed over my inventory, calculating what I needed for grocery money through the end of the month. Then I promptly doubled it.

"Fifteen." I waited for him to balk at me.

He didn't even blink. "Can you deliver? I didn't drive."

"Sure." I fought to appear casual at the amount of money he just dropped so that I could eat with him. I filed away the backhanded invitation to his place while I stood and gathered my things. Both of the brothers pitched in to help me close up shop, stacking frames and assisting while I packed up. As I glanced up from my cash box, they both shot me hot matching bookend smiles that pushed me even further toward the edge of my nympho cliff. My fingers rapidly flew over the screen of my phone as I texted Jayse an S.O.S. My body's lusty response to Sam gave me pause, and I was starting to have second thoughts about letting Trip out of the friend zone, since the slope seemed to be a wee bit more slippery than I remembered.

Me: I need a chastity belt, STAT.

Jayse's response was swift and 100% in character.

You just need to get laid, Miss Thang!

After stuffing the trunk and nearly half of the back seat of my car with the frames, the three of us crossed the street and made our way to Vic's. As we weaved through the crowded sidewalks, a startling feeling of foreboding crept over me. I assumed I was reacting to the weird vibes that the brothers were exuding. It was obvious listening to them attempt small talk that though Trip was ecstatic to see Sam, the brothers had issues. It wasn't anything that either of them verbalized per se, but more what they *didn't* say. Sam seemed to avoid all eye contact with Trip. Conversely, Trip seemed to be working extra hard to engage Sam in conversation. Sam's answers were brusque, and the conversation seemed obnoxiously one sided. The whole scene was stupendously awkward for me, and it wasn't long before I began to feel sorry for Trip.

By the time we entered the restaurant, I was incredibly fidgety and edgy. I struggled to understand the sudden shift in my mood. Until that morning, I'd felt really relaxed with Trip and was on the brink of asking *him* out. But now, in the company of *both* Sam and Trip, I felt all twisty and confused. There was something about their body language that jostled my instincts like tiny rumblings that might barely register on the Richter scale. As I watched Sam's poorly disguised apprehension as they walked side by side, I had a premonition that my appetite would be ruined long before the entrees came.

As we entered Vic's, a pretty brunette hostess glanced up from her schedule. Her metamorphosis from harsh and businesslike to dumbstruck when she saw my two companions was undeniably entertaining. She seemed especially flustered when her eyes rested on Trip. She pointedly turned away from him and zeroed in on Sam.

"Sa....Mr. Beaumont. It's been a while! Your usual table?" Her panicked eyes flit from Sam to Trip, and then back to her schedule. She pushed up her designer glasses and set her jaw, as if determined to get them seated before retreating to the ladies room to hide in a stall and cry.

"We'll take whatever works for you, Jen." Sam dismissively looked away, running a hand over his stubble. Had it not been obvious that there was some sordid story behind the exchange, I would have jumped down his throat. Having busted my ass in the industry for years, his condescension to the girl instinctively made me want to slap him in the back of the head.

"Right this way." She nearly tripped over her own feet, but somehow pulled herself together and led us into the main dining room, seating us by the windows. Peering around at the clientele confirmed that I was indeed underdressed. I consoled myself with the fact that Trip and Sam were also in jeans. I picked up the menu and nearly choked on my water when I saw the prices, which were pretty steep for a student. Trip glanced up from his menu, his eyes soft like a caress from gentle fingertips.

"It's about time you let me take you out." He smiled knowingly at me. Then he turned to Sam. "So what's the story with the hostess, bro? Did ya love her and leave her?"

Sam blinked blankly at Trip over his menu then narrowed his startling eyes. "Something like that."

"My brother is a bit of a ladies man, Annie. Consider yourself warned." Trip shot me a good natured smile. I was having a hard time understanding Trip's signals. Was this or was this not a date? Unsure how to respond to the loaded statement, I awkwardly shifted my gaze to the wall behind him, which consisted of floor to ceiling wine racks.

I sure could use one of those bottles about now...

I glanced at Sam, whose jaw clenched. His eye flicked to mine apologetically, and he quickly vanished behind his menu.

"I saw Randall last week." Trip continued after taking a sip of his water. "He says you got lazy up north and that he's had to kick your ass a couple of times to properly motivate you."

Sam scoffed at the obvious bait tactic, but the corner of his mouth twitched despite his best efforts. He tossed down his menu and glanced at me. Trip snorted with a sly grin. Registering the confusion on my face, Sam sighed.

"I box. Randall's my trainer. And he loves to exaggerate. He got in a lucky shot, that's all." Sam blushed and seemed to have trouble maintaining eye contact with either of us. Boxing explained the bandage on his eyebrow. I tried not to fidget as I willed my face not to reflect my renewed interest in his muscular shoulders and arms.

Finally, our waiter arrived. Sam wasted no time ordering a vodka tonic and I asked for a glass of chardonnay. Trip asked a couple of questions about appetizers, and then ordered the Oysters Rockefeller, fried green tomatoes and an iced tea.

After the waiter vanished, Sam turned doubtful

eyes at Trip. "Didn't you mean to order a Long Island Iced Tea?"

"You're not the only quitter in this family, Sam." Trip proudly pulled out his cigarettes and an emerald token, which he tossed to Sam. Sam caught it out of the air. I recognized it immediately, and my stomach sank to the floor. This new item instantly catapulted to number one on my KYPO list, and his club soda orders at the piano bar certainly made a lot more sense.

"Three month sobriety chip." Sam read emotionlessly as he flipped the medallion over. He wore no discernable expression. His apathy seemed cruel, and I felt like I was invading what should have been a private conversation.

"Yep." Trip's earnest smile seemed wasted on Sam, but it tugged at my heartstrings.

"90 days. Is this a joke?" When Sam finally looked Trip in the eye, it wasn't pride or love I saw on his face, but outright disbelief. The way Trip's eyes flickered with thinly disguised pain at Sam's belligerent tone made me want to throw my drink in Sam's face. Under the circumstances doing so seemed highly inappropriate.

"Five months, actually. I got this one a while back." Trip instantly recovered from Sam's lack of enthusiasm. He was trying so hard to win Sam's approval it made me feel sorry for him. Trip stood and began to pack his cigarettes. "I'll be right back.

I need a breath of fresh air."

Sam shook his head and huffed. I waited for Trip to be out of earshot before tossing down my menu.

"Well, for someone who doesn't say a whole lot, you sure choose your words for shit." I snapped, and if I offended him, you'd never know if from the blank expression he wore.

"Excuse me?" This wasn't so much a question as a filler line that he seemed to deliver on autopilot.

"That was mighty supportive of you, Bro." I waved after Trip while glaring daggers at Sam. As I reached for the stem of my wineglass, the irony of my momentary need for liquid courage was not lost on me. Sam's unapologetic nature annoyed me. He came off to me as the polar opposite of his brother: rude, antisocial, and judgmental.

"It's a bold-faced lie." Sam shrugged casually and took a long swallow of his drink. He set down his glass and folded his hands, fixing me with a look that dared me to challenge him. I frowned at him and shook my head.

"What on earth makes you think that?"

"I know Trip. He can't go a day without a drink."

"Is that so? 'Cause I've known him for months and I've never seen him drinking, let alone drunk."

His eyes narrowed and though he seemed to be

staring at me, I was pretty sure he didn't really see me. It was as if he were miles away.

I pressed on. "What's the deal with the two of you? It must be pretty bad if you can't even pretend to be excited for him."

Sam leaned his elbows on the table. His perfectly etched jaw and raw energy was distracting, but the intensity of his stare almost made me flinch. "Listen carefully, Annabelle. Don't be fooled by the act. Prince Charming is a toxic monster."

I can't really say if it was the harsh cadence of his voice or the overwhelming sadness I saw brimming under the surface of his cool facade, but I swear he curdled my blood. I searched his features for signs of malice and found nothing. What I did find was that I felt uncomfortable with the way his eyes penetrated mine, and I turned away and took a sip of my wine.

"Don't you think he deserves a second chance?" I forced myself to look at him. I was so fascinated by his beautiful features that it stung when he threw his head back and chuckled at me in a conciliatory manner.

"Do you think he deserves a seventh or eighth chance? Because if you plan to spend any amount of time with Trip, you'll have to ask yourself that question...and soon." He delivered this speech without emotion, as if he were stating that he took his coffee with cream and two sugars. He seemed practiced at the art of shutting down, stuffing his emotions in a trunk and locking them away for later examination. Unfortunately, I'd met his type many times before. Most friends and family of addicts wore a similar expression when their wounds were fresh. I was pretty sure I wore that exact expression when I was in a room with my mom. But Trip was nothing like my mom. I could feel it. Since Sam was a virtual stranger, I grasped for something insightful to say, but the usual platitudes seemed too cheesy to bother with.

Our waiter had been hovering nearby, blatantly eavesdropping. When he approached the table with the tomatoes and oysters, I glared pointedly at him. He smiled broadly back at me, as if our "table tension" was giving him a contact high. His nosiness pissed me off, but his interruption bought me time to gather my wits. After weeks of talking myself out of messing around with Trip and the last week talking myself back into it, Sam and his revelations were particularly unwelcome. My mom was an addict, and I'd ridden that roller-coaster enough to see that Trip definitely needed to work the twelve steps with Sam. I glared at the waiter as he leisurely refilled Trip's water glass.

"Enjoying the show?" I sneered. Sam's eyebrows shot to his hairline at my snarky remark to the man. As the chastised waiter fled as if his pants were on fire, I turned both barrels on my table companion. "Tell me this... if Trip's so unredeemable, why come to lunch with us?"

His near lavender eyes swept me with a frigid detachment. I saw a flicker of something...some twisted mournful...something. "So I could have *this* conversation with you. I wanted to spare you the trouble that follows Trip around. I guess I'm still my brother's keeper, whether I want the job or not."

I blinked in surprise, but his conflicted behavior made a hell of a lot more sense. He'd come here solely to warn me off. Sam's handsome, angular features were set in a manner that suggested he took no pleasure in what he was about to say. I braced myself when he glanced around and leaned in closer to me.

"That hostess...Jen? She hooked up with Trip once. This was shortly after Trip's wife left him, and he checked himself out of rehab. He called me and said he'd picked up some chick and was going out to this bonfire on Tybee Island and wanted to know if I'd like to come along. So I went. I wanted to be sure he wasn't going to drink and drive again. Trip spent most of the party off in a back bedroom with Jen. But he got so trashed that he ended up in the E.R., and I had to drive her home. She sobbed the entire time. She even showed up at the hospital the next day to see him. And he doesn't even remember her."

As I processed what he'd told me, my eyes

drifted to the view through the windows. I saw Trip across the street smoking. He leaned carelessly on a lamppost, bobbing his head in time to a street musician's tune. His wide smile as he applauded along with the tourists contradicted Sam's clinical description of him. I continued to observe Trip thoughtfully as he shook hands with the guitar player and dropped some cash in his open case.

"People are capable of change, Sam. Maybe he's finally ready to clean up his act." This hadn't exactly been my experience, and I wasn't sure if I said this to challenge Sam or to make myself feel better.

He heaved a sigh and tossed his napkin on the table. He glanced at me, then lifted his drink to his lips and muttered "Forgive my lack of optimism. I'd love to be wrong. But I very much doubt that I am."

I found myself reexamining Sam as he pulled out his phone and scrolled through the screens. Except for the stubble and denim, he looked like a prep school darling. The epitome of "white collar". How could he claim to be his brother's keeper when he'd been gone for months and hadn't seen him in such a long time? I wondered how much of his animosity toward Trip was about his brother's past skeletons and how much was just old sibling rivalry bathed in the juice of sour grapes. I was just about to ask why he'd dropped out of law school when Trip reappeared and hastily took his seat.

"Oysters! Fantastic." He smiled broadly and scooted his plate in my direction. "You know what they say about oysters-don't ya, Angel?"

CHAPTER THREE
Sam

A silent spectator, I brooded over lunch as my brother sprinkled compliments all over Annabelle like unholy water. To my horror, she seemed to drink in his attention like a lost soul gulping down sand at a desert mirage. If anything, she seemed *more* into him than before our conversation. From the moment I saw Trip kiss her cheek, she was off limits. I vowed to wash my hands of the en-tire mess, but I had a wriggling feeling that doing so would be easier said than done.

First impressions are Trip's specialty. He is a legend when it comes to making people fall in love with him, and if a competition existed for this tal-ent, he'd flawlessly land the dismount. Unfortunate-ly, his charm wasn't a sustainable resource these days. I hoped for Annabelle's sake he'd show her his true nature before she invested too much time in him and that his inevitable fuck-up wouldn't leave permanent scars. Though my dream girl had turned out to be a delusional, know-it-all Yankee, she didn't deserve to drown wearing Trip's designer cement shoes.

As the waiter removed our plates, Annabelle turned to Trip. Determination shone in her dazzling eyes, and her full lips curved in an impish grin.

"Alright, I'll do it." A light, musical laugh erupted from her that nearly shattered me.

"Do what?" Trip wiped his mouth with his napkin, and I could tell by the lascivious twinkle in his eyes he had a good idea what she meant.

"I'll pose for you." When Trip chuckled devilishly, she held up her hands, blushing. "On one condition. I'm wearing my bra and panties. Take it or leave it."

The image of her in a bra and panties just about made me spit my drink all over the table. Focused completely on each other, neither of my companions noticed. Trip let the silence hang in the air just long enough for dramatic effect. "Fair enough."

I was racked with sudden indigestion.

I chose to blame the vodka tonic.

As the heinous luncheon came to a close, I tried to make a break for it, but Trip guilted me into coming along to his new place to help carry in his purchases. Tension constricted every muscle in my neck and shoulders caused partly by their incessant flirting as Annabelle drove us past lush Forsythe Park, skirting the edge of the Victorian District. I could tell by the subtle expressions Trip wore when he looked at her that he had a soft spot for Annie. Bad blood or not, he was my only brother, so this placed her immediately in the "off limits" category. Though by now it was obvious I wasn't her type, I still found myself disappointed.

A block later, we pulled up alongside the curb of an immaculate Victorian. I couldn't help but notice this address was still within stumbling distance of Violet's place. My mood lifted a little. I covered a smirk with my hand, taking odd comfort in the fact that some things never changed.

As we entered Trip's condo, I fought to contain my surprise. The home had been painstakingly remodeled with impressive crown molding, meticulously restored hardwoods, and modern light fixtures. As we passed by the kitchen, I noticed a new butcher-block island and stainless steel appliances. Other than scattered charcoal pencils, sketch pads, and other various artistic accoutrements, the place was tidy and lacked the frat house feel of his previous bachelor pads.

"This place is amazing," Annabelle gasped, moving toward the ornate fireplace for a closer look at a painting of Trip's daughter, Maisie. It was a fine piece, much more of a literal interpretation than his usual work and understandably deserved this place of prominence in his home.

Trip shrugged and looked pleased by her response. "I like it. Lots of natural light."

I could feel him looking at me, as if he were expecting some sort of reaction. I refused to look in his direction.

"Any trouble with the neighbors?" It came out before I could stop myself. Though I knew my attitude would lead nowhere good, I found myself back in the role of the bitter nonbeliever. Annabelle's fiery eyes bore into me.

"No, I own it. I live in the front half and use the back half as a studio and storage," Trip responded, and at that, not only did I look at him, I gaped. He'd finally invested in real estate after a couple of years deluding himself that he'd reconcile with Violet. I was more astonished by this revelation than the sobriety chip, and doubt began to gnaw at me. It had been eons since I'd dared to hope my brother would climb out of the bottle. I honestly never thought we'd find ourselves having a sensible conversation about owning property and natural light. Wondering why Mama hadn't told me about Trip's journey of self-help, I crossed to the windows and admired the impressive view.

As I puzzled over whether my brother was actually clean and sober, I heard Trip mutter something about being a bad host and leaving the room. I felt Annie next to me before I saw her out of the corner of my eye. Her sudden nearness had my body on high alert, and the hair on the back of my neck stood on end. She looked out onto Forsythe Park as if searching the tree line for something. I cleared my throat nervously, and she turned toward me.

"Your brother has a pretty impressive home." Her delicate features contrasted with her bold eyes, which double-dared me to challenge her.

"Yes. He does," I conceded.

"Looks like the home of a man with his shit together to me." She muttered under her breath. Against my better judgment, I chuckled. Her smart mouth would have totally been attractive if her bite weren't directed at me. She quickly shot me a look and then relaxed when she saw I was not laughing at her, but in appreciation of her. The deli-cious apple scent of her hair made it somehow hard for me to catch my breath. She locked eyes with me for a blissful moment, and I was able to take in her exquisite face unchallenged. I'd never stood so close to such flawlessness, and she stunned me si-lent. Physically, I couldn't have found a more at-tractive package. I'm not sure how long I stared at her, but I could have happily continued to do so for days. But there was something else that pulled me to her. Underneath her undeniable surface beauty, I could just make out a lost little girl. As if she'd caught me reading her diary, Annabelle frowned and blinked rapidly like she was trying to clear her head. With visible effort, she coerced her perfect features into a harsh expression and turned back to the view of the park. Guilt gripped me, and I forced myself to look away. My brother liked this girl, really liked her. Then I remembered Violet, and that crushing weight of guilt vanished from my shoulders.

"Water?" Trip asked from behind us. I definitely needed something to quench my thirst, but I suspected a cold shower would have been considerably more helpful. We both took a bottle from him. The water was painfully cold and I couldn't suppress a grin when Annie practically chugged hers.

"What the hell are you going to do with all these, Trip?" She asked as she ran her long fingers across a framed rubbing nearby.

"Hang them in the bathroom...or maybe on the ceiling over my bed." His gold-medal caliber grin scored a perfect ten as she giggled that melodious laugh of hers.

"Classy," she chirped. "I really want to see the studio. Do we get a tour? "

Annabelle twirled a strand of her long, wheat blonde hair as she waited for a response. Her enthusiasm felt almost childlike and her clipped, rapid speech must have seemed exotic to Trip, who'd never spent time up north like I had. His face softened in response to her request, reminding me of the look he wore the morning he stole Violet from me. Maybe that explained my sudden bout of nausea.

Violet Duchamp was the only girl Trip and I ever fought over. And did we *fight*. He ended up with two black eyes, a broken nose and a bloody lip. I had to have six stitches and pissed blood for a week. Violet wouldn't speak to either of us for a month. It's funny because Trip and I usually attracted very different types of women. He usually lured the kind who chased after the "life of the party." I usually nailed those who sought out the shy guy. I met Violet first, but unfortunately for everyone involved, *Trip* ended up being her type.

A seventh generation Savannahian, Violet had all the breeding expected of a Beaumont wife. She'd been sent off to boarding school as a child, a fact which probably accounted for some of the glaring differences between her and the Georgia Peaches we were so accustomed to. Violet knew all the rules in the blue-blood handbook and broke them with spectacular panache. Though her family was notorious for having more money than brains, she was definitely an exception. Yes, indeed. Violet had vision. Pursuing a degree in business, the night we met she informed me she intended to be a buyer for Saks Fifth Avenue. Three weeks later, I introduced her to Trip and that was the nail in the proverbial coffin of our romance.

Trip, who had just started grad school at the time, planned to do restoration work for museums after finishing school. He'd been a track star in high school *and* continued to compete in college; his exceptional talent and unearthly charisma made him very popular with the ladies. Vi, it seemed, was no exception, and he was instantly enamored with her. I'd never seen my brother so consumed by a woman, and it was clear to me from the moment I introduced them that I was seeing the beginning of something monumental. They were the talk of the town when they started dating: a perfect blend of good looks, old money, and lofty ambition. My parents adored Violet, especially Cosmo, who remarked many times that Vi reminded her of a younger version of herself. After a whirlwind romance, Trip bought her an obnoxiously large diamond, and they threw an opulent engagement party that was the talk of the Savannah society columns. Their future seemed to overflow with infinite promise.

Then everything went down with Daddy, and my brother cracked and splintered, only to later resurface as a crumpled version of his former self. Violet inexplicably married him anyhow. I suppose she believed, as all of us did, that once he'd had time to properly mourn, he'd eventually return to the exceptional Renaissance man he'd been before Daddy's death. We were all idiots.

Violet was the last to realize that holding out hope for Trip was wasted energy. Watching her transform from a cheeky spitfire into a bitter whis-key widow was maddening for me. I pleaded with her to leave him. I know that sounds messed up, but I swear it wasn't because I wanted her back. I'd moved on long before that. They'd had a child, and it was my firm position that I would be damned if Trip's new brand of bullshit would destroy an inno-cent life. Thankfully, the same pioneer spirit that had attracted us both to Violet helped her to wriggle free from Trip's issues which were tethered around her neck like an anchor.

Trip offered his hand to Annabelle and I felt the past and present collide around me. My chest ached when she took it, and I struggled to understand why. My response to their chemistry was downright an-noying, and I presumed it was all just echoes of his betrayal with Vi. He led Annabelle out of the door, and I followed robotically. As I stepped back out into the heat, I was tempted to continue up the street away from my brother and our tumultuous past. But something told me to join them on the studio tour, so along I went.

As we crossed the threshold into the studio, the smell of paint thinner stirred my adrenaline, and I was instantly energized. As a kid, my brother's gift for painting always blew me away. I could barely draw stick people, so watching my brother's genius with a brush was like watching a magician pull a rabbit out of a hat. When we both still lived at home, I'd be in my room studying or in the rec room training at the speed bag, and the scent of fresh paint thinner would permeate the house, calling to me. I'd drop everything I was doing to see what amazing creation Trip was pulling out of the thin air. That was really how it seemed, like he had some exclusive third eye that allowed him to somehow see what belonged on that empty, creamy canvas.

I entered the studio in time to hear Annabelle gasp and immediately understood her reaction. Paintings overtook the room – dozens of them. They hung from the walls and leaned in bunches against the sparse furniture. Unlike the melancholy paintings that hung in my mother's foyer, these were bright, vibrant pieces. Bold, colorful and brilliant. The kind he *used* to paint.

Old school Trip Beaumont.

Sober Trip.

Trip and Annie had moved on to the next room, but I was stuck as if the wood beneath my feet were quicksand. Goosebumps erupted on my arms, and I gaped as I slowly turned 360 degrees. Seeing those paintings was like glimpsing into the past through a peephole, and I was floored by my emotions as a lump rose in my throat. My eyes stung and when I finally inhaled, it was more like a heave. My physical response embarrassed me, and I felt juvenile…vulnerable. I was suddenly very glad they'd left me alone. A tiny part of me dared to wonder if Trip had finally managed to follow the trail of breadcrumbs out of the twisted forest he'd been lost in for so long.

When I was finally able to propel myself on-ward, I joined them in the back room which I took to be his work room. A man-sized canvas loomed in the center of it, facing away from me toward the widows. Annabelle stood to one side, examining its contents with wide-eyed wonder. Trip stood on the other side, arms folded with his thumb to his lips. His eyebrows were critically drawn together as he examined his own handiwork. Curiosity gripped me and I rushed around the mammoth easel to see what it held.

The subject of his painting was a narrow road canopied by draping oaks and Spanish moss. Shades of green dominated the large canvas. Though one side was only three-fourths completed, the detail was already phenomenal. As with the bounty of canvases in the first room, Trip had chosen dynamic shades of color. It didn't escape me that the avenue that tunneled down the center of the painting stood conspicuously empty.

"So you're going to paint me naked...onto this?" Annabelle's genuine awe charmed me, and had I not been so disturbed by the location he'd chosen for his subject, I would've chuckled.

He shook his head. "Sorry to disappoint you,

but I'd like you to wear a white dress, if that's alright."

Trip seemed to be a million miles away, his voice reflecting a quiet thoughtfulness. As I beheld his Technicolor depiction of the avenue at Wormsloe Plantation, I was awestruck by its perfect detail and optimistic vibrancy. This picture was practically a snapshot of the spot where he proposed to Violet; however, the startling colors gave it an otherworldly feel, as if the viewer were the Mad Hatter peering through the looking glass. I felt a familiar weighty pressure in my chest, and my blossoming hope for Trip's recovery blinked out of existence.

CHAPTER FOUR
Annie

I chewed aggressively on the inside of my lip as Sam and I drove in silence. Just as we were leaving Trip's place, the ashen sky dumped torrential rain down on us, and I'd insisted on giving Sam a ride. Though he'd been nothing but a master douche-lord all day, I didn't want his catching pneumonia on my conscience.

Trip's jaw-dropping talent intimidated the hell out of me, but I was psyched about being a part of his latest creation. He'd told me he'd need a few days to finish the background and detail work and that he'd call me about dress shopping later in the week. Imagining hours alone with Trip intrigued me, but the way Sam was telegraphing his angst, I knew he had a lot more to say about the matter.

"Why'd you leave law school?" Keen to redirect him, I took the opportunity to satisfy my curiosity.

I could feel his eyes boring into me, but even

with the wipers on full blast, visibility sucked. I trained my sights on the road ahead, and I heard him exhale.

"I hated it. It was a soul-sucking bore." He sounded tired, and I snickered.

"A bore? Well, duh. What the hell did you expect?" I stopped at a red light, and then turned to look at him. He was way too good looking. Trip had that ruffled around the edges quality, but even with his stubble Sam looked immaculate…airbrushed. I knew something had to be terribly wrong with him. "Were you failing?"

"What?" His response was practically a whisper. He looked distracted, and he seemed to be fixated on my mouth. The way his eyes locked on my lips was incredibly hot, and I felt like my face was on fire.

"Were you flunking out?" I pointedly enunciated each word. He met my eyes, and I spied some inner struggle bubbling beneath his polished exterior. He ripped his eyes away and turned to face forward.

"Green light," he informed me, so I turned away from his perfect profile and pressed the gas. "No. It actually came really easily to me."

"Then you *are* an idiot," I scoffed. I've never been known to hold my tongue well, and it seemed our charming little car ride would be no exception.

"What?" His shocked response came out with a

laugh.

I flipped my hair out of my face. "If you were away from the family drama and doing well in school, dropping out was pretty moronic."

"Thanks a lot, Annabelle." His drawl engulfed my name as if he were a chocolate fountain at a decadent buffet. Rich, sweet, and incredibly bad for me. The way his wet hair clung to his tanned skin was hypnotic, and I greedily stole a sideways glance at him. I involuntarily pursed my lips and pressed on.

"You think pharmacy school is fun? Talk about dry reading! But you know what? It's better than working at 7-11…and when I'm finished I'll have a career that's important."

"Hey, now." He mockingly objected. "Buying my daily Slurpee at 7-11 is *very* important to me."

"You know what I mean…impacts the world around me in a meaningful way. And *that's* motivation worth busting your ass for."

"Sounds like you have a real passion for it." I couldn't tell if this was more of his tell-tale sarcasm or not, but I blundered on as if he was serious.

"Someone's got to do it."

"Well the world has plenty of lawyers. No one's gonna miss me."

I shook my head at his flippant words. "Wasted opportunity has always pissed me off. Dropping out of a school people would kill to get into? It's bullshit."

"Interesting philosophy. *I'm* a piece of shit for changing my mind, *but* Trip should be embraced in all of his rum-soaked glory." His bitterness lashed back at me like a whip. I paused, debating with myself. Deciding this battle was worth fighting, I pushed forward.

"Alcoholism is a disease, Sam. Lack of drive is not. You got into Harvard Law. If I ditched out after accomplishing that, I'd be embarrassed as hell…not cracking jokes about it. All that wasted time and money…" Speculating about the tuition costs of an Ivy League school made me cringe.

"The time was mine to waste. The money, too." I glanced at him and saw that his clenched jaw didn't match the carefree delivery of his words. He was so polished, like a born politician. I could sense something stewing under his cool exterior – something hostile. I wondered if he was just cynical about life in general. His negativity was a major buzzkill, and I would have dropped the subject, but I really didn't want to discuss Trip and had no idea what else to make conversation about. I hated the tension between us, but neither of us spoke for the next couple of blocks.

Finally, I cleared the gigantic frog blocking my throat. "What are you gonna do now? Since you aren't planning to finish, I mean."

"I have no idea." He sighed, sounding like a

lost little boy, and it overwhelmed me with sadness to hear such defeat in his voice. I couldn't comprehend why I felt so empathetic toward him when he was clearly his only obstacle. I refused to look in his direction.

We rode in silence after that, but the air in the car was still heavy. Frustration radiated from him, yet when I finally peeked at him, his face was as placid as a lake at sunrise. I barely knew this man, so I figured it was best not to push him more. He exhaled loudly, and it was plain to me that he wanted to say something.

"What?" I blurted after his third dramatic sigh.

"You shouldn't pose for him. It's a trap. That's how he'll lure you in."

"Maybe I want to be *lured in*." My voice sounded playful as I imitated his drawl. We stopped at another stoplight and I turned to him. I saw frustration and my own exasperation reflected in his features.

Those lavender-blue eyes were on mine again. "You'll regret it."

"Sam, pipe down. It's not Playboy." I snorted.

His joking mood had vanished. He didn't laugh or even crack a smile. "You have no idea how bad he can get. I do. "

"I know a thing or two about addicts." I mumbled, looking away and busying myself with the radio. He reached out and covered my hand with his. I shot him an apprehensive glance and tried to ignore the spark that shot from his touch and circulated throughout my entire body.

"Calling Trip's drinking an addiction issue is like calling the Grand Canyon a hole in the ground. He's an exceptional drunk." His eyes, which were locked on mine, narrowed thoughtfully. "I swear it's all the Savannah inbreeding."

"But you're his brother, and you're *normal*." I countered, pulling my hand away from the radio and from his.

Sam paused and looked thoughtfully out of the windshield. "Maybe I only have one kidney, and I just don't know it yet. I'm sure some congenital abnormality will haunt me later."

"Maybe he *is* on the right path. With all due respect, Sam, you aren't exactly up on current events around here." The light turned green, and I hit the accelerator.

"And why do you think that is, Annabelle?" Every time he said my name, it was like an intimate caress. My heart raced as I felt him watching me. I wanted to face him head on, but in the confined space of the car, my responses to him were…troubling.

"So he screwed up. Don't we all? I'm sure you aren't perfect either. He seems like he's doing really well. Cut him some slack. As for me…I can take care of myself."

An awful cackle erupted from him, and it was possibly one of the most uninviting sounds I'd ever heard. "You must be really fucked up. You're so ready to hop in the sack with a total fucking train wreck? Jesus. Your daddy issues must be epic."

I sucked in a loud breath. My vision blurred, as if someone had pulled down a red shade in front of my eyes. Rage coursed through my veins, and I jammed my foot onto the brake with such force that it's amazing we didn't both have whiplash.

"Get out." I heard my voice tremble as the words left my lips. There was a pregnant pause, and the rhythmic sound of the rain beat in time with my hammering heart.

"Annie…," he whispered, both gentle and contrite. I whipped my head in his direction. His eyes widened at whatever he saw emanating from me.

"I said get the hell out of my car, Sam. Now!"

Without further delay, Sam clambered out of my car and was drenched before he shut the door. As I peeled away, I heard him exclaim when my tires threw more water up on him, but I was way too pissed to laugh about it.

My blood boiled the rest of the way home. Goddamn right I had "daddy issues!" My biological father ditched us when I was only three years old. Knowing my mom, he had plenty of reasons. I didn't really blame him, but I often wondered why he didn't take me with him. I liked to think I got my levelheadedness from him, but since I didn't remember him at all, I couldn't be sure.

After he left, my mom may as well have had a revolving door on her bedroom. She got knocked up twice more after me – by different men, no less. I always took bizarre pride at being the only non-bastard of her litter. During her third pregnancy, she finally settled down with the "baby daddy" for nearly five long years, and he turned out to be a pervert.

Drenched and feeling like utter crap, I sloshed up the stairs to my apartment and burst through the door. Jayse, who lounged on the couch watching Bravo, uttered a melodramatic gasp and grabbed his chest.

"Helena Bonham Carter!" He theatrically exclaimed, as if the actress's name were a swear word. "You scared the hell out of me!"

"Sorry." I muttered, flinging open the fridge and scouring its contents for something bad for me.

"What are you doing home so early?"

"I live here."

"No shit, Cuntzilla. Did they close The Marketplace early because of the weather?" Jayse could sense drama like some people could divine water using a forked stick. He snatched up his pita chips and hummus from the coffee table. His blonde curls bounced as he frolicked into the kitchen, offering me some of his snack.

"No. I closed down early. Trip took me to

Vic's." I scooped a huge amount of hummus onto a chip and popped it into my mouth. Jayse's brown eyes twinkled as he graced me with a scandalous, dimpled grin.

"You *filthy* little social climber! Blowing off your booth for a nooner with a Beaumont? Don't let me down, Fancy. This is your one chance!"

"Calm down. I just gave him a ride to his place. His brother was with us the whole time."

"Oooo...ménage de Beaumont. Très trampy! I've taught you well, Young Grasshopper." He clapped his hands enthusiastically, and I gave him a dirty look as I snatched a bag of cheese puffs out of the cupboard. He must have seen something telling on my face: his smile vanished, and he immediately shifted into "Supportive Jayse" mode.

"So no three-way. Boo...hiss. But that's hardly a reason to put on ten pounds, Annie."

"I told Trip that I'd pose for him," I said, crunching on a mouth full of saturated fat.

"About time. And all the more reason not to become a fatty." Jayse snatched the cheese puffs from me and tossed the bag on top of the fridge. "Okay, focus. Trip's brother: is he hot?"

"He's...ok." My mind flashed to Sam's scorching violet-blue eyes and the lanky way he towered over me by the windows at Trip's place. I flung open the freezer, moving things around until I found my stash of thin mints.

"Mmmmhmmmm…" Jayse's sardonic reply accompanied his outstretched hand. I took three cookies out of the package and grudgingly handed it to him. He closed the freezer bag and swiftly stuffed them back in the freezer. "Alright, spill it, Sistah. Why ya' trippin'? No pun intended."

"It turns out that Trip's an alcoholic." I bit into a cookie and peeked up at him from under my lashes.

"Keep your panties on," Jayse deadpanned, the smile disappearing from his eyes. My weakness for bad boys and foolish choices was the stuff of legend. Though Jayse often commented that I needed to loosen up, he wasn't about to let me move directly from training wheels to base jumping.

"He's in A.A.…and his brother is a *total* asshole. If I *never* see him again it will be way too soon," I huffed, and Jayse pulled a bottle of wine out of the fridge.

"Deep cleansing breaths, Annie. Let's get buzzed, and you can tell me everything," Jayse instructed, producing the wine bottle opener out of thin air. We moved to the couch with our glasses, and I explained the events of my day.

"Well," he sighed thoughtfully, after a full minute of silent contemplation, "let's be realistic. You won't find many thirty- year-olds without baggage. And as for Sam, he sounds like a sexy good time. Are you sure he's straight?"

"A good time?" I snapped, after nearly choking on my wine.

"He sounds like a decent guy." He sat forward a bit, as if he were trying to explain a complicated issue to a confused halfwit. I squinted at him.

"You're joking, right?" I felt angry all over again.

Jayse rolled his eyes. "He's trying to keep you from getting mixed up with a brother who he believes will screw up your life and hurt you. As for his theories about your daddy issues...he just fucking met you, Annie. You can't hate the man for being a good guesser."

"Maybe not. But I can hate him for laughing at me and basically calling me a whore." The image of Sam's amazing arms and lavender eyes flickered in my mind, and I angrily shoved my hair away from my face. Jayse seemed to scrutinize me.

"Whatever blows your skirt up, Lovergirl." He sat back and flipped the TV back on. "Just tell me who we're mad at, and you know I'll play along."

Jayse and I didn't get to talk much the rest of the week. We were both buried in a blur of studying, classes, and tests. I got 97% on the Pharmokinetics test I'd crammed for, so all was right with the world as far as I was concerned. The rain continued its relentless assault on Savannah, and I didn't even bother to ride my bike to the cemetery, knowing it would have been an absolutely pointless endeavor.

The piano bar was completely dead on Wednesday, and I got sent home from work early. I was pretty damn happy I'd overcharged Trip for the rubbings because the missing tips would have squeezed my infinitesimal budget pretty hard. I had hoped Black Keys would be busier Thursday because I adored that place and didn't want to have to quit and go to some shitty sports bar out by the mall. I loved the classy music and the location in the historic part of town. As lame as it sounds, working at such an upscale place somehow made me feel like I'd come a long way.

Fortunately, Black Keys was slammed on Thursday night, so I had nothing to fear. The pianist was wildly popular, a foul-mouthed bit of a local legend. He told bawdy stories between numbers, and the crowd gobbled it up like kids at a build-your-own-sundae bar. They drank bucket after bucket of beer and tipped as if it were their last night on earth.

While I was settling the tab of a snotty table of country club widows/divorcees, I caught sight of Trip seated in his regular corner booth. Sitting across from him was a pretty blonde, and they appeared to be having a very animated conversation. With her heart-shaped face, she rocked a pixie haircut and she had an hourglass figure that Jayse would have described as "va va va voom." I tried not to feel like a gangly giraffe as I assessed her and wondered who the hell she was.

After clearing the table of aging "mean girls" and pocketing their lame excuse for a tip, I approached my boss, Martin. Hyper as always, he shuffled behind the bar, nearly salivating as he opened the cash register. Martin was an easy guy to work for. He never objectified me, and he'd been in the industry for longer than I'd been alive. Consequently, he knew almost everyone in town. Since he loved to name drop, I knew it was likely he'd have intel I needed.

"Hey," I whispered to him, "who's the blonde sitting with Trip Beaumont?"

Martin barely looked up from the tall pile of receipts as his savvy eyes peered at their corner. "Violet Duchamp. His ex. She's a class act. Those two were really something back in the day."

"What happened?" Unable to keep my eyes from searching the former couple for clues, I observed that Violet seemed unable to talk without using her hands. In the few months that I'd know Trip, I'd never seen so much emotion on his face. At that particular moment, he looked surprised and disturbed, like when Sam mentioned leaving law school, but ten times more so.

Martin paused and blinked at me uncomfortably. I may not have been able to read Trip, but I *could* read Martin like a book. He'd seen me talking to Trip on more than one occasion, and he wasn't sure how much he should say. "Trip's a wee bit too much like his father."

I felt a shiver down my spine, though I had no idea what he meant by the statement. Martin, as a character witness, was *way* further removed from the source and therefore much more reliable than Sam in my book. Hearing him corroborate that Trip had problems not only raised a red flag, it illuminated my KYPO list with all the wattage of the Fremont Street Experience in Vegas.

"Truth is, they were doomed from the start. A classic tale of a couple that burned too hot not to fry out. Now, enough chit chat. Go and take them their drinks."

I raised my eyebrows as he handed me a tray with a club soda and a frou frou umbrella drink perched on it. Dread poured over me like the nearby water wall as I approached them. Violet's arms were folded across her voluptuous chest, and Trip seemed to be raving at her. Still, their chemistry was palpable from fifteen feet away.

This is the opening act that I'm supposed to follow? Seriously?

As I approached, I heard Violet rail back at him. "Well of course you 'only hurt the ones you love', Reg. That's because they're the only ones who give a shit about you!"

I saw Trip's lips moving, but I couldn't make out a word he was saying. Violet noticed me approaching and held up a hand to shush him. Trip turned mid rant and snapped his mouth shut when he saw me.

"Sweetheart, you read my mind," Violet purred to me as she snatched the umbrella drink from my tray and placed the glass to her full lips.

"Angel…" Trip's nickname for me sounded like a question. Violet's lovely, big eyes grew even bigger, and she raked me with a haughty once over.

"I don't think we've met," she trilled, sounding all old south and hoopskirts. "I'm Violet."

"Hi, I'm Annie." I replied, handing Trip his drink. Her earthy green eyes blinked rapidly, and I could see the wheels behind them whirling like a pinwheel in a gale storm when she realized my name wasn't actually 'Angel.' She took another sip, this one slightly longer than the first. In fact, it was more like a gulp.

"Annie. This is my *ex-wife*, Violet." Trip's explanation spewed from his lips like a bath tub faucet flipped on at full strength. I looked from Violet to Trip and knew my expression was significantly more composed than it would have been if Martin hadn't just given me a head's up.

"A pleasure to meet you." I smiled my well-practiced customer service face.

"Likewise," she managed between dazzling gritted teeth.

"So, are you ready for me yet?" I asked Trip,

marking my territory swiftly and harshly. Out of the corner of my eye, I saw Violet slump back against the padded pleather of the booth.

"Yes, I am. In fact, I came here to ask if you are available to go shopping on Saturday. Then I ran into Violet."

"And I informed him that I'm engaged." Violet cooed, toying with the umbrella in her drink and staring at Trip. Trip's stunning eyes regarded her in a weird mix of disbelief and despondence. It was painfully obvious he was crestfallen. That was the moment I should have walked away, but we all love to tell ourselves all manner of lies, don't we?

"Congrats." I tilted my head toward her and plastered on a smile. She winked at me and lifted her glass in salute.

There was a moment of silence as Trip looked from Violet to me. The corner of his mouth twitched upward, and he spoke. "So? Saturday? "

"It's a date," I replied. I'd already decided on the way to their table that being his rebound girl suited my needs perfectly. I was officially bored, and he was sex incarnate. Besides, I didn't have time for anything serious anyway.

"Well, you'll have to pick him up. He lost his license years ago. It's a charming story. I'm sure he'd love to tell it to you." Violet's snarky remark was masked in the heavy perfume of magnolias. She gracefully removed herself from the booth and I realized I had several inches on her. I'm 5'7", and though some women might have felt powerful in that scenario, I slouched to appear more feminine. She grinned up at me confidently, placing a French manicured hand on her shapely hip.

"Have fun, y'all. I'm sure you'll love whatever he picks out, Annie. Reg has always had excellent taste."

CHAPTER FIVE
Sam

"Get up, you pussy," Randall bellowed from around his mouth guard. I blinked wildly, trying to clear the stars from my vision. For the record: I'm fast. My footwork is *way* above average. And my former trainer, who was now in his mid-thirties, had just connected with a killer right hook, knocking me flat on my ass.

"Focus, Sammy." He grabbed both sides of my sparring head gear with his gloved hands. His hard, dark eyes glared into mine. "*Do not* embarrass me, White Boy."

He had every right to be pissed. Randall had several guys touring the gym today and had been talking me up earlier as one of his success stories. The rich white kid from Ardsley Park who'd won fight after fight, despite having a silver spoon shoved up his ass. And here I was, sitting on the mat, looking like a little bitch.

In my defense, I was completely stuffed and a

little buzzed. I'd just gorged myself on a gourmet lunch, and I had no idea Randall was planning for me to perform an exhibition. Mama had lured both Trip and me to The Chatham Club. I hadn't been to the club since coming back to town, and I was torn about going when she suggested it. The club was the one place besides his study that really reminded me of Daddy.

Daddy. Thinking about him still wrecked me. He'd always been the fun one…the life of the party everywhere he went. Trip had always been a lot like him, actually. My father had always been a joker, constantly laughing and making others laugh in return. And the Chatham Club was his favorite place to eat; he'd get as excited about their brunch as a little kid on his first visit to Disneyworld.

After a bit of private deliberation, I decided that if I was going to live in Savannah, I needed to face the club head on. Knowing Cosmo, she was scheming to fix one (or both) of us up with some well-bred ex-debutante, but she'd scheme Machiavellian-style whether I brunched or not, and a man has to eat.

It was a clear day, so the dining room's panoramic windows offered an unencumbered view of Savannah's famed historic district and the river. Seeing the river made me think of Annabelle, and I wondered if she'd ever speak to me again. I'd never seen anyone as angry as she'd been in the car when

I'd wedged my foot squarely in my mouth. If looks could kill, Cosmo would have been burying my ass at sea. I'd gone way too far with what I'd said, and it was evident I'd leapt across some amorphous line of hers. I wasn't sure if she held a grudge, but based on my single afternoon with her, she certainly seemed like the type. If by some sort of fluke Annabelle and Trip turned into something lasting, her hostility toward me was sure to make for some awkward family Christmases.

When the entrees arrived, Trip mentioned that he and Annie were going out to get a dress later that afternoon. Mama seemed peeved that I knew who he was referring to and demanded to know who this "Annie person" was and why she hadn't yet met her. Meanwhile, I downed my whisky sour, reveling at the burn in my chest and belly. The mental image of Annie in a changing room in various stages of undress was mighty distracting. It irked me that I had given her a second thought. But now that I had, I found it impossible not to give her a third…and a fourth…

When it became evident that Annie's family was of no importance and that Trip had no plans to introduce the two of them, Cosmo promptly changed the subject.

"Tell me, Son. Has Violet agreed to let you have Maisie for Halloween? I've found her the perfect costume." Mama's eyes sparkled youthfully when she spoke Trip's daughter's name. Though she'd never admit it, I have no doubt that Mama had always wished I'd been a girl. When Violet and Trip found out they were expecting a daughter, I swear Mama was transformed. For the first time in my life, she exuded an undeniably nurturing aura. She smiled more easily and laughed for the first time since we'd buried Daddy.

It was undeniably the "girl factor." At long last, she had an excuse to buy frilly pink underwear and ostentatious dresses no toddler could actually play in. Little Maisie gave her purpose – a tiny blonde "sugar bean" that she could spoil rotten. Maisie was instrumental to keeping Cosmo relevant in Trip's life, and she knew it all too well.

I watched as Trip's features clouded over. The subject of his daughter obviously troubled him. His answer was brief.

"Yep."

"You don't look very pleased about it," I chimed in and Trip's frazzled eyes met mine.

"She's letting me have her for the entire week-end." He stated with the solemnness of a prison guard at an execution. I wondered if he was up for having a three-year-old for two hours, much less two days.

"Why, Trip! That's marvelous news!" Cosmo gushed. Trip's eyes narrowed. He gave her a cool sideways glance, and his expression shifted to one of grandiose distaste.

Considering Trip had always been Cosmo's favorite, his responses to her were downright frigid, even compared to my own. My brother had always been generous to a fault, notorious in his drinking days for buying rounds for the house to the tune of thousands of dollars in one night. The fact that Mama had been hocking antiques from the family estate spoke volumes about Trip's lack of financial assistance to her.

I pondered the mystery of their falling out as I slowly chewed my Kobe beef. When Trip had turned twenty-five, he'd been granted total access to his trust fund. Since before Daddy died, he'd had the means to set Mama up for life in the style she was accustomed to without making a dent in his fortune. Yet as far as I knew, he hadn't given her a dime. Earlier that morning, he'd made it clear on the phone that the only reason he'd come to lunch with her was because I would be there.

Their current lack of relationship absolutely perplexed me. They'd always been close when we were growing up. In fact, I'd kind of been jealous of the all attention and adoration she gave him. My earliest childhood memories all involved some sort of Tripapalooza with Mama fawning all over him. Not long before Daddy died, things eroded between Trip and Mama. I always wondered if it was some kooky Oedipus thing since he was marrying Violet, but Cosmo liked Vi, so it didn't really add up.

Come to think of it, I always sensed that Trip was also Daddy's favorite. It seemed like he took him everywhere he went. I tell myself it was because Trip was five years older than me, but that could just be my adult mind glossing over the facts. Even my nanny, Athena, noticed that neither of my parents had much interest in me. She always let me tag along with her; I can only assume this was because she felt sorry for me. That's how I ended up meeting Randall. Athena's son was a boxer at his gym. Of course, Hard Knocks was Randall's father's gym back then, but Randall was already an assistant trainer. I can still recall the fascination I had at the antique steam heat radiators and the rank smell of determination emanating from the place. The rhythmic sound of fists beating against heavy bags had me entranced before I'd even seen my first fight.

Mama was appalled when I asked to train as a boxer, but Daddy quickly countered that "colored kids using me as a punching bag" would help me to become "a real man." When Cosmo realized this was not just a passing fancy of mine, she finally conceded. Even at the tender age of eleven, I could be exceptionally persuasive when properly motivated. I knew I would never have Trip's artistic talent, nor would I break his state record in the four hundred meter hurdles. So instead of trying, I chose to blaze my own trail.

"How is Violet these days?" Memories of my lonely childhood fanned my envy, so I intentionally pressed my thumb into the open wound Vi had left in our family. Both Mama and Trip trained sharp blue eyes on me.

"She's well. Engaged to a banker from Charleston. They're announcing it in a couple of weeks." Trip stared down at the table and spoke as if the words tasted like curdled milk on his tongue. Cosmo placed an impeccably manicured hand to her chest, and her expertly painted eyes bugged out, giving her a cartoonish appearance.

"So I suppose she thinks she's just going to uproot Maisie and move to Charleston?" Though Mama's question sounded legit, her expression already seemed to be calculating her next move on the chessboard.

"No, Mama. She's going to leave Maisie behind… in a closet. With a bag of Doritos." I shook my head snidely, downed the rest of my drink, and waved my empty glass at the waiter. Cosmo shot me an icy scowl, but I watched her expression morph to one of shock as she gaped over my shoulder. Her lips parted in surprise. and it was as if she'd completely forgotten what we'd been discussing. Unable to resist, I shifted in my seat to see who or what had struck my verbose mother speechless.

At the table behind me sat a Heisman trophy

winner, a big hulk of a black man. At first, I thought Mama was being racist (a black in *our* club not carrying a tray? God forbid!), and I was ready to wring her wrinkled neck. Then my eyes were drawn to a dashing older gentleman that seemed to be holding court at the same table. He wore navy Armani that nearly matched his shrewd eyes and contrasted dramatically with his salt and pepper hair. There were two men hovering behind him who could have passed for secret service. The man's confident mannerisms demanded my focus, and it took me a full minute to even notice he was also dining with the mayor of Savannah and the owner of the local paper. He simply *outshone* all of them. It occurred to me that I'd seen him somewhere before (he'd be pretty damned hard to forget), but I just couldn't place him. He wore a wry smile and regarded my mother in a familiar, almost filthy manner that immediately got under my skin.

"Who the hell is that?" I scoffed, turning back to her. She had paled visibly, and this alarmed me. Cosmo is a ball- breaking hard ass and usually pretty unflappable. My instinct was to grab her by the arm and drag her the hell out of there. I turned to Trip for moral support and saw that he looked worse than Mama did. He stared fixedly at his lap, drained of color and trembling.

Mama seemed to find her voice. "Who?"

"The skeevy guy in the navy suit."

"Sebastian Wakefield," Mama practically whispered his name, and her voice sounded like it was coming from miles away. "He was your father's business partner."

I shot Trip a curious glance. He looked at me grimly; the skin around his mouth looked almost gray, and he packed his cigarettes with visibly shaking hands. A moment later, he shot to his feet and mumbled something about meeting us outside. As he passed their table, Mr. Wakefield shot a knowing smile at Trip, but Trip didn't even look in his direction. I looked on as Trip tore out of the main dining area and noticed with surprise that Wakefield was now focusing on me, but his smile had vanished. He nodded at me thoughtfully, and I turned back to Mama, perplexed.

"Business partner? In which company?" The Beaumonts were major shareholders in companies all over the southeast United States when my father was my age. Unfortunately, it was common knowledge that my father had no head for business and never grew the family fortune like his father before him. Thankfully, he hadn't lost his shirt; he'd just let the dynasty become a bit dusty and stagnant.

"He served on several of the board of directors. He and your Daddy were fraternity brothers. He sold his shares and moved west years ago."

I swirled the ice in my glass thoughtfully. "He looks familiar."

"He comes back to Savannah from time to time." Her eyes flitted back in Mr. Wakefield's direction, and something about her expression made me feel like a Peeping Tom. This time, I opted not to look over my shoulder.

So it wasn't much of a leap to say I was distracted by my family's bizarre behavior and a little under the influence when Randall and I were putting on our exhibition.

"Are you drunk?" Randall demanded once the others were gone and we were headed into the locker room. He frowned at me disapprovingly and folded his monstrous arms across his chest. I knew I'd better explain myself, or he'd promptly kick my ass as only a best friend can.

"I had a couple of sours at lunch," I blurted.

"At *lunch*? Okay, Trip Junior. What the hell is wrong with you?"

"It's not like that, Randall." My overall exasperation at being judged had reached an all-time high.

"Oh yeah? What *is* it like, exactly? Dropping out of school...couch surfing at your mom's... drinking hard liquor *during the day*! They teach you that shit at Harvard, Sam?" Randall's brown cheeks had a red under glow to them. His fury was obvious, and I had no plausible explana-tion for my out of character lackadaisical behavior. I felt my shoulders sag, and I stopped mid-act while unlacing my shoe.

"I don't know what I'm doing." I confessed, staring at the cracked cement floor.

"Well that much is painfully obvious. You need to get a grip, Beaumont." Randall pontificated. When I didn't argue or even respond, his tone and volume softened. "Maybe you should apply to a law school closer to home…"

"No. I'm done. I don't have the stomach for that kind of life." Randall and I had already discussed school until I was blue in the face. When I set out for Harvard, I'd intended to honor Daddy's wishes and specialize in corporate law. Even though he paid little attention to me in my youth, when I shone on the debate team and later graduated valedictorian, he started bragging about me to his cronies. He claimed I was "a shark" and often compared me to his father. It sounds pathetic now, but back then I took great pride in the comparison to the original Reginald Beaumont, who'd been single handedly responsible for doubling the family's net worth. So I'd had designs on working for the family corporation, but I soon found I had no appetite for screwing people over. I discovered that studying economic torts made me loathe my legacy. Regardless of my family name, I had no desire to follow in the footsteps of slave owners who'd once cornered the market on cotton. The more law school I experienced, the more obvious it was that Harvard and I were through. With all my apprehension and uncertainty about where I was headed, that was one fact I was certain about.

Seeming to comprehend just how lost I was, Randall appeared momentarily sympathetic, but that expression disappeared just as quickly. "Well then, what's next? Are you gonna just sit around and sip high balls all day on your yacht with your brother?"

"Trip quit drinking." The words tumbled out of my mouth, and I was shocked at how defensive I sounded. It seemed I was still capable of sticking up for Trip, and that surprised the shit out of me. I knew Randall was onto something, though, and it stung.

"Good for him. So are you auditioning for the vacant role of town drunk?" His fierce eyes dared me to argue, but we both knew he wasn't wrong. I had been acting pretty foolish, and the whole booze thing was a slippery slope. Time to nip it in the bud, hard and fast

"Alright, alright. Enough. Message received, asshole." I glowered at him, and he seemed satisfied – at least temporarily – with my response.

"So what the hell have you been doing with your time? 'Cause I *know* you ain't been working out." He took a seat next to me on the bench. He was a couple of inches shorter than I, but damn! That dude is *big*! And even now that I was a grown man, his attitude made him seem large than life.

"Not a lot. I met a girl…but she's into Trip."

"Jesus. Not again. Can't he find his own dates?" His snarky backdoor reference to Violet made me laugh.

"Nice. No, this time I'm the one who's late to the party. Her name's Annabelle. She really hot, but she's a royal pain in the ass. I'm pretty sure she doesn't think much of me, anyway." I stood and kicked off my shoes.

"I like her already." He flashed a pearly smile and motioned for me to continue.

"She told me I'm a dumbass for quitting school. And apparently I'm also a tool for not singing 'Kumbaya' at Al-Anon meetings with Trip." I shed my sweat-drenched shirt and headed for the showers.

"So she's hot *and* insightful. Next time you see this Annabelle, give her my number!" he called after me. I rolled my eyes, but couldn't contain an amused grin. God, I'd missed that son of a bitch. One goal was clear in my mind: I was going to knock *him* square on *his* ass. And soon.

CHAPTER SIX
Annie

I bounced my knee up and down nervously as I waited for the light to turn green. I would be at Trip's house in less than five minutes, and I was operating on only four hours of sleep. My therapist used to tell me that sleep disorders were common in people with a history like mine and had prescribed me several different pills to turn my brain off at night. Last night I'd had a particularly disturbing dream, so I'd been up reading since 3:45.

It was one of those gauzy dreams that felt as if you were viewing everything through a lens smeared with Vaseline, like in the old movies. Things aren't clear or chronological, just a bunch of disjointed images and sensations. I recall that I was in a warm bubble bath and that I wasn't alone. I could feel a rock hard man behind me, his torso against my back, his erection pressed deliciously against my backside. Large masculine hands stroked every inch of my slick skin. Wildly aroused,

I turned over in the tub to face my dream guy, and my head nearly exploded when I realized it was Sam Fucking Beaumont.

I awoke with a gasp, confused and sexually frustrated. The ache between my legs was ferocious. Apparently my subconscious is a filthy little slut.

I tried to read a novel, hoping to fall back to sleep, but it was a steamy romance, and my mind kept wandering back to the dream. Sam's reticent eyes were the one image that was not at all fuzzy. Preoccupied, I tossed my e-reader aside and stared at the ceiling, barely visible by the light of the nearly full moon. I wondered what my therapist would say about all of this and came to the conclusion it was time to find a new one here in Savannah. Hypnotherapy had made a huge difference for me in the past, but I'd slacked off and hadn't been to any sort of counseling since moving to Georgia. I'd managed to wean myself off of the anxiety meds, and for the most part, I found my ability to survive on four to five hours of sleep helpful as a student. I knew the antidepressants were a must. I was a lifer on those, no doubt about it. But some nights I just craved sleep, and that night was one of them. So once the sun rose, I'd layered on too much concealer to cover the dark circles under my eyes. By the time I arrived at Trip's, I'd had way too much coffee and entirely too much salacious advice from Jayse.

My nerves were a live wire when I parked my freshly cleaned car in front of his place. I forced myself to stop and take three deep breaths. Casual and simple. That's what I needed. No drama. If I was going to get through the day, I needed to stop obsessing about the way Trip looked at his ex-wife *and* the way Sam looked at me. As I climbed out of the car and made my way up the walk, I caught myself wringing my hands and I forced them to my sides. I was just about to tap on the front door, when I realized that the loud music I heard was leaking from the studio at the back of the house.

Three times I knocked on the studio door, each time louder than the last. Finally I pushed my way in, and wandered through the maze of canvases to his workroom, which was obviously the source of the eclectic music. Trip had turned the canvas around since I'd last seen it, and I presumed the change had to do with the time of day and the way the light entered his makeshift studio.

His back was to me, and he balanced a painter's palette in his left hand. He held multiple brushes in his right hand, using a tiny one to tweak "the avenue of oaks" painting, which to my amateur eyes had no need for alteration. He stood shirtless, his broad shoulders tapering perfectly to his narrow hips. My eyebrows twitched as I admired how his jeans hung dangerously low on his hips. I drew nearer, and the light changed enough that I noticed a large faded scar that spanned from his right shoulder, down to his elbow, and over to his mid back. I sucked in my breath, but the loud music masked my presence from him. At some point in his life, he'd been badly burned, and against all reason, I had the overwhelming urge to reach out and touch his damaged flesh. I saw that his opposite arm and shoulder blade displayed large, vibrant tattoos, and I wondered if their presence was a result of Trip's artistic compulsion for symmetry.

Feeling voyeuristic, my guilty conscience compelled me to make my presence known. I inched closer to him and gently placed my hand on his scarred shoulder. He flinched, dropping his palette and brushes and instinctively shielded his face with wide, terrified eyes. He nearly missed knocking the easel over, as he came to a stop against the wall five feet away from me. The panic-stricken expression he wore reminded me of my little sister Becca's face when we used to hide in the closet during her father's drunken rampages.

"Hey…it's just me." I managed a soft, gentle tone, though I'd nearly shrieked. Trip peeked at me over his tattooed shoulder, and his mask of calm returned in the blink of an eye. Relief softened him, and the corner of his mouth curled upward. If he was self-conscious about his reaction or his damaged exposed skin, he hid it with the skill of 007.

I watched as his entire body relaxed. He

straightened to his full height and squinting as if he'd just noticed how loud the music was, he leaned over swatting at the volume of the blaring sound system. He succeeded in turning it way down and graced me with his crooked grin, as if nothing bizarre had just happened. "Sigur Ros. Music to dream by."

"Never heard of them." I replied, shaking my head with a frown. His ability to shift gears so quickly disturbed me. As I opened my mouth to ask about his dramatic reaction, his eyes implored me to leave it alone. I shut my mouth and nodded. He broke into a wide, boyish smile.

My traitorous eyes took in the impeccable front half of his exposed body. Not a single burn, scar, or blemish marred his chiseled arms, chest, or abs. And I was looking…really hard. Thankfully, he knelt to pick up his palette and brushes and wiped off his hands while I ogled him, so I didn't humiliate myself.

To my disappointment, he snagged a black shirt off a nearby chair and tossed it over his head.

"Ready?" Though his smile was still in place, his face seemed blotchy and his eyes appeared puffy. I could tell something was up with him, something beyond my surprise arrival.

"Yes. Trip…are you Ok?"

"Yeah," He spoke the word, but the way he looked away toward the carpet told a different story.

"Bullshit," I contradicted him, placing my hand delicately on his arm.

His face fell into an uneasy grimace, and he placed his hand on top of mine. "It's been a rough day. I ran into someone from my past."

"Violet?" The question was out before I'd formed it. His surprise gave way to a look of understanding.

"No. Much, much worse. Let's just say it's been a long time since I've had to call my sponsor before five o'clock." He raked a hand through his tousled hair and chuckled without a hint of mirth. He seemed to pause when he looked at the expression on my face, and he brushed a loose tendril of my hair off of my cheek. He was standing dangerously close to me, and we silently studied each other's eyes. For a second, I thought he might kiss me and realized I wasn't sure it was what I wanted. Something about the darkness in him seemed like more than I could handle. When he didn't, relief hit me like an avalanche. I struggled to make sense of what my instincts were trying to tell me. I decided to stop psychoanalyzing, to take the path my gut told me to and keep my hands to myself – for now. Unsure of what else to do, I patted him on the cheek with a rueful grin.

"Let's go get that dress. Then you can take me to dinner. But I'm picking the place this time. And believe it or not, I can be an excellent listener when

I set my mind to it."

With Trip sprawled carelessly in the passenger seat, we made our way toward Broughton Street. My curiosity ate at me like a starving piranha, and finally I worked up the moxie to begin my overdue inquisition.

"How did you lose your license?" I could tell I'd caught him off guard and he paused.

"I don't think you'd continue to like me much if you knew." He sounded resigned, as if he knew we were going to have the conversation one way or the other.

"Try me."

"It was a dark time, Angel. I was very drunk and got it into my head to drive to Mama's and yell at her. I didn't get more than a couple of blocks from home before I ran into a tree. Fortunately, I wasn't going fast." He stopped, licking his lips nervously. "Maisie was in the back seat. Blitzed as I was, I had her fastened in the car seat, thank God. "

My stomach dropped, and I thought about the blistering look in Violet's eyes when she'd brought up Trip losing his license. I didn't blame her at all. Drunk driving with her little girl in the car! If he'd been my husband, I would have put him in traction.

"That was the second time Sam had to drive me to rehab. He railed on me for the entire car ride. He told me I needed to 'get my shit straight' or he'd disown me. Ever since the night of the accident, he treats me like a stranger. And he's not the only one. Violet served me divorce papers while I was in rehab."

Conflicted, I grasped for something to say. I relished that he'd trusted me enough to confide in me, but I began to understand and even respect Sam's hesitation about Trip. I'd been burned by my mother's selfishness and felt the shame when I'd fallen for her false promises to "do better." At age fourteen, I'd spent several nights in budget-planning classes, courtesy of Gambler's Anonymous, while she was out pissing away our child support. That ever-present, ingrained leeriness rumbled around inside me and probably always would. That said, I was burdened by the openness I recognized on Trip's face, and my mind raced for an appropriate response. He seemed as if he were waiting for a well-deserved slap in the face that he had no intention of blocking. I felt compelled to speak, so I blurted the first thing that came to mind.

"Thank you for telling me." I watched as a storm gathered behind his eyes.

"Grant me the serenity to accept the things I cannot change...yadda yadda," he muttered crossly, pointing out a prime parking spot.

When I opened the car door, he was there to offer me his hand. I reached out for it, and he pulled me up. We stepped onto the sidewalk and began the hunt. As the afternoon progressed, we wandered through some rather upscale shops. Wherever we went, Trip seemed to silently command a sort of awe from the shopkeepers, who brushed their employees aside in an effort to serve him themselves. It was evident that they knew him by sight and that the name Beaumont meant something serious in Savannah. At one point, he leaned in and whispered in my ear.

"Thanks for treating me like a normal person." He squeezed my hand tighter, and I looked at him wide-eyed. It surprised me that Trip knew how unusual their treatment of him was, especially since he'd been born into the good life. As the day wore on, we got cozier, walking arm in arm or with his arm around me. We held hands often, and I sometimes got the feeling he was using me as a human shield. The younger shop girls (and one of the shop boys) openly regarded me with jealousy. Trip had mastered the art of cool, but I was starting to see small cracks in his façade, like a china doll that had been painstakingly repaired, but would never quite look the same. His money and status made him powerful, but also very anxious and wary. Try as I might not to feel it, it was hard not to be drunk with power by osmosis. Being pampered and doted on was incredibly addictive.

By the time we neared the entrance to Marc by Marc Jacobs, we had several bags of goodies, including a stuffed kitty for his daughter and a pair of sterling silver cufflinks shaped like boxing gloves for his asshole brother's twenty-fifth birthday. Trip mentioned that the anniversary of the blessed event of Sam's birth was at the end of the December. But still, we had no dress. Trip paused on our way into the store.

"Is all the groveling annoying you as much as it is me?" He ran a hand through his messy hair, looking outright flustered for the first time all day long.

"I'll live," I replied with a tired sigh. He tilted my chin up and seemed to assess my level of fatigue. His smooth confidence returned, and I smirked. My contribution to his ability to seize control of himself aroused me. I suppressed a shudder that had threatened to surface.

"If we can't find something suitable here, I'll have a dress made for you. I have an excellent tailor, but it'll delay the sitting, so I was hoping to avoid it."

I had no response, as I was a total fish out of water, so I merely nodded. Who has a tailor? Stinking-rich Beaumonts do, apparently. The air conditioning felt lovely as we crossed the threshold. The vast store stood nearly empty, as it was 5:30 and most shoppers were clamoring for a dinner table at one of the nearby restaurants. The overly accommodating manager enlisted all available employees to pull every potential white dress, skirt and blouse in the joint. Trip immediately insisted they remove all the skirts and blouses and take them away. When they brought us both an unrequested glass of wine, Trip gently waved the stemware away and asked for Cokes instead. When the manager returned with two frosty bottles, he unceremoniously dismissed her and told her to take her employees with her. Considering how uncomfortable the VIP treatment had made him all day, he certainly knew how to play the game. I took my Coke into the dressing room and tried on two dresses, which I modeled for him. Neither of us was particularly impressed with either of them.

At that point, my lack of food and sleep began to cripple me. I started to feel petulant and bored, like a small child long overdue for her afternoon nap. I pulled a plunging silk gown from its hanger and stepped into it. The zipper was unreachable, and I poked my head out of the dressing room. The store's speakers pumped a seductive beat, and I saw Trip lounging on a nearby sofa. His bored expression changed when he looked at my body in the unsecured dress. He slowly sat forward unconsciously, as if about to pounce. The look of rapt attention he wore had me suddenly feeling playful. I glanced around, noticing no one else in sight.

"Can you zip me?" I asked, afraid to step out of the room for fear of falling completely out of the open gown.

"I'm at your service." He drawled, climbing to

his feet and sauntering in my direction. I licked my lips at the sight of his cocky swagger, and when he was close, I turned to present my bare back to him. I released the dress from my grasp, and could feel the slick material expose me in the back all the way down to my waist. I looked over my shoulder at him and saw his eyebrows rise and his lip curl in a testosterone-fueled smile.

"That's one hell of a dress." His voice sounded husky, and I felt him take the zipper in his hands. He paused, and his fingertip grazed the length of my spine, slowly... admirably. On impulse, I turned and pulled him into the dressing room by his shirt collar.

He pulled back a bit, apprehension plastered on his face.

No. That won't do. Not at all.

I attempted to lure him in with a sly smile, beckoning with my finger for him to come closer. His eyes flashed hungrily, and he responded to my invitation by swiftly swinging the door shut and pinning me against the wall of the dressing room. He held me with his heated gaze, his finger slowly trailing all the way from the hollow of my neck to the area between my breasts. I gasped as the need for his touch overruled my judgment. I reveled in the power I had over him, at the blatant fascination in his cobalt eyes.

A small voice cried out in the back of my mind,

begging and demanding me to stop. My compulsive need to have his undivided attention won out, and I slammed shut the vault on that voice, spinning the lock. My hands were in his rakish hair, as I tugged at it to pull his mouth closer to mine. Our lips locked in a scorching kiss, and he tasted like a naughty mix of nicotine and salty goodness. His talented hands easily brushed aside the unsecured straps of the gown, exposing my bare breasts. He pulled his lips from mine and his lustful eyes roamed my flesh. I sighed and closed my eyes victoriously, knowing I held all the cards as his skillful mouth trailed down my ear to my collarbone. As I leaned my head against the wall of the dressing room, that old familiar numbness slowly trickled over me. Like my own unique morphine taking hold, it was like I was hovering outside of my body looking down on us. Trip's lips were on mine again, and my thoughts drifted to my past sexual mishaps. I suppose I could thank my childhood monster for grooming me to be a world-class fuck up.

A collage of my transgressions flashed on the blank screen of my closed eyelids like one of those war propaganda news reels from World War II. My carnal misconduct....my fucking inability to stop myself from jumping into a situation crotch first. Moment by moment, I recounted the sepia highlights of my necrotic sex life. Unprotected sex with my amateur tattoo artist, Nick... inappropriate behavior my senior year with an innocent freshman boy...my filthy tryst with a married T.A. when I was an undergrad. Even as I scolded myself, I felt my hands grasp the button of Trip's jeans on autopilot.

He grabbed both of my wrists suddenly, stopping me millimeters short of my goal. He pulled back, and his conflicted expression both infuriated and humiliated me. He seemed to analyze every pore on my face, and I felt bare and exposed under his scrutiny... and not in a good way. I darted my eyes away, suddenly feeling like a child who'd been caught with her hand in the cookie jar.

"Annie." Trip's voice was a hushed whisper, and his Adam's apple bobbed as he swallowed with far too much effort. Humiliation at my own tawdry behavior had already shoved arousal aside. I had a feeling whatever was going to come out of his mouth next would be bad news, and if I hadn't been half naked, I probably would have fled. "You're amazing. I have no doubt we could have all sorts of fun. But I need to be completely honest with you."

My anger dissipated as mercurially as it had appeared and shame took its place. I had been trained to recognize and understand my behavior. This scenario was far from new. I was "acting out sexually" as my therapist often called it. It was bad enough when I pulled crap like this with some unsuspecting schmuck at a bar, but Trip? It was so uncool of me. He was trying to get better. The last thing he needed was me to drop my matching baggage on him.

That's you, Ugly Mutt. You could fuck up a wet dream.

I was failing spectacularly, letting my body get ahead of my brain. Zero to 100 miles per hour, gone in 60 seconds. Messing with him was such a bad, *bad* idea.

"I can't start a new relationship—not at this point in my recovery." An expression of exasperated grief was etched on his handsome face, and he raked through his near-black hair with one hand. "And…and I still love Violet. Dammit, I wish to God I didn't. But it's out of my control."

This was his huge revelation? My gaze met his, and he seemed to be waiting for me to punch him or claw out his eyes. He may as well have told me the sky was blue, or water was wet. "I know, Trip."

Wide eyed, he seemed confused by my reaction, but pressed on. "She's my soul's better half. I think you deserve to have that. I'm not anywhere near ready for a fraction of that. Honestly, I'm pretty sure it's not a future possibility. That kind of thing only comes around once." He looked ill, and it was obvious that his frankness was harder on him than it was on me. Overwhelmed with pity for him, it was hard not to admire his seemingly limitless courage.

Reality seeped back into my cloudy brain. I had a zen-like moment of clarity as I calmly considered the facts. None of this was meant to be, and for once I had the opportunity to make the healthy call. I surprised myself when I proceeded to do just that.

"You're right. I do deserve more. So do you." I awkwardly pulled away from him and returned my gown to its rightful position. Feeling uncomfortable with my state of exposure on more than just a physical level, I shielded myself, crossing my arms in front of me. Suddenly sheepish, I turned away from him with my face on fire.

So this is a normal response to a virtual stranger seeing you half dressed. How about that?

Way to go, 'Ho.

"I'm sorry," Trip offered, and when I glanced over my shoulder, I noticed his eyes closed. He shook his head, wearing a look of remorse that wasn't warranted.

"Trip, I'm not some school girl with a crush. I'm not going to cry and beg you to love me." He looked relieved at my reply and placed his palms on his eyes with a frustrated groan.

"This whole thing sucks, Annie. You're so beautiful…and I really like hanging out with you. " He removed his hands, but kept his eyes locked on my face, studiously ignoring me from the neck down. His contrite expression really seemed over the top, and I had to roll my eyes. Our current predicament struck me as preposterous, and I couldn't suppress a giggle.

"Oh, for fuck's sake, we can still be friends, Trip. In fact, I insist on it. Now zip up this damn dress. I'm starving." I turned away and felt his shaking hands fumble with the zipper. I brushed past him and left the dressing room to look at myself in the tri-fold mirrors. I tried not to look as impressed as I felt at my own appearance, which reminded me of a Greek goddess in old picture books from when I was a kid. Trip's eyes met mine in the mirror.

"That's the dress, alright," he concurred, as if reading my mind.

"Great. Buy it, already. I'm craving a cheeseburger."

Trip smirked at me and pulled out his cigarettes in anticipation of leaving the confines of the retail world. "Yes, Ma'am."

Twenty minutes later we were kicked back in a booth at B&D's. It was my kind of restaurant-- casual with unpretentious, yet supremely delectable, food. On my way in the door, I'd spotted Jayse's boyfriend, Dale, seated on the opposite side of the restaurant. He was eating in a booth with his parents. Thankfully, they didn't seem to notice us; I was in no mood to explain my fledgling relationship—or lack thereof – with anyone.

We ordered mozzarella sticks and guzzled

sweet tea. Finally, I broke what was rapidly becoming an awkward silence.

"How did you get that scar on your back?" The question didn't appear to offend him, which was a relief after our recent emotional upheaval.

He paused in chewing, and then recovered, washing down the bite of cheese with a swig of tea. "I stumbled into a bonfire."

I blinked in surprise. Another image of Trip's drunken adventures flashed before me. Wincing at the violence of my mental picture, I wondered if this was "the Tybee incident" Sam told me about the day we met.

"Sam saved my life. If he hadn't been right there beside me, we wouldn't be having this conversation. He got some minor burns on his hands trying to put the fire out."

"Jesus," I blurted, and my eyes felt like they were ready to fall out of my head. It was beginning to sound like Sam had spent a lot of time babysitting an adult-sized toddler without the luxury of an oversized baby gate.

"I was in the hospital for several months. They stapled skin grafts into me, the whole nine yards. The burn baths were the worst. Sheer torture. Nothing like how Penthouse portrays a sponge bath from a nurse, I can assure you. My little stint in the Burn Unit was one hell of a detox. You'd think with all that pain and all those weeks without alcohol that I would have quit drinking for good."

"You mean to tell me that *that* wasn't your rock bottom?" Our waitress arrived just then, dropping off our burgers and quickly moving on. He seemed to consider my question carefully before he replied. Then he nodded.

"It was the beginning of the end. I never really got *drunk* again, but I did have a few drinks. I started playing little games with myself. Like, 'I'll just have a couple tonight' or 'I'll have one an hour.' I knew I was headed back in that direction, and I knew I couldn't stop – at least not on my own. That's when I found myself in a church basement at an A.A. meeting."

"Good for you." I nodded and took a huge bite of my burger. B&D's made possibly the best food I'd eaten since being in Savannah, and I was overjoyed at the basic pleasure after our excruciating day. For a few minutes we ate in silence. I saw Dale leaving with his parents. He winked at me and gave me a 'thumbs up.' I rolled my eyes. Trip noticed and glanced over his shoulder in time to see nothing but the door closing behind Dale. He turned back to his food.

"I have a lot of apologies to make. But trying to make amends to Vi...it's virtually hopeless. It was hard on her. I was hard on her." He frowned, and I couldn't shake the thought that he looked like a tragic hero plucked from an epic movie and tossed into a bar and grill. "Now she's shut me out completely; go figure. I totally deserve it, but that doesn't make it any easier to face. I'd give anything for her to give me a second chance, but she's made it clear there's no fixing us. Some things you just can't undo."

It's a little known fact that deep down I'm a hopeless romantic. Don't get me wrong, I *am* a glass-half-empty girl. Not a pessimist, per se. I like to think of it as being pragmatic. A realist, *reasonable*. So it seems like a giant contradiction for me to bawl when I watch *Braveheart* or even *The Little Mermaid*, but the idea of true love gets me every time.

Maybe it's all the years of obsessive reading, but I totally believe in soul-mates. I feel, down deep in my marrow, that when something is right, it's unstoppable. There is no fighting the heart when it wants what it wants. Though I had never found anything remotely like it in my own life, I have the ability to sense connections between others. I kind of suspect that's why my gay-dar is so damned accurate. All that said, from the moment I set eyes on Violet, I *knew* that she and Trip were far from over.

"Does she still love you?" I needed to gauge his thoughts on the matter. That question seemed to jolt him. He practically snickered.

"Of course not. She divorced me." His expression told me he really believed the thought was preposterous.

"Because of your drinking and all the bullshit that went along with it." I remembered Violet's body language at Black Keys and her wide eyes when she heard him call me Angel. "Trip, I saw you two together. And I think you're wrong."

"She was the love of my life. And I drove her away." He looked positively grim at his own declaration.

"So get her back." My words sounded harsh, but I'd only meant them to be firm.

His eyes shot toward the ceiling and then settled on mine. "She's engaged, Annie. She's moved on."

"She's *trying* to move on. But it's not over yet. All's fair until they actually say 'I do'. "

"You don't know Vi. When she settles a subject, she dots the i's and crosses the t's *in permanent marker*." Trip dropped his burger onto his plate as if he'd lost his appetite.

"You mean like when she married you?" I knew I sounded sassy, but he needed a reality check; I happened to be there, so what the hell? "Trip, what if she still loves you and you let her go off and marry someone else without fighting for her? Is that a possibility you're prepared to live with?"

I watched my words take root and start to germinate. I felt like I was catching a glimpse of the

Trip who must have existed before booze destroyed so many of his relationships and brain cells. It was as if my notion lit a pilot light somewhere in his chest, and for a brief instant I prayed I wasn't wildly off base about Violet and that I hadn't overstepped my bounds.

"Hell no." His eyes were downright fierce and his posture declared he was ready for war.

"Well, then," I replied, as I felt a self-satisfied smile overtake me. "I have an idea."

CHAPTER SEVEN
Trip

The coffee here is shit.

Everything else about the meeting room charmed me, from its musty smell and tattered American flag to the warped hardwood floors. There was even a fantastically kitschy painting of black Jesus on the far wall. I tilted my head to the side and really scrutinized the aggressive brush strokes. Whoever the artist was, he or she wasn't half bad.

My need to romanticize the details of the room probably wouldn't have surprised my shrink one bit. After all, this was where I took the first step toward saving my own life – what little there was left to save. But the coffee tasted like motor oil with a side of ass. I made up my mind to anonymously donate a high quality coffee machine and a few cases of the good stuff. Just because we were a bunch of drunks didn't mean our taste buds deserved punishment.

I watched as several of the usual suspects filed

in and each began to claim folding chairs scattered randomly throughout the room. There were a couple of new faces, but for the most part it was the regular diehard contingent of warriors fighting for sobriety. I felt like I knew most of these people better than I knew my own family. And these people most assuredly knew me *much* better than my family did.

As the meeting chairman shuffled papers around at the podium, I decided that I would not share that day. My mood was all over the place, and my attitude completely sucked. Now that I'd had time to consider Annie's proposal, I thought the odds of her plan succeeding were less than one percent.

Annie's entrance into my life had been well timed. I'd just attended my first few meetings and was looking for a reason to swim, not sink. Her exceptional looks captured my attention-I'm a red blooded man, after all-but her exuberant nature helped to lift me from my shadowy prison back into the sun. Annie reminded me a lot of Vi. More accurate-ly, her *aura* reminded me of Vi's aura. They shared a ferocious lust for life and meeting Annie was an inspiration when I needed it the most. When I first spotted her in the cemetery that day, I'd been toiling with whether sobriety was worth fighting for, or whether I should just go buy out a liquor store and let the intoxicating undertow drown me. Then she smiled in that playful way that she does, and it was like I'd been sent a guardian angel. Every encounter I had with her made me feel good about me, and that had been an addiction that matched alcoholism shot for shot. Even now that I'd come to my senses about taking up with her, her enthusiasm in regards to me fighting for my family had been virulently infectious. Now with only myself as a cheering section, deep down in my heart I was sure I'd nuked that bridge when I'd crossed it.

I pulled out my wallet and slid out the picture of Vi holding Maisie when she was a newborn. Violet looked so serene that it took my breath away, but the fact was, Maisie's birth was the beginning of our end. My drinking severely escalated after she arrived. Not because I regretted having her: I wanted that child more than anything, and I adore her. Hell, I'm the one who took Vi's birth control pills and threw them out the window on our honeymoon. The memory of her hysterical laughter when I'd done it caused a crushing pain in my chest, and for a moment I thought I was going to have to leave the meeting before it even began.

Simply put, becoming a father really punctuated the absence of my own. And his death was a subject I dealt with poorly. It triggered depression on a level I'd never experienced before, and rather than see it for what it was, I buried my head in the sand and self-medicated with liquor. One might even say I overdosed more often than not.

But these days I was getting professional help. My A.A. sponsor, Vanessa, had suggested (some might say she *demanded*) I start seeing a shrink a couple of months back. A seasoned nurse, Vanessa had a way of delivering orders that made me agree to them before I knew what I was doing. Vanessa was the perfect sponsor for me. Too young to be a mother figure, she was like the bossy older sister I never had.

Now that I was going to therapy, the good doctor and I were making some real progress in our sessions. My diagnosis of clinical depression came as no surprise, but the secondary diagnosis of PTSD shocked the hell out of me. I looked it up on the internet, ready to prove him wrong. I scrolled through the signs and symptoms, astonished at how much of a textbook case I was.

He put me on some medication and had me coming to talk therapy twice a week. So when Sam wandered back into town, I had the tools to be able to take it on the chin when he lashed out at me with well-deserved hostility. Instead of turning it into a huge fight or reaching for a nearby bottle, I just shut my mouth and listened. But when I'd seen Sebastian Wakefield's sorry ass at the club I ran outside and hid like a coward. Then I puked in the bushes, smoked three cigarettes down to the butt, and called my sponsor. Vanessa's advice was to take a deep breath and to get to a damn meeting.

I'm such a fucking loser. I'm not going to beat this thing. Violet deserves someone a hell of a lot better than me.

But her new fiancé, Dashul Stein, wasn't any better than me. He and I had crossed paths on more than one occasion. Though he lived in Charleston now, he was originally from Savannah and I knew him from sports back in high school. He'd been a pompous, skirt-chaser back then, and he came from a family that would eventually drive Violet nuts with their avid civil war re-enactments and their antiquated beliefs that the fairer sex should stay at home and keep the hearth burning. The thought of Maisie being brought up around that sorry lot of throwbacks made me grit my teeth.

As everyone in the room stood to say the serenity prayer, I tucked the picture of my absent family back into my wallet.

When Violet told me she'd started dating Stein, I'd hired a private detective to follow him. It was shitty, I know. But I don't regret it in the slightest. All I regret is that he hadn't found a damn thing that was useful.

"He likes to drink. " The P.I. revealed, handing me pictures of Stein in various bars.

Wow. Really?

He proceeded to run down the highlights of Dash's life in a nutshell. He worked forty hours a week and attended the Methodist church on Sundays. He liked to blow a lot of money getting manscaped and having massages at the spa. When he wasn't getting metero-sexualized, he spent the rest of his free time sailing, playing racket ball, and going to the occasional strip club with his friends.

Scandalous.

Alright, fine. Maybe he was a better human being than I was, but he wasn't better for Violet. Violet was the kind of girl who's born once a millennium, and she'd be nothing more than a trophy wife to him, like some damaged can of peas marked down at a supermarket. I could almost hear his smug voice as he told his buddy over cigars how she came with baggage, but that baggage was Gucci, so they'd manage somehow.

No. I simply wouldn't allow it.

But if I wanted to win Violet back, it looked like it wouldn't be by incriminating her fiancé.

The loud sniffling sound from Slutty Lara pulled me back to the meeting. I hadn't heard a word anyone had said so far, and Vanessa shot me an irritated look from across the room. I sat up and attempted to focus on Lara's gripping tale about a one night stand she'd just woken up from. I wasn't trying to judge her, but based on the way she was always hanging all over me after meetings, I kind of thought she was a whore whether she was drinking or not.

Unable to listen to another of her "did I or

didn't I use protection" tale, I allowed my mind to wander once more. Annie's idea to pretend that we were a couple had merit. Meeting her seemed to set Violet off that night at Black Keys. Vi could definitely be the jealous type. One time during my drinking days, she'd physically dragged me out of the bar when some girl kissed me on the mouth for buying a round. I hadn't dated anyone else since we'd split, so exaggerating my relationship with Annie, and acting like we were getting all steamy and serious just might get her attention. It certainly couldn't hurt. She was a hair's breadth away from marrying Stein and taking my daughter to a neighboring state, making me an "every other weekend" dad. What the hell did I have to lose by fighting fire with fire?

My nerves were frayed, and I wanted a drink in a way I hadn't in a very long time. So when the chairman asked if anyone else wanted to share, I stood and walked purposefully to the front of the room. It was times like this, when I wanted to find the nearest bar and close the place down, that I needed to jump in with both feet. Or in my case, to just belly flop.

I cleared my throat as I gripped the podium with sweaty palms. "Hi. My name's Trip, and I'm an alcoholic."

CHAPTER EIGHT
Sam

In my silver-gray Hugo Boss suit, I felt like Wall Street's answer to a Cherokee warrior painted for battle. I sat back in the leather chair enviously watching as families enjoyed the emerald garden of Forsythe Park. Meanwhile, I was forced to endure the cloying air conditioning of Armstrong House, home of the law firm which employed the attorneys who served as trustees for both of my trust funds. My twenty-fifth birthday loomed a mere month away, the mythical date when I was suddenly considered mature and capable of managing my own affairs. My lawyers and I had scheduled a series of meetings over the next couple of weeks to hammer out the details of my inheritance. I needed to dig deep and channel my inner counselor. I may not buy into all the "polite society" schlock, but I was not about to be swindled, nor would I squander my portfolio simply because I wasn't in the mood to be indoors.

Hours later, I left Armstrong House confident in my team, but not in myself. They'd done a consummate job of managing my affairs, but they'd raised some tough questions about my future plans for the company and the family estate. All of it had to be sorted out. And soon. I needed a sounding board, needed to hash it all out, and the only person who could truly help in any real way was Trip.

Since he lived so close by, I left the Mercedes where it was and strolled across Forsythe Park. I desperately needed to stretch my legs after all of those hours behind a desk. As I drew close to his front door, I heard music drifting out the open windows of his studio, so I bypassed the front door all together.

"Come in!" I heard a female voice call, and felt all of the air escape my lungs. I was both excited and anxious when I realized Annabelle was on the other side of the door. I caught myself straightening my tie and rolled my eyes at my own behavior before entering his workroom. I was greeted by the sight of my shirtless, paint covered brother and his breathtaking subject.

She lived up to the role of muse in every possible way, from her upswept honey hair to her red painted toes that peeked out from underneath her silky floor-length gown. I felt blood rushing away from my brain, and I tried to ignore the unwelcome pressure in my pants when she turned her azure eyes in my direction. As she scrutinized me, I nearly came unglued. "The south" was indeed rising again. I'd taken off my suit coat halfway across Forsythe Park, and was grateful that I had it to drape in front of my traitorous member.

Trip grinned as he gave my attire an amused once-over and whistled a taunt at my expense. "Every girl's crazy 'bout a sharp dressed man."

"Ha ha," I replied sardonically as I sauntered over to appraise his progress. He'd chosen to position Annabelle squarely in the foreground, and though her image was nowhere near finished, I saw by the outline of her he'd constructed, that in the finished product, she would be nearly three-feet tall.

"What's up?" Trip asked, returning his brush to the canvas. Annie stretched her neck and then resumed an uncomfortable-looking pose. She stared fixedly at a nearby mirror marked with tape, presumably to help her maintain her position and recreate it from day to day. She dropped the pose long enough to place an ear bud in one ear, and fiddle with her I-Pod. It was a relief to know she was preoccupied. It was bad enough to need help from Trip, let alone have my lack of self-sufficiency witnessed.

I proceeded to launch into the broad stokes of my meeting. Trip nodded thoughtfully and then asked some surprisingly appropriate questions. I rattled off the answers regarding projected profits to the best of my recollection. As he continued to create a startlingly accurate visage of Annabelle, we exchanged some general thoughts on different companies in which I would soon be a major shareholder. Trip paused in his task and handed Annabelle a bottle of water out of a cooler, then asked about the current values of certain shares. I mentioned I was thinking of selling my shares in a particularly unimpressive company in order to pay cash for my own place.

Trip stopped painting and turned to me, surprised.

"Finally leaving Cosmo in 'the big house' all by her lonesome? Have you picked a house yet?"

"No, but I found something near the waterfront that I'm considering. I have a couple of appointments with Marybeth next week."

"Marybeth Dutton? She's your realtor? Don't forget to bring condoms." Trip snickered and offered his hand which I mindlessly high fived. As I lowered my hand to its rightful position at my side, I had a moment to register surprise at how automatically I had fallen back into the rhythm of our pre-drinking-binge rapport. It was like I'd wanted so badly to go back to the way things used to be that my superego had lost the ability to catch up.

"Yeah…she seems a bit…deprived," I snorted, and I noticed Annie glance our way. She saw me watching her and quickly stuck in her second ear bud, adjusting the settings on her I-Pod.

"Depraved, maybe…but I doubt that woman is deprived. She practically raped me when I toured this place," Trip murmured in a hushed tone, as if to spare Annabelle the gory details of his past conquests. "Fortunately you can't rape the willing, and well…you know me. But back to business. You really think selling that stock will pay for something on the river?"

"Oh yeah. Current market value on that amount of shares should get me roughly 1.3 million." I shrugged, and Annie spit out her water, narrowly missing both her dress and the canvas. She openly gaped at us both. From the look on her face, I surmised that, though she had her ear buds in her ears, she must have turned the I-Pod off.

"You alright, Angel?"

"So let me get this straight: this *shitty* stock that you *need* to unload is worth 1.3 million dollars?"

Trip and I exchanged confused and somewhat petrified glances, and I nodded with no small amount of hesitation. She rolled her eyes, clearly exasperated and plopped rather ungracefully into a nearby chair, pulling her legs underneath her, Indian-style. That position seemed so unnatural in her formal gown and yet somehow her unpretentiousness endeared her to me. Her mouth, on the other hand…well, I guess looking at her mouth kind of endeared her to me as well. Too bad I couldn't control it with a mute button.

"And I thought *I* had first-world problems!" Her acrid remark was the last thing I needed after the eternal and pretentious day I'd had.

"These are real issues I need to deal with, if you don't mind. And Trip and I have some serious family business to discuss."

She squinted at me, then shrugged. "All that money is wasted on you."

"Is that so?" I folded my arms and glanced at Trip. "I can't wait to hear this."

Annie scoffed. "If I had a quarter of the money and time to burn that the two of you do, I could change the world."

"Could you now? Just how would you do that?" I asked, unable to fight the urge to engage her, since her disdain was clearly aimed at me. As if preparing for a test of endurance, she took another long pull from her water bottle which allowed me a glorious view of her long golden brown throat. I traced her flesh downward with my eyes, briefly resting on the spot just above the plunging neckline. She blinked thoughtfully at me and then blew out a loud breath that disturbed the bangs draping her forehead.

"Didn't you ever have a dream? Back when you were a kid, maybe? Something that inspired you? Can't you think of any way to spread some of that money around and be a part of the community instead of looking down at it from a penthouse view?"

Again, her words cut me to the quick. Annabelle had an uncanny knack for seeing beneath my carefully crafted façade. However, my response to her today was different. Rather than feeling violated by this knack of hers, I felt…invigorated. Trip and I glanced at one another, and I saw that his face mirrored my epiphanic expression.

"I have to go." She sounded apologetic as she turned to Trip. "I have a shift at Black Keys tonight. Some of us wage slaves have to keep society going for y'all. Thanks for the idea about recording my lectures. It's a way better use of my time than listening to your freaky-ass music."

Trip chuckled good-naturedly at her scathing comment. She grinned fondly at him and turned, presenting her zipper to him. I don't think I've ever wanted to be my brother quite so ferociously in my life. He unzipped her, and I was blessed with the vision of a black tribal style rose on her gorgeous right shoulder blade. Feeling like a voyeur, I struggled to avert my eyes as she whipped around perched onto her tiptoes planting a loud kiss on his cheek.

"See ya on Sunday?" Trip asked her. To my delight, Annie fumbled to hold her gown across her chest. Wow, her body was preternaturally perfect.

"You know I have to be at the Marketplace. My crap isn't going to sell itself. It'll have to be Monday."

Trip groaned.

"Paint something else," she replied, bumping him with her hip playfully and heading toward the restroom. "Paint that realtor of yours."

A sly smile spread across Trip's face, and he glanced at me. I couldn't help but grin in return and shake my head.

"You filthy little eavesdropper," Trip called after her with a mix of admiration and amusement.

"Said the skanky man-whore," she replied in a sing-song tone over her perfect tattooed shoulder.

"Mmmm mmm. That girl's the real deal." Trip shook his head as we both admired the view. I thought I noticed a note of regret in his voice, but when I turned his way, he'd ditched his painting gear and was wiping his hands off.

"So...I take it things are going well on *that* front." I nodded to the door she'd just exited. I didn't want details on the Annie situation, but at the same time, I needed to hear his answer.

Trip wore a cautious smile and paused like he had a secret he very badly wanted to share. "We have an understanding."

What the hell does that mean? Is she a booty call, a friend with benefits? A ball-gag wearing submissive? What the hell?

I had the overwhelming urge to choke him.

"I just wish she had more time, so we could get

this painting finished. That girl is way over-scheduled."

"You still have those rubbings of hers?"

"Yep," Trip replied, cocking an eyebrow at me.

As he continued to dab his brush onto the canvas, I laid an idea on him. He seemed pleased at my plan to help Annabelle, thereby helping himself. We worked out the logistics, I made a phone call, and that was that.

Later, my brother tossed his supplies around carelessly, evidently done painting for the day. "So…I suppose you're really here about the Mama and the mansion?"

I nodded and took Annabelle's recently vacated chair, spinning it around backwards and taking a seat. "Yep. Sharing ownership is…awkward. And pointless as far as I'm concerned. Let me start out by saying that I don't want it."

"Neither do I." He responded, turning down the music. His previously lively attitude vanished. He looked positively gloomy as he always did when we even skirted the subject of Daddy. I pressed on.

"We just need to settle it. I say we just sign it over to Cosmo and be done with it. Thoughts?"

I didn't expect an argument. I expected the same distant disinterest he usually displayed when it came to the family business. He'd never had any intention of actively participating in Beaumont affairs, even before Daddy's death. To my astonishment, I watched a dizzying array of emotions battle their way through my brother's features. This went on longer than I was comfortable with, and I felt my stomach sinking slowly toward my knees. He shook his head slowly as if trying to clear it and actually slapped himself on the temple at one point.

Well, this is a whole new flavor of crazy. What fresh hell have I stumbled upon now?

"Trip?" I asked slowly, my voice surprisingly solid considering how much he was creeping me out.

His eyes shot to mine as if I'd snapped my fingers and broken his trance.

"Maybe we should just sell it." He retorted icily. He turned on the faucet and began rinsing out his brushes.

"That's certainly an option, I suppose…but I thought if Mama wanted to stay—"

"I'll think it over." He flipped off the sink with an authoritative voice that stopped me from pressing him. I hadn't heard him sound so commanding since before…Daddy. It was refreshing, but also more than a little confusing. I held my hands up in concession.

"Fine. But don't take too long."

CHAPTER NINE
Annie

I turned my face skyward, basking in the glorious sunshine as Jayse and I walked arm in arm down Broughton Street. Nervous energy had me practically crawling out of my skin. Trip had called me with the news that his mother was hosting a charity event and Violet would be there. We finally had an opportunity to put our surreptitious plan into action. I was sure if we pretended to be dating, she'd become outrageously jealous, and I could help him to get her back.

So for the second time in less than two weeks, I was dress shopping. Trying on clothes really wasn't my thing, but thankfully I had Jayse on my side. When I asked him for fashion advice, he insisted we make a day long extravaganza of it. Or, in his words, "day of complete and total happiness". We began with a decadent brunch at The Firefly Café and had booked pedicures and chair massages for the late afternoon. In the meantime, I needed a dress that, in Trip's words, was "both classy and hot at the same time".

Fuck.

I suspected I'd look a bit like Leo Dicaprio at dinner in *Titanic* during this event, but making Violet jealous had been my idea, so I had no one to blame but myself. Jayse, in typical Jayse fashion, seemed oblivious to my internal nervous breakdown. He prattled on, discussing simple accessories and insisting I have a clutch purse and shoes that match. He had "a vision of the look" I needed, and since his *a capella* group had coincidentally been asked to perform at the same fundraiser, he felt it was his duty to make sure I reflected well *on him*. Thriving in his natural "retail therapy" habitat, he practically floated down the sidewalk, chattering about the amazing set list his group had assembled for the event.

As I half-listened, I thought about Sam. Trip had also invited me to Sam's birthday weekend. I had a little time to decide. It wasn't until the weekend before Christmas. He was having it at Trip's beach house on Tybee Island. I argued that I wouldn't know anyone but Sam and that Sam and I were not exactly friendly, Trip encouraged me to bring Jayse along. I reluctantly agreed, though this would just complicate matters. Jayse still believed – like everyone else did – that Trip and I were an item. Jayse was sure to balk at the sleeping arrangements if I stayed with him, and I could *not* share a room with Trip and guarantee I wouldn't misbehave. Though I knew it was highly unlikely, I hoped we'd have Trip and Violet reunited by that time, and then the whole charade could be over.

Jayse had been teasing me all day about having "a sugar daddy with oceanfront property." I really wanted to spill my guts and tell him that I was still pathetically single, but for all of this to work, he had to believe the ruse. Jayse was physically incapable of keeping a secret, and no one could know Trip and I weren't together. It was all an essential part of our scheme.

I knew I should pick up a gift for Sam while we were out and about, since I never get time to shop. I couldn't help but feel very apprehensive about the idea. What do you get the man who literally has, or at least has the money to have, *everything*? But how awkward would it be to go to a birthday bash for him and be the only one who didn't have a gift?

What the hell do you get a guy who has millions of dollars to toss around on any little thing he likes?

I thought about the cuff links that Trip bought him and decided to give the gift a little bit more thought before lamely resorting to an impulse buy. Besides, today I was carrying around Trip's cash and was on a specific mission. We'd had a wicked fight about his giving me money, but he'd insisted on paying for my outfit for the event. It was probably for the best; I may have ended up in a gown borrowed from a drag queen or a vintage dress from the Salvation Army.

"This one." Jayse yanked a lavender gown off the rack and held it up in front of me critically. It had a halter top and a straight skirt with a side slit. I had to say, color-wise, Jayse knew his stuff.

"I don't know, it looks awfully clingy."

"The skirt and color are conservative. Balance, my dear girl. Try it on. I'll look for shoes."

After paying for Jayse's selection, we decided to take a much-needed food break. In the spirit of our "perfect day" theme, we went to B&D's for lunch. We sat in the same side of the booth, as we always did, so that we could watch people come in the door and dissect them in our typical snarky manner. Blissful bitchiness over double cheese burgers. I had just ripped on a yuppie couple and had Jayse laughing appreciatively when the door chimed again and Sam Beaumont walked through it.

Sam looked incredible, as always. His bright eyes seemed to match his aubergine sweater, which stretched across his sinewy shoulders and arms as if tailored specifically for him. Based on Trip's comment about his "tailor," maybe it was. I felt the smile vanish from my face. Those bedroom eyes of his scanned the room and met mine. He slowed his stride for a moment and shifted his gaze to Jayse, whose approval for Sam's appearance was expressed in a wordless vocalization that sounded as if he'd just bit into a salted caramel.

"Mmmm…" He murmured narrowing his eyes at Sam and turning to me with a sexy grin. The grin faltered when he saw my face, which suddenly felt all tingly and splotchy. "You know him?"

"Sam. Beaumont," I managed, with the talent of a ventriloquist. Jayse whipped his head back in Sam's direction, his blonde curls bouncing chaotically. Sam wore his frosty politician's face now as he proceeded past us to the bar where he was greeted by an attractive black man whose grin lit up the restaurant. Sam took the seat next to him, and the man slapped him on the back in a familiar manner.

"Oooo. Yummy! Tell me you know *him*, too!" Jayse drooled.

"Nope. Sorry."

"Damn."

Our food arrived, but I noticed my appetite had vanished. I could hear Sam's friend exclaim, and I peeked over my shoulder at them. Sam gesticulated with his hands as he spoke, and his friend seemed to listen with surprise and fascination. As Sam continued, the man continued to nod emphatically. Sam lifted his drink to his lips and glanced in my direction. I whipped around and practically ducked down in the booth on instinct.

"Smooth, Annie." Jayse snorted and tossed

some cash on the table and stood. "Stop drooling over your boyfriend's brother and eat something. I'm running to that shoe shop next door. I'll be back in five."

Panicked at being abandoned in the same vicinity as my attractive nemesis, I hissed Jayse's name. He pretended not to hear me and sashayed out the door. I took a few cleansing breathes, trying to push my bathtub wet dream out of my mind. The way Sam had stared at me in Trip's studio last week, like I had nothing on at all, still had me tossing and turning. I shook my head at my own craziness, then cut my burger in half and took a bite. It was so good, I took an even bigger bite, and that's when I saw Sam's friend pass by my booth. He cast me a curious glance and then beamed at me. As I watched him head into the men's room, I felt my shoulders tense as I waited for Sam to pass by. I just wanted to avoid another awkward confrontation. Trying to look deeply involved in my food, I reached for the condiments. The top of the ketchup bottle popped off, dumping its entire contents on my plate. I swore around my half chewed beef and grabbed a handful of napkins just as Sam slid into the seat across from me.

"Big ketchup fan?" His greeting sounded playful, but his posture was as uptight as they come. I choked down my oversized mouthful and washed it down with a drink.

"Hello, Sam. What brings you to B&D's? Slumming?"

He scoffed at my suggestion. "This happens to be my favorite restaurant. What about you? Hot date?" His jaw muscles worked overtime. I felt the sides of my mouth twitch at the thought.

"You could call it that." My obvious amusement seemed to infuriate him, but he somehow managed to stuff it all back inside, as always.

"I thought you were with Trip. What's with the blonde dude?" He deadpanned, almost sounding carefree and curious. Almost. I toyed with my straw and took another drink.

"Who? Jayse?" I smiled naughtily, enjoying that someone as intelligent as Sam could be so imperceptive.

"Are you a couple?"

I started giggling, which quickly progressed into a full throated chuckle. "A couple of what?"

Sam's expression remained unchanged, but his entire face turned scarlet.

"I'll take that as a no. So why's this guy giving me dirty looks?" Sam continued when my laughter died down. I started cackling again because Jayse had most assuredly been giving him dirty looks, but not in the way Sam meant. Sam rolled his eyes, but he seemed mildly entertained by my reaction. It was at that moment that Jayse reappeared beside the booth.

"Sam, this is my roommate, Jayse." I managed, attempting to conceal my amusement.

"Hello." Sam began in an oh-so-Sam-like way. All polite and guarded and scrumptiously southern.

"Charmed, I'm sure." Jayse's effeminate lilt caused Sam's eyes to widen in surprise. Jayse turned back to me with jazz hands. He was so excited he practically sang his words. "Guess what I found? Beige 'fuck me' pumps!"

He placed his hands on his hips as if waiting for the accolades.

"Yay! How much?" I reached for my wallet.

"Eighty." He replied and I winced, pulling out a 100 dollar bill which I handed to him. He waved it in the air and practically skipped out the door.

"I see." Sam stammered, looking after Jayse with shocked awe, as if he were some mythical beast. I simply nodded, relishing the humiliated expression he wore. "Listen. I think we got off on the wrong foot."

"Which time?" My retort tasted overly harsh, but I held his gaze anyway. I'd moved beyond his "daddy issues" comment, but I'd be damned if *I* was going to blink first!

"Take your pick." He didn't flinch at my question, just smiled wryly. There was a pause as he glanced at the table top as if looking at notecards for what to say next. When he spoke again, he leaned forward slightly, fixing his impressive eyes on me.

"Dealing with Trip has been…challenging the last few years. He tends to bring out the worst in me. I just wanted to say that I'm sorry for what I said in the car. I was way out of line. I hope you'll accept my apology, especially since it looks like we'll be crossing paths a lot."

It wasn't until I exhaled that I realized I'd been holding my breath the entire time he spoke. I'd had a lot of time to think about his intentions the day we met, as well as Trip's revelations about his past exploits. Though I knew what Trip had confessed was likely just the tip of a gargantuan iceberg, knowing even that much allowed real sympathy for Sam. And I was actually starting to like him. *A lot.*

Oh shit.

I was afraid. Like jittery-trying-to-get-your-keys-to-unlock-the-car-door-when-you-hear-footsteps-behind-you-in-a-dark-parking-lot afraid. What the hell was it about Sam that freaked me out so much?

You aren't afraid of him, Annie. You're afraid of you.

A feeling of serenity settled over me, and I wanted to tell Sam that I was over our little war. That Trip and I weren't seeing each other. That I'd had a naughty dream about him and that I *ached* to watch his reaction as I described it in explicit detail. I wanted to explain that I'd been a megabitch the day we met and that I would very much like to start over, too.

But I needed to help Trip and stick to our plan. I wished I could find a way to convince Sam that Trip wasn't permanently broken. If I could just get Sam to listen to reason and give Trip one more chance...

One more chance. Would Trip make the most of it? Would he just tumble off the wagon if Violet ignored our little show and went and got married anyway? I considered how many times I'd foolishly bought my mother's promises to change. On reflex, I flashed back to the day I told my grandparents that my mom's boyfriend was touching me. The abject terror I felt when they confronted her was nothing compared to the rage when she proceeded to betray me. I listened in horror as my mom calmly explained that I'd been on cough medicine with codeine and that I'd hallucinated the entire thing. And even as I felt my blood boil and my temples throb like they might explode, I didn't argue. Why bother? I could see by the looks on my grandparents faces that they wanted, no *needed,* it to be true. After all, wouldn't it be a relief if they didn't have to worry about me being irreparably damaged? Wouldn't it be easier to *not* call the police and not have to take in three kids when my mom and the pervert ended up in jail? The sudden, crystal-clear memory racked me with nausea. I dropped my fork and covered my mouth with my napkin as tears sprung into my eyes. I felt Sam reach across the table and place his hand softly on my arm.

"Annabelle?" he murmured, concern plastered all over his handsome face. I closed my eyes and yanked away from his grasp on instinct. The last thing I wanted was to be touched. He pulled back from me, but I couldn't look at him yet. I stared at my plate, fighting through the urge to vomit. After what seemed like forever, I tossed my wad of napkins onto my barely-touched, ketchup covered plate.

"It's all good," I croaked out the words and then looked up at him from under my lashes. He narrowed his eyes at me, a mixture of disbelief and concern battling on his face. "Really. We're cool."

"This must be Annie." Sam's handsome friend had materialized at the perfect moment to save me from having to explain myself. "I thought I'd introduce myself since it looks like Sam doesn't plan to. I'm Randall."

"Randall." I took the hand he offered me and shook it. Then I made the connection and felt a coy smile overtake my lips. "Sam's trainer. The one who kicked his ass."

Sam slumped back in his seat with an irritated groan as Randall threw back his head and laughed. "One and the same."

"Well then, it's truly a pleasure to meet you. I would have *loved* to see that." I took a sip of my Coke and winked at Sam who slanted his eyes sideways at me, but failed to suppress a smirk.

"Come by any Monday, Wednesday, or Friday at four. His ass has a standing date with my mat." Randall handed me his card. He looked me over like he'd heard all about me and was deciding if I lived up to the hype. By his expression, I was guessing the jury was still out.

"Good to know," I replied and looked over his shoulder out of the window. Jayse had a beige pump out of the box and was gesturing to it like one of the bathing suit models on *The Price is Right*. The murmurs of the other customers were escalating to a dull roar, and I feared that if I didn't join him outside, he'd get us banned from B&D's.

"If you'll excuse me gentlemen, I have to go."

As I headed for the door, I heard Randall blurt, "You weren't exaggerating about her hotness."

"Shut up, Randall." I heard Sam snap and I tingled all the way to my toes.

CHAPTER TEN
Sam

Black tie. Just thinking about those two little words exhausts me. A man's preparatory ritual for these occasions is typically eclipsed by that of a woman's, but ladies, I can assure you, it's laborious. Pros like me, however, have it down to a science. As with all things, it helps to have the right tools for the job. A well-fitted, well-tailored tux can be surprisingly comfortable, especially if you're used to wearing one and know how to move in it. And I was and I did. Like most of the men I grew up around, several tuxedos hang in my closet and that night I leaned on the doorframe, staring blankly at them.

First I had a choice to make: midnight blue or black. Usually, I just closed my eyes and yanked one out of the closet, but tonight, that simply wouldn't do. Tonight while Cosmo played Queen Hostess Supreme to Savannah's upper echelon, I planned to get laid. Even with daily trips to the gym, I couldn't seem to blow off enough steam to suppress my taxed libido. It had been far too long since I'd gotten some, and I needed to look my best for tonight's meat market of debutantes Mama so graciously assembled for me. I feared that if I waited much longer to find a playmate, I'd fall prey (like my brother before me) to my gold-digging realtor, the cougarlicious Marybeth Dutton.

As if it had a mind of its own, my hand shot out and pulled the black tux from the closet. If memory served, the black one had a slightly higher success rate for "sealing the deal." I performed my pre-ball ritual: showering, exfoliating, shaving, silk shirt, suspenders, cuff links, money clip. An hour after I began, I hopped in the Mercedes and leisurely maneuvered the turns of Washington Square.

As I headed toward the river, my mind drifted in the unwelcome direction of Annabelle. We'd had a moment at B&D's; that was *not* just my imagination. She had looked at me with the same heat, the same emotional entanglement, the same conflicted frustration that I felt for her. How anyone who looked like her could seem so uncomfortable in her own skin was beyond me, but this was a blatant truth about her. For a fraction of a second after my apology, I'd thought things might have shifted between us. That maybe, like in my wild dreams, she might tell Trip she couldn't see him anymore. That she wanted to see me instead. But her extreme reaction when I touched her—like I'd scalded her with a brand – made me realize that I'd been deluding myself.

She'd made her choice, and it wasn't me. I knew from experience that this familiar sting would fester if I let it. So I'd spent the week bracing myself for a glamorous night of watching her dance in my brother's arms.

Christ.

I was already sexually frustrated enough without that mental picture. With any luck, Cosmo would have all the debs lined up at the entrance awaiting my arrival, like the madam of a Nevada whorehouse. Then I could just grab the first one who caught my eye and drag her upstairs to the nearest bed.

Being a traditionalist, Mama had selected the Marriot Riverfront for her charity ball. I had to hand it to her: Cosmo really knew her stuff. In a few weeks the hotel would host the Christmas Cotillion, and tonight's charity gala was sure to help build the anticipation and rile everyone up for the season. This wasn't accidental. There were no coincidences in Imogene Moore Beaumont's world. The sky wouldn't shed a drop of rain during a garden party unless she allowed it.

After tossing my keys to the valet, I plastered on a game-show-host smile and made my way to the lobby. I came to an abrupt stop, and the smile vanished at the sight of the atrium. Mama had truly outdone herself. I'd been to many functions at the Marriot, and I'd never seen it look better.

Stars shone through the glass ceiling mirroring the sparkling white lights and gauzy silver table cloths below. White flowers and candle light garnished every surface, and champagne fountains framed the large stage at the far side of the space. Jeremy Davis and the Fabulous Equinox Orchestra had already claimed the stage and were in full swing, entertaining enthusiastic throngs of socialites. I veered left and made for the relative sanctuary of the bar, cautiously scanning the crowd for a familiar face. The first person I made eye contact with just happened to be Violet.

It'd been at least six month since I'd last seen her, and she looked better than ever. Her pale skin and fair hair glowed in the candlelight, and her low cut gown was a wardrobe malfunction waiting to happen. She'd already spotted me and was moving purposefully in my direction.

"Sam Beaumont, as I live and breathe..." Her eyebrow twitched just slightly and I broke into a genuine smile. Vi was an incorrigible flirt and she'd never stopped, even after she married my brother. That accent of hers sounded affected and dramatically sweet, but I knew she genuinely liked me, no matter how messy things had been with Trip. I still harbored some guilt for introducing her to him, but I had no more control over their love affair than a sailor has over a mid-Atlantic swell.

She'd never given me reason to think she blamed me. Violet and I had established our own relationship in the years following Daddy's suicide and its disastrous fall out. Like two passengers who'd bailed on a sinking ship, we'd survived a terrible experience together and would somehow be forever bonded by it. Violet stepped forward and made the motion of kissing me on both cheeks. She would never have actually kissed me at a social event like this; she'd been brought up right. Messing up her perfectly glossed lips would be unthinkable. "I heard you were back in town. Why am I *just now* laying eyes on you?"

"Lookin' good, Vi. That haircut suits you," I responded to her rhetorical question.

"Well, I don't have time to screw around with long hair now that Maisie has the ability to run into the street and climb out of windows." Her dry response made me realize just how much I'd missed her and that I was still mourning her loss. I'd always thought divorce had to be worse than death. One still has to see the ex…or at least know they're still out there wandering around in the world.

"How are things?" My face was neutral, but she paused long enough for me understand this was more than a casual question.

"Marvelous." She winked at me coquettishly as I watched her wash the lie down with a chaser of

champagne. "God, I'm glad you're here. I can finally relax now that a real human being has arrived.
Oh! Guess what? I'm leaving Macy's."

"What the hell? I thought you loved it there."
Her career as a buyer was the one thing she still had
left from her "picket fence" plans for the future.

"Of course I do. But I'm leaving them for Sak's
Fifth Avenue!" Her excitement was infectious and
remembering the dreams of the freshman girl I'd
once had a crush on, I grinned.

"That's wonderful. I'm really happy for you." I
replied, and as I basked in the contact high from her
achievement, my mind wandered back to Annabelle's pointed question in the studio weeks before.

Didn't you ever have a dream?

Though I'd tried to thrust both her and her
words from my mind, her questions clung to me like
a spider web. After a couple of days of trying to
brush her away, I actually stopped to consider the
validity of her query. And I *remembered.*

Memories soon led to an idea, and that idea
bloomed and sprouted into a mission. In a matter of
hours, I realized how I could put my plan into action. I'd found a way to give back to the world and
occupy my time with something meaningful and
productive. But I had needed a sounding board –
someone who knew me and was grounded. So I
called Randall and we met for lunch to discuss my
idea. As fate would have it, Annabelle had been sit-

ting fifteen feet away when I dropped my plan on him.

I'm pretty sure he was stunned speechless at first. Not that I didn't have a good idea (he knows I have at least a half a brain), but at how passionate I was about it. When he'd recovered from his initial shock, he said he was thrilled with my suggestion, and he'd agreed to help me out. Psyched to finally have a focus, I wanted to keep the entire thing under wraps until I was ready to surprise my family with it.

"Of course, it's the Sak's in Charleston. You *have* heard my other news, haven't you?" Violet pulled me out of myself and back to the real world.

"About your engagement? Yeah, Trip told me." Her reaction when I spoke his name was fleeting and might have been missed by anyone but me.

"Congrats."

"Ah, thanks, Sam." She leaned in to give me a real hug and whispered in my ear. "You know, you're the only one in that family of yours that was ever worth a damn."

I felt an unwelcome lump in my throat at her kind words, though I knew she was lying to herself. "That fiancé of yours is one lucky man."

"I want you to meet him! He's here some-where." She linked arms with me and gently tugged me into the crowd. Cringing inwardly, I felt like a man walking to the gallows. Meeting this amorphous character was about to usher in the end of an era for me. We simultaneously plucked flutes of champagne from a passing tray, and Violet giggled playfully. I nodded to a few familiar faces as we weaved our way through clusters of haute couture. I could smell her lavender perfume, the same she always wore, and I closed my eyes as the scent propelled me down memory lane. A steady stream of gossip flowed from Violet's shimmering lips, and I was struck by the realization that this could have been any one of dozens of parties we'd been to since we'd met. Same people, same stories, same music, same caterers. For a fleeting moment, I allowed myself the illusion that Daddy hadn't blown his brains out and Trip hadn't destroyed his own life. But when Violet released me from her grip and walked into the arms of a dark-haired stranger, all pretending came to a halt, and my homespun illusion dissipated.

"Dash, I have someone I want you to meet," I heard Violet say as I exchanged uncomfortable nods with the collective group of men gathered around her date. I recognized only one of them, and it was Hank Fredrickson. An old classmate of mine, Hank was a racist tool to whom I'd given two black eyes in the ninth grade. He'd been the class bully since elementary school, but when a boy half your size pummels you in front of the entire student body, your street cred takes a serious blow. Formerly a classic muscle-head, Hank had really let himself go. If this dude was an example of who Vi's fiancé hung with, I figured it was unlikely we'd become yachting buddies.

Joy to the world.

Violet pulled away from her fiancé, and I tried not to gawk. He looked like a movie star – one who would be cast as a gladiator or possibly a Greek God. He smiled at me with polite curiosity. "Sam, I'd like you to meet my fiancé, Dashul Stein. Dash, this is Sam Beaumont."

As expected, his smile evaporated at my surname. His eyes widened slightly, and then he blinked rapidly. "Beaumont?"

"Yep. Ex-brother in law. Nice to meet you anyhow," I quipped, offering my hand. Dashul took it in a very business-appropriate manner. His jaw tightened, and he pressed his lips into a thin, pale line. The entire mood of the group shifted, and the tension was palpable. I silently wondered what I'd done to piss Violet off enough to put me in this predicament. Her smile faltered, but she looked perplexed. She was usually pretty socially savvy, so I wondered if she was tipsy.

"Sam. You're a hell of a lot bigger than your brother." Dashul had evidently recovered from his initial shock, and as he spoke, he wore a disingenuous grin. I shrugged, unsure how to respond to his evaluation. Hank snorted, looking very much like the bulldog mascot of the University of Georgia, and I fixed him with a stone-cold glare. Hank was the kind of guy you had to take out at the knees immediately, before he got any wild ideas. It worked instantly, and he was suddenly very interested in the ice cubes in his scotch. This seemed to set off a couple of his pals, who started to get their hackles up like wolves around a piece of raw meat. One of them stood up in anticipation of a brawl, and I waited for him to start beating on his chest like a silverback gorilla. I turned my glare on him deducing that I could easily take him and that I'd probably come out unscathed, but I didn't want to cause a scene for Violet or put a wrinkle in Cosmo's latest societal triumph. As irritating as Mama was, she needed this as much as starving children in Africa need a dollar a day.

"Sam? Sam Beaumont! Why, there you are; we've been looking *everywhere* for you!" Like my fairy godfather, Annie's flaming pal from the restaurant pushed through the men without a backward glance at them. His impeccable tux contrasted with his unruly blonde curls. Lurking behind him was a small red-haired pretty boy, peeking eagerly at the scene.

"J…Jayse?" I stammered, surprised as hell to see him in this setting.

"Excuse me, gentlemen, but this man's mother is our hostess, and she has requested his presence,"

Jayse gesticulated wildly, speaking about three notches on the volume control louder than necessary. I nodded neutrally, but inside I was overjoyed to be extracted from the tense situation.

"You'd better save a dance for me, Sam Beaumont!" Violet called after us as Jayse unceremoniously yanked me away by the arm.

"Thanks," I muttered when we were out of earshot.

"Anytime. I can spot Neanderthals in heat from twenty paces. We can't have that delicious face of yours pummeled so early in the evening. Oh. This is my boyfriend, Dale." I nodded in greeting to the diminutive ginger who fell in step with us as we made our way back toward the neutral territory of the bar. "Your mother really is looking for you, by the way. When I told her I knew you, she dispatched me on a mission to bring you around. I think she has some hoochie Mama she wants you to meet."

"I don't doubt that." Though I'd barely even exchanged two words with Jayse prior to this conversation, I wasn't at all offended by his overly familiar manner. I liked frank people; they were a refreshingly exotic breed in my universe. It probably didn't hurt that he lived with Annabelle, a concept that I found fascinating. But the prospect of dealing with Cosmo seemed daunting at the moment. I knew I had to go kiss her ring at some point, but I really needed another drink to stomach that pomp and circumstance.

"Jayse, we have to warm up in five," Dale said in a hushed tone as if this were a state secret. I must have looked as confused as I felt because he quickly began to explain. "We're in Noteable. We're performing tonight."

I nodded like I knew what that meant.

"When Annie gets here, let her know I'm in room one-fifteen." Jayse ordered and strutted off with Dale scampering after him.

I shook my head at their abrupt departure. After a tension breaking sigh, I ordered a scotch on the rocks. I was fixated on the bartender's fluid motions, when I felt a tap on my shoulder. Glancing in the mirror behind the bar, I saw my realtor, Marybeth, lurking behind me like a succubus in a medieval tome.

*You have **got** to be kidding me.*

"Hello, stranger." She attempted to dazzle me with a shark-like grin. Pounds of thick black hair were skillfully piled on top of her head, and she apparently lived in a tanning bed. Her gown would have been scandalous on a woman twenty years younger, but on her it may as well have been a welcome mat. I had to give her credit; through genes, exercise, and most likely plastic surgery, she could definitely pull it off.

"Marybeth." I took a long pull off my glass and

contemplated my aforementioned plan to get my pipes cleaned by any means necessary.

"Ready to come back to my office and make an offer?" Her voice made her a shoo-in for a second career as a phone sex operator. I blushed at her double entendre.

"I loved the Bay Street condo, but I have a bigger deal I want your help with first," I responded. She raised a suggestive eyebrow and leaned back against the bar. I gawked at her considerable cleavage, unable to figure out how she kept the flimsy material strategically positioned over her ample chest. I suspected it involved smoke and mirrors.

"Hmmm...I bet you do." She purred. When I simply blinked at her, she straightened up, her megawatt smile fading. I had a front row seat to her seamless transformation from man-eater to shrewd businesswoman. "Oh. You're serious. What did you have in mind?"

I pulled out my wallet and handed her an address. She frowned as she read it and cast cautious eyes at me.

"What the hell do you want with that old place?" She cocked her head to the side, and the bartender slid another drink in front of me.

I sipped it nonchalantly. "That's my business. And I want it for 20,000 less than they are asking. Can you broker the deal?"

She scoffed. "Are there mustaches in Mexico?

Are you sure you want it? It's awfully close to the ghetto."

An eye-roll threatened to escape me, but I managed to suppress it. The neighborhood wasn't that bad. I was certain that for Marybeth, anything that wasn't Ardsley Park or Hilton Head was "the ghetto." She was still eyeing me as if trying to remember the combination of her high school locker. "How serious are you?"

"I'll pay for it in cash," I replied. "And I want to take possession no later than Christmas. If you can make that happen, I'll buy the Bay Street condo as well—for full asking price."

Ms. Dutton's dark eyes danced with the prospect. "Consider it done."

As she sashayed away, I was unable to restrain myself from admiring her heart-shaped ass. Feeling overheated, I loosened my tie as I started to turn back to the bar. I caught sight of Violet, who was yanking her arm out of Dash's grip. He looked amused, but she seemed furious. As she strutted away from him, he shrugged and turned back to his friends. Violet made a beeline for the ladies room. I started after her, but noticed her immediately slow her step and gape at the entrance. My eyes followed her gaze and landed on Trip. He saw me and waved with a friendly smile. He wore black on black, and seeing him dressed to the nines gave me a disturbing sense of déjà vu. By all appearances, he seemed well rested and remarkably happy. I altered my course in his direction, all the while surveying the crowd for his date. When I finally spotted Annabelle, my heart stopped.

As always, her beauty nearly knocked me over. Every curve of her body was showcased in strapless satin, and as she walked toward her date, I saw one perfectly shaped leg peek out from underneath the slit in her silky material. She carried herself with cocky confidence that made the corners of my mouth lift skyward. Though I suspected this sort of engagement was not her typical Saturday night affair, she looked nearly as at home as everyone else did. Annabelle glanced in Violet's direction with a self-satisfied smirk. Violet's porcelain face marred with a frown, and she looked once more at Trip before vanishing into the ladies room.

I resumed moving toward my brother, but I was caught off guard as I realized Annabelle's eyes were on me. Her smug look had vanished, but I wasn't able to pinpoint what emotion lay behind the expression that replaced it. Time seemed to slow down as we drew nearer to one another, and I felt like my limbs were trudging through wet sand. Her skin seemed to shimmer in the low light, giving her an ethereal quality. Her long flaxen hair cascaded over one bare shoulder, and I caught a glimpse of a little black heart tattoo just up and to the left of where her actual heart resided. I could smell the fruity scent of her hair as she and I both reached Trip simultaneously.

"Fashionably late, I see." I forced my eyes in Trip's direction, and he shrugged nonchalantly.

"You know me: I like to make an entrance. Especially with such an enchanting creature on my arm." Annabelle rolled her eyes, but beamed at his compliment. That smile of hers was liquid sunshine.

"You *do* look amazing." It was out of my mouth before my big brain caught up with my smaller, south-of-the-border one. I felt heat rise in my cheeks, but I kept my eyes firmly on hers. I didn't want to look at Trip, afraid my crush on his date was etched on my face. Annabelle blinked twice, and her plum-shaded lips parted in surprise. She awkwardly cast her gaze to the hem of her floor length gown, and then peeked up at me from under impossibly long eyelashes.

"So do you," she replied quietly, and though I grinned like a fool on the inside, I simply nodded once.

"She's gonna turn some heads, alright." Trip chimed in, but he wasn't looking at either of us. He was obviously distracted, scanning the crowd.

"Violet had a front row seat to your grand entrance. She ran off to the restroom like Annie spilled punch on her at the junior high dance," I remarked and watched as Trip turned to Annie with a sly smile. She smiled back with a nod of confirmation. A mysterious look passed between them, and I decided it was probably some private joke of theirs that I most likely didn't want to be privy to.

I swiftly changed the subject. "I'm glad you're finally here. Word on the street is that Cosmo is looking for us."

It was Trip's turn to produce an eye roll, but his didn't come with a side order of smiles.

"Naturally." He looked like I'd just proposed a rectal exam. "Let's get this over with."

I took the lead, guiding them through the swelling crowd. We skirted the dance floor, heading in the opposite direction from the way Vi and I had traveled. As frustrating as it was to see my brother with Annabelle, the solution was not to steer him directly to Hank, Dash, and their douchebag convention.

It wasn't hard to find Mama. She presented herself as the center of attention—more so than the 22 piece band across the room. Standing elevated two feet above the crowd, Cosmo radiated superiority in her shimmering silver gown. Flanked by polished debutantes, it seemed that she was treating the risers (connected to ramps on both sides) as her own personal receiving line.

What a saint. My mother, the ever-selfless philanthropist.

She flitted from person to person like the world's oldest butterfly, exchanging haughty air

kisses with the mayor's wife and whispering something in the ear of an infamous businessman. As
they both chuckled, I marveled at her chameleon
nature and secretly wished I had inherited it. Unfortunately, I'd been born with a soul, so it seemed I
was doomed to a life of blissful mediocrity.

Like the good little soldiers we were, Trip and I
moved into line, readying ourselves to play our
roles as courtiers to the Red Queen. I paused when I
noticed Annabelle release Trip's hand and pull back
from the line. The look she wore could best be described as abject terror. Trip reached out to her, and
she regarded his hand as if it might sprout fangs and
bite her. Another strange wordless exchange occurred, and I saw her shoulders heave with a large
inhale. Her eyes were on mine suddenly, and they
seemed to ask me if this was going to hurt. I gave
her a reassuring smile that even I didn't quite believe. She reluctantly stepped forward, taking her
place at Trip's side. Trip pulled her hand to his lips
and kissed it. It seemed showy and over the top—
Trip's typical M.O.

Soon I stood toe to toe with Mama. She gave
me a Cheshire grin and turned to a pretty, young
brunette beside her.

"Here he is, Jenny. This is Samson."

"Samson!" I heard Annabelle blurt behind me
and then giggle in her melodious way. I purposely
acted as if I hadn't heard her, but noticed Mama's

reptilian eyes shift unblinkingly to the couple behind me. The smile never left her face as she continued.

"Jenny is a Tri-Delt at the University of Georgia." She presented Jenny as if she were a tie that I
might like to try on. Earlier in the evening, I would
have been game, but now I was painfully aware of
Annabelle's eyes burning two holes into the back of
my head. Deciding to give the little pain in my ass a
show as payback for making fun of my name, I took
Jenny's gloved hand and kissed it.

Then I panicked, realizing I had no idea what to
say to the girl. The uncomfortable silence was
growing longer by the second. I urgently grasped at
the fact that we had the same alma mater.

"Go Dawgs," I murmured semi-sarcastically. I
heard Trip snort behind me.

"Damn good dog!" Jenny cheered as if she had
a pair of pom poms hidden somewhere in that
slinky dress of hers.

"I *thought* the two of you might have a lot to
talk about," Cosmo prompted me as if I were a
small child and it was my first time at the play-
ground. Jenny seemed more than willing to over-
look my obvious idiocy, presumably since Mama
had showed her a spreadsheet showcasing my net
worth. I glanced at her green eyes and olive skin
and suppressed a "what-the-hell" shrug. I offered
my arm to her, and as we moved to go down the

ramp, I noticed Sebastian Wakefield and his ever-present bodyguards step out of our path. Wakefield was holding two glasses of champagne. He grinned and gave me a semi-mocking half bow. I searched him with a puzzled frown. My instinct was to lure him into a corner somewhere and interrogate him, but about what, I had no idea. I glanced back over my shoulder as Jenny pulled me toward the dance floor and watched him ascend the ramp and take his spot beside my mother. The realization that he was Mama's escort seemed to hit Trip and me at the same time. Wakefield smiled at Trip in a predatory manner and went to shake his hand. Trip glared at him and ignored his outstretched hand as if it belonged to a leper. I froze, and the physics of my clumsy move caused Jenny to stumble backward into me. I'd never seen Trip look at anyone with such open hatred. He was one of those people who always found the goodness in others, not a card-carrying cynic like me. That was one of the reasons that his spiral into drunken depression was so devastating to those around him.

As I gaped at the exchange, I felt two arms wrap around my chest.

"They say you can tell what a man's like in bed by how he leads," Jenny whispered in my ear from behind. Then she spun me toward her and pulled me onto the dance floor by my lapels.

CHAPTER ELEVEN
Annie

I tried not to fidget as I watched Sam's mother throw a girl at him as if he were a wrathful volcano and she a virgin sacrifice. Witnessing his enthusiasm as he kissed the hand of Princess Nosejob caused prickly needles throughout my entire upper body. This sensation was so fierce and unexpected, I wondered if my hair was visibly standing on end. Imagine my astonishment when I realized I was jealous. And we're not talking just a bit of envy. Oh, no. Neon green jealousy of a magnitude I hadn't felt since I was in high school.

Sure, I'd been jealous of the kids whose back-to-school clothes weren't from garage sales or Goodwill. And of those whose parents showed up to teacher's conferences or remembered to pick them up after school. But I'd only felt that way about a boy once before in my life. And to say that it ended badly was the understatement of the century.

I had just turned 16, and my mom was long

gone by then. We'd moved in with my grandparents, and though I went to therapy twice a week, I
acted up constantly—not coming home on the
weekends, cutting class and taking a bus back to my
hometown to hang with my friends. My grandma
claims I was simply "high spirited." I now understand I was craving attention and approval from
someone...anyone. And I didn't have to look far to
get it.

I thought Nick was a kindred spirit and mistak-
enly assumed he was as damaged and screwed up as
me. Of course it was all costuming, but by the time
I figured that out, I was in a locked ward on a sev-
enty-two-hour hold. I became so infatuated with his
shaggy black Goth hair and sullen demeanor that
within a month of knowing him, I let him tattoo me
and take my virginity. It only took him two clumsy
times in the back of his car to knock me up. My
grandparents were so disappointed, but his parents
were furious. When I insisted on keeping the baby,
Mr. Perfect stood right beside me in total agreement. It was all so romantic, like a pierced Romeo
and Juliet.

A month later when the cramping and heavy
bleeding started, I kind of fell apart. Not everyone
was as distraught; Nick's mother actually jumped
up and down and clapped her hands when the doctor told them there was no longer a heartbeat. While
his family celebrated outside in the hall, I sat alone

in my hospital bed crying for my dead baby. After a quickie D&C, the doctor said I'd "dodged a bullet" and pretty much shoved me out the door. Three days later, Nick dumped me over the phone. He didn't love me anymore and wasn't sure he ever did. My friend Ashley called to say he'd started seeing someone else a week after that. After hanging up with her, I locked myself in the bathroom and downed a couple of bottles of pills.

I was startled out of my morose trip down memory lane by Sam's new friend shouting 'damn good dog!' Trip and I exchanged wide-eyed, amused looks, and I was suddenly a lot less concerned about Sam running off with her to Atlantic City.

"Tri-Delts. *Everyone* else has," Trip whispered. I was so busy trying to stifle a hysterical giggling fit that I was completely caught off guard when Trip's mother cleared her throat. I spun around to see Sam and Nosejob vanishing onto the dance floor, and Mrs. Beaumont gazing expectantly at us. The statuesque woman swept me with an icy glance, and I instantly felt underdressed. I figured she was in her early fifties, but she wore her age like a champ. Her hair was a youthful shade of light brown, and her elegant poise commanded admiration. I had to beat back the urge to curtsy.

"Well, Trip? Aren't you going to introduce me to your *friend*?" As she spoke the last word through gritted teeth, she turned to me and surveyed me like a tract of land. Blinking rapidly, she looked as if she hoped I was an optical illusion and I just might vanish if she rubbed her eyes, but she couldn't take the chance of smudging her mascara.

Trip smiled mirthlessly. "Mama, it's my pleasure to introduce you to Annabelle Clarke. Annie, this is my mother, Imogene Moore Beaumont."

Her three-name introduction seemed to call for some sort of reverence and I nearly said 'ooooo' like I was watching a fireworks display. Thankfully I hadn't had a drop of alcohol, or I'm sure it would have slipped out. I simply smiled and turned to my date. I recognized Trip's terse body language and expression in his mother's presence. The tension was almost identical to the way Sam had reacted to Trip the first day I met him.

"Tell me... Annabelle, is it?" his mother began, her face frozen in a frightening pageant smile that didn't make it past the lower half of her face.

"You can call me Annie," I responded out of habit. Then I tried on a pageant smile like hers. My face hurt instantly.

"Very well. Annie. Where are you from?" Her drawl was like molasses.

"Minnesota. Well, the Midwest...everywhere, I guess. We moved around a lot." I neglected to add that our nomadic existence was in response to my mom being banned from one casino after another.

How do you get banned from a casino, you might ask? Trust me, it's possible. But she just picked up and moved closer to another one. 'Gotta go where the queen of jacks takes you', she always used to say. Like everything that came out of that woman's mouth, it was meaningless bullshit.

"How nice," she replied, and her eyes shifted from me to Trip, then back again. I'd never heard so much sarcasm expertly poured into two little words. When I'd agreed to help Trip get Violet back, I didn't figure on having to meet his mother or explain anything about my past. I had a feeling that this oversight was an enormous tactical error. I stared at Trip, trying to silently hint to him my need for an escape, but he was too busy glaring over my shoulder to pick up on the signal. I glanced behind me, expecting to see a troll eating a baby. Instead, I saw that a dashing older gentleman had emerged from the crowd below, holding two champagne glasses. He presented one to Mrs. Beaumont, and she took it with what appeared to be her first genuine smile since laying eyes on me.

"Sebastian, this is my oldest son, Trip and his date, Annie. Trip, I'm not sure if you remember your father's friend, Mr. Wakefield—"

"Oh, we've met," Sebastian interjected with a sly grin, holding out his hand for Trip to shake. He wore a pinky ring that was worth more than my car. Mr. Wakefield's expression made me want to flinch, but I wasn't sure where the instinct came from. It was as if he was *daring* Trip to shake his hand. Trip said nothing, and silently refused to acknowledge Sebastian's outstretched palm. If looks could kill, I'm pretty sure Imogene Moore Beaumont might have dismembered Trip. But Trip was younger and more agile, so the death-stare he gave her in return could have taken her down before she had the chance to wield her machete. When Trip continued to glower at them both, his mother's expression converted from anger to disbelief.

"Reginald?" She seemed as genuinely shocked by his blatant hostility as I was. Though I'd always known Trip was a nickname, hearing him called Reginald so soon on the heels of "the Samson incident" caused me to let out a nervous cackle. I slapped both my hands over my mouth. It was my turn to get a homicidal glare from Her Royal Highness.

Mr. Wakefield gave Lady Beaumont a pacifying rub on the shoulder. The gesture was innocent, but not the way he executed it. I felt dirty just standing next to them, and I could feel Trip bristle beside me.

"It's alright, Geenie." He soothed her, and then turned a playful expression at Trip. "No matter how old they are, it's startling for children to see their parents dating again."

Trip's face turned such an awful shade of purple that I thought he might be allergic to my perfume. He opened and closed his mouth twice before practically dragging me down the ramp away from them. He pulled me into his arms at the edge of the dance floor as the band began to play. I know nothing about formal dancing, but thankfully it was a ballad and all I had to do was sway back and forth in a customary manner.

He had one of my hands in his and the other on my waist, like in an old Bogart movie. I could see that he was still frothing with unexplained anger, and I noticed Violet dancing nearby, so I wrapped my arms around his neck and stroked his hair in a soothing way. I felt his shoulders relax a fraction of an inch, and I placed one of my hands on his freshly shaved cheek. He lowered his apprehensive eyes to mine.

"Care to tell me what the hell that was all about?" I was dying of curiosity. But selfish motives aside, he was my friend and it seemed like he needed to vent. Trip pursed his lips with a knitted brow and then blew out a sharp breath.

"That man was *not* my father's friend. He's a fucking vulture. He's been out to destroy my family for years," he seethed, seeming so passionate in his hatred that I wanted to grab a torch and start a lynch mob with him.

"Start talking, Trip."

His eyes shifted from side to side, and when he

seemed satisfied that no one was eavesdropping, he continued. "It's a long-ass story, Angel. You sure you wanna hear it?"

I was about to demand answers when Violet waltzed by in the arms of a guy who looked like a male model. She smiled up at her date, but when she caught sight of us, she stumbled. Abercrombie and Fitch caught her easily, masking her clumsiness in a dramatic dip. She blushed and gave us a sideways glance. Her date turned, and seemed to recognize Trip. His cover model face twisted in aversion. A dreadful gleam in his dark eyes, he smoothly guided her in our direction. Violet seemed to drag her heels, and I thought she was about to protest, but she snapped her mouth shut when she noticed me watching their approach.

"Well! Look what the cat dragged in!" The man boomed, and I scanned the area to see if we had an audience. Thankfully, it seemed the acoustics of the atrium and the big band's volume provided plenty of cover. No one even looked in our direction.

"Dash!" Violet snapped, and I watched a silent conversation take place between them in the span of three seconds. From the panicked look on her face, I got the impression that Violet usually won their arguments, but that Dash was feeling a bit uppity this evening. Trip casually pulled me closer, catching my eye. His unspoken message may as well have been in skywriting.

Showtime.

"Dashul. Violet." Trip managed to sound carefree, and in light of what had just happened with his mother's date, I was impressed.

Dashul? Were all southern mothers drunk when they named their kids, or just the wealthy ones?

"How'd your mother lure you here tonight? Was it with the promise of an open bar?" Dashul's impossibly square jaw clenched as he drawled his ugly insult at Trip. Violet yanked out of his arms and covered her mouth with her hand. Trip seemed to take it all in stride, most likely due to spending the last few weeks in Sam's presence. I, however, was fuming.

"Classy future husband you have there, Violet." The words slipped from my lips like a bar of soap in a prison shower room.

"And who might this be? Tell me, dahlin', what hole in the wall did he drag you out of?" he sneered, looking me up and down as if I were a cocktail waitress at a strip club. I nearly punched him in the nose, but just that second I saw him sway slightly on his feet. I found his intoxication ironically comical, so I laughed in his face. His eyes flew wide in unabashed surprise.

"You watch your mouth," Trip snapped at him. He sounded convincingly offended, and for a minute, I forgot he was acting. I saw the fire behind Violet's eyes as she looked at him, and the sight of it had me celebrating victory on the inside.

"Relax, Trip. Judging by that mouth, I'm guessing lots of guys talk to her like that. Don't they, Shug?" His clipped speech had an especially biting edge, and he eyed me in a way that made me offended *for Violet*. I'm terrible about making snap judgments, and I was baffled that Violet would divorce Trip for his drinking and then proceed to hook up with this hot mess. I figured his behavior was pretty out of character, based on Violet's responses to him and the deer in headlights look she wore.

Trip faced him head on. "I think you owe Annie an apology."

"I'm so sorry...he's been doing shots with the boys," Violet directed at me as she stepped forward, acting as a barrier between us and her man. Dashul appeared perturbed at her graceful attempt to make excuses for him.

"Where's your sense of humor, Beaumont? Why don't you go get yourself a drink?" her charming beau chimed in, grabbing Violet's shoulder and pulling her back. The force of it was hard enough to make her wince. Trip advanced on him grabbing him by both lapels. They were toe to toe. Though Dashul towered over Trip, my gut told me that good old Dash was headed for the E.R.

That's when Sam appeared. He thrust himself between the two angry men so quickly that I wanted an instant replay.

"Trip, go get Annabelle some punch," Sam ordered calmly and then faced Violet. His grim eyes fixed her with a resolved stare. "Violet…reconsider your future."

"Hey!" Dashul scowled, shoving Violet out of the way and getting in Sam's face. "What the hell is *that* supposed to mean?"

"Dude. You don't want to come up against me. Walk away." Sam's deep voice was as cool as an ocean breeze. He inched forward, his unblinking eyes level with Dash's. Guests on our side of the dance floor had stopped to watch the sparking altercation.

"Let's go, Dash." Violet's voice was practically a whisper. Her large green eyes were on Trip's. The hopeless romantic in me swooned as I witnessed the poorly disguised passion in both of their eyes. Trip gave her a gentle smile and mouthed 'it's okay.' I could see that she was practically trembling as she pulled Dashul away to the far end of the dance floor.

Audibly exhaling, Sam turned to face us.

"Are you alright," he asked me, all puffed up and macho, as if he might chase Dashul down if I said I had a hangnail. I huffed in amusement.

"Sure. It's not the first time someone's treated

me like a lowlife slut." I instantly wanted to crawl into bed and pull the covers up over my head. It was an unintentional burn, and now I had no way to take it back. Sam winced as if I'd slapped him, and I watched his ego deflate like a balloon stabbed with an icepick. He turned away, and I allowed Trip to pull me back into his arms. My eyes never left Sam, and when he turned back to us, his flushed face telegraphed resolve.

"Can I cut in?" Stunned speechless by his boldness, I blinked at him in total disbelief. Trip shrugged, releasing me from his grasp. Sam and I just watched each other for a moment, and he suddenly looked as apprehensive as I felt. I saw Nosejob moving in our direction, but Trip deftly intercepted her, and before I had a chance to utter a syllable, he'd whisked her away toward a table filled with punch and hors d'oeuvres.

Sam approached me slowly, and then in one swift motion, he confidently pulled me into his arms. A small gasp escaped me as the full length of our bodies touched for the first time. Intense heat swept through me, and I fought to keep my breathing steady.

His eyes refused to release mine as he began to lead, somehow making me look like I actually knew how to dance. I helplessly searched those tempestuous eyes, completely ignoring my surroundings. He lowered his face toward mine, and I braced myself for the electrifying impact of his lips. I was severely disappointed when his mouth brushed my earlobe instead. I could feel his warm breath tickle my ear as he whispered.

"I meant it when I said I was sorry." I closed my eyes, relishing the sensation of his closeness. Ashamed that he still thought I was angry about the stupid argument in my car, I shook my head and smiled. I found it hard to speak; I was so incredibly turned on by his mouth hovering near my skin.

Before I could reply, he pressed his forehead to mine. Breathless, I forced my eyes open and looked up into his. His features had such perfect symmetry I could have stared at him all night long. It felt like telepathy, the way he seemed to see into me. Something dark in him called out to something deep inside me, recognizing one of its own. He was so maddening...so infuriating-and so damn overwhelming! Yet somehow he was just so *comfortable* at the same time. All of these sensations were alien to me, and I wanted to bolt, but I knew nowhere would feel as right as in his arms. I closed my eyes, unable to stand the intensity of our connection for one second longer.

"I know." It was lame, but it was all I could manage. We continued to dance in silence, trading frequent glances. The pensive expression he wore compelled me to break the tension. "I wish I knew what you were thinking."

"I wish you were here with me." His deep voice reverberated all around me, and my limbs felt like mush as I melted further into him.

I inhaled, greedy for oxygen. It's hard to explain, but I felt like I could *breathe* again, as if I'd been holding my breath for a month. I'd felt his attraction to me since the day we met, but it still made me weak in the knees when he said it out loud. Hearing him say those words thrilled and terrified me in equal measure. I wanted so badly to lead him off to a dark corner and show him I felt the same. When I spoke, my voice almost cracked: "I know that, too."

His lips lifted in a half smile. I had a wild urge to kiss him, needing to taste that taunting mouth of his. I felt my chest rising and falling a little too rapidly. He had to be aware of my strong attraction to him. His smoldering sky blue eyes held me prisoner, and I was about to tell him that Trip and I were just friends when the music stopped and everyone began to clap enthusiastically.

The singer nodded and bowed, all showmanship and flair. Then his voice boomed into the microphone. "And now, ladies and gentlemen: It's my pleasure to introduce Armstrong Atlantic's very own a cappella champions, Noteable!"

My eyes flew wide, and I stepped back from Sam, still holding his hand. "Shit! That's Jayse!" I turned on my heel and dragged him with me toward the stage.

CHAPTER TWELVE
Sam

The lights dimmed and the crowd murmured in hushed tones as Annabelle pulled me along through the crowd. I was tempted to throw her over my shoulder and head for the nearest exit, but Trip would put a price on my head, and Mama would call it gauche in the best of circumstances. In seconds we were at the stage. A crowd filled in around us, and I offered my front row spot to a very short girl, who eagerly took it. As people jostled for a better view, I found myself pushed up against Annabelle's back. My mouth watered when I noticed her second tattoo—the black rose – peeking out of the top of her dress. She glanced over her perfect shoulder at me, her delicate features clearly conflicted. I had to beat down the urge to wrap my arms around her and plant my lips on her gorgeous naked collarbone.

I wondered where Trip was and worried that he was pissed if he'd been watching us dance. I hadn't been able to keep a platonic distance from Annabelle; hell, I'd nearly kissed her right there on the dance floor! I'd known my confession wouldn't surprise her, but it felt good to finally come clean about my intentions. If she still chose to be with Trip, I wouldn't look back one day and wonder if it was because I was too much of a coward to even enter the race.

A group of men took the stage and when the spotlights popped on, I spotted both Jayse and Dale near the center. They began to sing in six part harmony, slow and solemn, but the song quickly shifted into an upbeat, cheerful number. Jayse pranced forward to solo, mic in hand, and proceeded to throw himself into the number with all his flaming might. He worked the stage like it was Silly Putty, and the crowd around me seemed simultaneously riveted and unsure how to handle the situation. His impressive vocal skills were undeniable, but lyrically, the song sounded as though it were written for a woman, and some of the notes he hit could have shattered crystal. I couldn't help but smile at his campy showmanship. I wished I could see Annabelle's reaction to her friend, but her back was still to me.

As the song continued, I heard a loud whoop of support from ten feet away, and when I turned in that direction, I realized it had come from Violet. She grinned from ear to ear and saluted Jayse with a raised martini glass. As if she'd given them permission to admit they enjoyed him, several of the younger partiers joined in with whistles and enthusiasm. As I turned back to the stage, I saw that Annabelle had also turned to see who the upstart was. She put a hand to her lips, her eyes wide in disbelief. I shook my head at her and shrugged. She burst out laughing. I reached out and put my hand on her shoulder and then pulled it away, fighting my baser instincts yet again.

Jayse seemed to feed off the crowd's growing energy and hammed it up even more, flying his freak flag for all of Savannah society. Marybeth Dutton cheered wildly in the front row a few feet to our left, and he pointed at her and then gyrated Elvis-style perilously close to her face. I covered my eyes with one hand, remembering that Mama knew he was an associate of mine. It should be noted that the fair Ms. Dutton didn't seem to mind a bit.

When the song came to its dramatic conclusion, the crowd erupted with pockets of wild enthusiasm. Annie catcalled and cheered at the top of her lungs. Jayse bowed to the crowd with all the aplomb of an R & B diva.

Three short (much less entertaining) songs later, Noteable finished their set. All of the soloists were talented, but none of them had Jayse's star quality and range. As they dismounted the stage, Annabelle and I fought counter current to the rest of the crowd, who made their way to the tables where dinner would be served. Trip and Jenny met us along the way, and Jenny snaked her arm through mine, leaning her head on my shoulder as if we were betrothed. Trip put his arm around Annabelle and whispered in her ear. Whatever he said must have been funny because she let loose with that laugh that was sure to haunt my dreams. I felt my night go from moderately promising to dismal in that one simple moment.

I had just noticed Jayse and Dale approaching when I saw Annabelle lift her skirt slightly and run into Jayse's open arms. His permanently sassy expression softened as he somehow managed to receive her undignified flying hug with all the grace of Fred Astaire. Dale laughed as Jayse pretended she was too heavy and made like he was about to drop her. When he righted her, she slapped his arm in mock anger.

"Jayse, that was amazing," she gushed as Trip moved forward to greet Dale with a fist bump that told me they knew each other well.

"Awe, shucks." Jayse's voice dripped sarcasm, but a hint of a smile betrayed his pleasure at her approval.

Trip proceeded to introduce me to Dale, explaining that Dale was a fellow artist. Dale told Trip that we'd already met earlier when Jayse saved me from 'some tacky brutes.' Trip cocked his eyebrow at me as if waiting for an explanation, but I simply waved it off. Through the conversation that followed, I came to understand that Trip and Annie had become friends at one of Dale's gallery shows. All the while, Jenny kept stroking my arm like I was her pet tea-cup Chihuahua. I assume she was trying to be seductive, but frankly it was annoying. Violet approached our small group hesitantly. Dash was nowhere in sight, and she carried two martini glasses which contained some sort of orange elixir.

"Sam, I'm simply dying to meet your friend. Be a dear and help a sistah out?" she cooed as she approached Jayse. To his obvious shock, she handed him one of the martinis. He muttered a quick 'thanks,' and I used the moment as an excuse to untangle myself from the overly zealous Jenny.

"Jayse, this is Violet Beau—" I began and then cut myself off. I realized I wasn't sure what she was calling herself these days. I shifted my eyes sideways at her, wondering if I was about to wear her martini. Violet smiled at me sympathetically and jumped in.

"Violet Beaumont. Reg and I *used* to be married." She offered in her sweet-as-honey voice, nodding to, while fixedly ignoring, Trip. Trip, who stood two feet from her, did his best to look unconcerned.

"Jayse Monroe." He replied, grinning at her snarky remarks with unveiled admiration. She proceeded to take his arm and slowly herd him toward her dinner table. From the moment she'd opened her mouth, Jayse seemed drawn to Violet like a moth to a flame, and he ignored the fact that he was leaving the rest of us behind. His boyfriend seemed unsurprised as he continued his conversation with Trip. But Annabelle followed after them, a look of stunned petulance firmly in place. When Jayse took a seat at Vi's table across Violet and Dash, Annabelle ended her pursuit and waited for Trip to catch up to her. They took their seats at our table, and I trailed behind with Dale. Apparently, Jenny had decided I wasn't worth the effort and had thankfully disappeared without a trace.

"You like her, don't you?" Dale asked, nodding in the direction of Annabelle. I froze for a moment, then deciding it was laughable to deny it, I nodded.

He nodded back at me, and I didn't see any amusement on his freckled face as he continued to speak. "Annie's a good egg, sweeter than she'll ever let on. But she's been through a lot. I'm worried about her and Trip hooking up. The way I see it, they'll either help rebuild each other or rip one another's progress to shreds."

I had no idea what to say. I realized just how little I knew about Annabelle and felt foolish as hell. Like it or not, I felt like I *could* see her, see who she really was, past the posturing and the hard defensiveness. And I felt compelled, for whatever reason, to protect her, especially from Trip, though I believed he really had made commendable progress. I didn't think I could stand by and watch Annabelle act as training wheels while he learned to get back on the bike.

As my tablemates engaged each other in lively conversation, I ate dinner in a silent fog trying to sort out just how much I was deluding myself. After a few minutes, I actually contemplated leaving town. I'd walked this path once before with Trip and Violet, and I just couldn't force myself to lace up my hiking boots again. After my birthday, there was nothing stopping me from going anywhere I wanted to. Maybe I'd go buy a house in the Keys and have Randall oversee my Savannah project while I went deep sea fishing and drowned my sorrows in margaritas.

Somehow the subject of Mama came up, and Annabelle turned to Trip.

"You never got to finish telling me what the deal is with Mr. Wakefield," I heard her say. Trip whipped his head in my direction as if worried I would hear her, and I raised my eyebrows at him.

"I'm dying to hear this, too," I confessed. Until tonight, I hadn't realized Trip's reaction at the Chatham Club had anything to do with Wakefield. I assumed it was all about Violet's engagement, but after observing their confrontation in the receiving line, I viewed his urgent need to smoke during brunch in a different light.

"And I'm dying for a cigarette," Trip replied, pushing back from the table. He was on his feet and gone before I could speak. I shot Annabelle a "what the hell" look, and she shrugged in response, her expression mirroring my own.

I didn't want to press him. He was finally doing well, and stressing Trip out was the last thing on my to-do list. I was a lot more interested in getting Annabelle alone. But as I said before, Trip was not a hateful person. He wasn't snarky. He didn't hold grudges. In short, he was my polar opposite—yin to my yang. So as I sat pushing my desert around on my plate, I become more and more agitated until I dropped my fork and excused myself, tossing my napkin on the table

I headed toward the nearest exit on a hunt for my brother. As I stepped outside into the night air, the river and the humidity greeted me like an overly friendly neighbor waving hello. I wandered beyond the valet circle and squinted, looking left and right up the street. Seeing no sign of him, I went around the building to the river side of the Marriot. As I approached the steps, Annie exited a back door right into my path. I paused to acknowledge her, wondering why she was leaving the comfort of the air conditioning, and she gave me a sheepish shrug. Part of me was envious, but mostly I was glad to see Trip had another ally in his quest for well-being. I turned away to survey the river walk, and by the lights of the Talmudge Bridge, I could see Trip down near the river. He wasn't alone. I heard raised voices and recognized one of them as his. Remembering the altercation with Dashul Stein earlier that evening, I hurried in his direction.

As I drew near, my feet faltered when I realized that the three men with Trip were Sebastian Wakefield and his bodyguards, not the Dash the Douche Bag and his merry men. I wasn't sure whether to be relieved or alarmed. I was vaguely aware of Annabelle's heels clicking on the ground behind me, and I strained to make out what Trip was saying.

"You will not breathe a word of this to him," I heard him growl at Wakefield, yanking his arm out of the bigger bodyguard's grasp. "Don't even look in his direction, so help me God!"

Wakefield chuckled playfully at Trip as if he were a toddler throwing a tantrum in the toy aisle.

"Grow up, Trip. He's dead. Do us all a favor and just let it go."

Annie kicked off her shoes and went to descend the stairs in front of me, but I grabbed her by the arm. They hadn't spotted us yet, and I wanted to hear the rest of the conversation; I needed to finally understand what the hell was going on with this Wakefield character. Annie looked confused, but I heard Wakefield speaking again and there was no time to explain.

"He has a right to know, don't you think?" Wakefield asked, puffing on his cigar. Trip flicked his cigarette into the river and ran his hand through his hair.

"What purpose would that serve? It's not his fault his mother's a whore. It wasn't Daddy's either, though there was no convincing him of that once you were done mind-fucking him." Trip's words knocked the wind out of me. Suddenly I wanted to turn and go. I just wanted to walk. Away from the hotel, out of Savannah, and right on out of Georgia. But like a rubbernecker at the scene of a traffic accident, I was fixated on them. Annabelle had hold of my arm, and I heard her gasp beside me.

The four men below heard her as well. They all turned in our direction, and a wall of uncomfortable eyes stared up at us. With one last knowing glance at Trip, Wakefield approached the stairs followed by his entourage. He surveyed Annabelle casually, and then his eyes rested on mine. He appeared thoughtful and amused, but breezed past me without breaking his stride. Dazed, I watched him enter the hotel. Then I was descending the stairs.

"Sam..." I heard the slow delivery of my name...the faint note of caution in Annabelle's voice, but I ignored her and moved on toward Trip and the answers he possessed.

Trip lit another cigarette and aggressively shrugged out of his tuxedo coat.

"Trip?" I breathed out the humid air that felt like it was dry cleaning my lungs and waited.

"I promised not to tell you." He sounded low. As low as I'd ever heard him. Mournful.

I was starting to shake all over and felt like my stomach was turning itself inside out. "Promised who?"

"Daddy." He sounded very young, like a small child afraid of the dark.

"Tell me what?" I'm not an idiot. By this time, I suspected the answer, but it was time to have it out. No more cloak and dagger bullshit. No more hinting around or haughty glances across the parlor. It was truth time if I had to beat it out of him.

"God dammit, Sam!" Trip's voice broke, and he covered his eyes with his palms. He managed not to drop his cigarette, and I found myself focusing numbly on the burning cherry at the end.

I took a deep breath. My whole body felt foreign, like all of my limbs had fallen asleep. "Say it, Trip."

He turned to me, his cheeks flushed. Rage and fear seemed to batter him, and I saw tears standing in his eyes. "He's your fucking father, okay? Sebastian Wakefield's your father."

CHAPTER THIRTEEN
Annie

Trip's revelation seemed to suck the oxygen out of the atmosphere surrounding the three of us. The endless implications spiraled in my mind, but my feet seemed to have a mind of their own, and they carried me toward Sam. He hadn't moved or blinked, and his face set in a disbelieving frown. I was irrationally terrified that he might stay frozen that way forever.

A tear slipped down Trip's cheek, and he aggressively swiped at it with his arm. His labored breathing was the only sound breaking the maddening silence. I wanted to take some action, to say something diplomatic to them both, but I wasn't equipped. As well read as I was, I'd never reached the section in Emily Post that advised what to say when your fake boyfriend's brother (whom you lust after) finds out he's a bastard.

Sam blew out a slow breath and walked right past Trip to the railing overlooking the river. He gripped it with both hands as if it were his sanity he was trying to hold onto. All the while, the frown he wore hadn't moved a fraction of an inch. Trip glanced unhappily at me and then joined Sam. He seemed to steel himself, prepared to wait patiently for whatever fallout was coming. I stepped up to the rail and turned, leaning my elbow on it. I stared intently at them both and realized their profiles looked nothing alike. Their speech patterns, hair color, eye color, and smiles were practically identical, but everything else about them was wildly different. It was a marvel how quickly the simple power of suggestion had affected my perception of their resemblance.

"Wakefield outed the affair at my engagement party. I'm not sure what he said to Daddy exactly, but he more than implied he'd slept with Cosmo. I have no idea why he chose that night to tell him, or what brought it about. I might have never known about it at all, but I just happened to notice Daddy gone from the party and went looking for him. When I found him in his study, he was drinking scotch directly from the bottle." Trip took a drag from his cigarette, his eyes never leaving the river. "He kept pacing back and forth, completely fired up. Spouting off about defending Mama's 'good name' and that sort of thing. He told me he wanted to go to Wakefield's hotel and kick his ass. I tried to talk him out of it; I really did. I told him it was all total bullshit, that the dick was just a jealous nobody with some old axe to grind. But he'd have none of it. He was already drunk, and I'd never seen him so…crazed. It was pretty clear he was going with or without me, so I had no choice. I went along as the designated driver. My phone kept on buzzing the entire way there. I'd left the party without a word to Violet, and she kept calling and texting me. But what was I gonna say? 'Y'all will have to excuse me for a bit, Daddy and I have to go beat the shit out of someone. Go ahead and help yourselves to some more Prosecco?'"

I saw Sam's eyes dart to Trip and then back to the water. It was obvious to me that he felt cornered and he looked so lost that I thought I might cry if I didn't look away. He also looked like he'd rather jump the rail and dive into the river than hear the rest of the story, and I needed to keep an eye on him.

Trip swallowed hard and turned to Sam. His eyes flicked in my direction, and for a moment it seemed like he'd forgotten I was even there. "When we arrived at the hotel, Wakefield was sitting down to dinner. Obviously he wasn't the slightest bit surprised to see Daddy. He seemed caught off guard at my arrival, though. His body guard showed us in. He had his henchmen even back then. I suppose when you conduct yourself like he does, you need constant protection. He was sitting at the head of a dining table eating prime rib like the lord of the manor."

Sam seemed more and more restless with each passing sentence out of Trip's mouth. He turned away from the river and leaned against the railing with his arms crossed over his chest as if warding off Trip's words. He worked his jaw muscles so hard, I was concerned he might hurt himself. His attention fixed like a laser sight on his brother, and I saw him shift into self-defense mode—completely void of emotion. I had the distinct impression that the lost, panicked Sam from earlier would have been the better alternative. I could almost see him fortifying his walls and climbing into his suit of armor.

"Daddy didn't even sit down." Trip's voice was so hard he could have cut through inch thick glass. "He just said 'start talkin', Sebastian.' Wakefield had that stupid shit-eating grin on his face and started in on how nothing would have ever happened if Daddy had given Mama the attention she deserved. The icing on the cake was some comment about how idiotic he was to believe you were a month overdue. Daddy looked white as a sheet, and I got *pissed* and completely lost my shit. I put my cigarette out right on the table, ready to throw down. I was in his face, calling him a liar and a fucking slimeball. He laughed at me and said 'you're a real chip off the old block, Reggie boy. You Beaumonts are all bark and no bite.' So I punched him in the mouth. Then his goons were all over me. The next thing I knew, I was slamming into the wall and crawling on the ground, seeing double. One of his guys kicked me in the ribs, and I heard Daddy cry out in pain. I think that's when they broke his wrist. Then things got a bit fuzzy. I remember looking back at Wakefield as they were dragging me out. He dabbed at his bleeding lip with his napkin. Fucking psychopath. He didn't even put down his fork."

All the color had drained from Sam's face, and I reached out for his shoulder. He pulled away from me without looking in my direction, and I'd be lying if I said it didn't sting. As I pulled my hand back from him, I met Trip's eyes. I could tell he suspected how I felt about Sam, and his eyes seemed to tell me to back off and just let it go.

"On my way out of the suite, I got a good look at Daddy, and I knew the damage was already done. He believed Wakefield. Completely. And since he knew both Cosmo *and* Wakefield a hell of a lot better than I did, that was enough for me. And I could see that it crushed him. That asshole was Daddy's best friend, and he'd just ripped his beating heart from his fucking chest and tossed it at his feet. I'm no fighter; you know that. But I wanted to murder him with my bare hands for the defeated look on my father's face.

Right before they tossed me into the hall, I

heard him asking Daddy if he remembered the weekend he'd flown to Concord to sign contracts with some company. I sat dazed on the floor, trying to catch my breath and wondering if my ribs were broken. A few minutes later, Daddy came out of the suite and quietly pulled the door closed behind him. When we got to the car, he popped the trunk and took out a tire iron with his good hand. I watched for about ten minutes while he took out his frustrations out on the car. So help me God, I was unable to think of a single thing to say to comfort him. He didn't say a thing to me, either. Not even when we started for home. I can only imagine how embarrassed and defeated...he felt, on so many levels. I know I did.

When we turned onto Victory Drive, I looked over at him and saw tears rolling down his face. He told me if anyone asked, we'd been in a car accident and he finally looked at me for the first time since I'd been thrown out of the suite. He said 'no one can ever know about this, Trip.' He made me swear not to discuss any of it with anyone. Mama...Vi...you. I told him that it was madness, that we *needed* to at least tell you. But he wouldn't budge. So I promised him."

Trip was quiet for a long time, but I could tell he wasn't finished with his story. Just when I was sure I was mistaken and debating on what to say, he spoke. "He wasn't the same after that night. I never saw him smile after that. He quit going to social events altogether, and one night at the yacht club, his lawyer let it slip that he was skipping board meetings. I tried to talk to him about it and thought I got through when he made an appointment with the law firm. I figured it was a consult about a divorce. My guess is that was probably when he changed his will. Cosmo was so stinking busy opening Imogene's that she didn't notice a thing, and I couldn't think of a way to point out his...deterioration without breaking my word and violating his trust."

"You should have tried harder." Sam's voice sounded especially deep and thick. It frightened me, but not half as much as the shattered expression he was trying hard to hide.

Trip tossed his tux jacket onto the ground like it was a candy wrapper and ran both hands through his hair. "Jesus, Sam. Do you think I don't get that? Do you think I haven't reexamined my inaction from all angles while I got shitfaced at every fucking bar in Savannah? You have no fucking idea how much I regret my choices. I'm pretty Goddamned aware that I screwed up every single thing in my life!"

At some point during his story, I'd started crying, but I didn't realize it until that moment when I sniffed loudly. Sam's blue eyes swept over me, but they didn't seem to actually see me. His thoughts appeared to be a thousand miles away. Trip looked like he was about to fall apart completely. I crossed to Trip and put my hands on his shoulders. He regarded me uncomfortably, like I was about to dole out some punishment to him. It seemed like he was about to dissolve into tears right along with me.

"You need to quit punishing yourself. He was your father, and he asked you to keep a secret. I'm sure he had his reasons, but it wasn't fair for him to do that to you." I turned so that I could look at them both as I continued to speak. "Parents are just people, guys. They screw up all the time. It's an ugly truth that's hard to face, no matter how old you are. He shouldn't have asked you to cover it up in the first place. He really should have confronted your mom."

"This is not *Daddy's* fault," Sam snapped at me and then paused and barked out a semi hysterical laugh. "I guess I really shouldn't call him that anymore, huh?"

I turned away from Trip and tried to reach out to Sam. I wanted to wrap my arms around him, to hold him and comfort him. He moved away from me again, but I was done playing at that point. I launched myself into his personal space and took his face in my hands, forcing him to look at me. I could feel him trembling beneath my palms, and the dead look in his eyes made me afraid enough to tremble right along with him. "Don't be ridiculous, Sam. Your father didn't want you to know about it.

He obviously loved you very much."

Neither of them spoke after that. Trip stared at the ground, his hands on his hips. Sam looked away from me, still leaning against the rail as if we were discussing Georgia's odds against Florida State. I saw right through his act, and for the first time since we'd met, I wished I wasn't so intuitive about him. That I couldn't peek behind that curtain of his. It was too damned hard to watch him hurting. My heart went out to them both. To Trip, for the lives he'd destroyed simply trying to do right by his dad. And to Sam, for the unimaginable loss of his entire reality, the veritable collapse of his identity.

Sam shook his head slowly, his eyes darting back and forth as if reviewing a transcript of the scene Trip had just described to us.

"I think I could use some time alone," Sam murmured, and he pushed off from the rail and took off, but not in the direction of the hotel. At first I just watched him go. His pace was moderate, but he seemed to be fixated on the ground in front of him, as if putting one foot in front of the other took incredible focus. My instincts told me not to let him wander off alone, and this time I wasn't going to ignore my hunch. I hurriedly picked up my discarded shoes and went after him.

As I chased after Sam, I heard Trip mumble to himself behind me. He sounded as bad as he looked. "I could really use a shot of Patrón."

I didn't even turn around. I felt awful ditching him like that, but my heart said Sam needed me more.

CHAPTER FOURTEEN
Violet

Why is he being such an incomprehensible prick?

Dash had been in rare form from the instant we arrived at the Marriot. I leveled with him on the ride over that Imogene was hosting the gala, and as with all things remotely related to Reg, Dash had immediately sprouted a giant chip on his shoulder.

"Wanna do a body shot, Vi?" Dash grinned hazily at me. I watched as he and Hank snickered and downed one more shot of tequila. Suppressing a sigh, I glanced at the clock on my phone. It was only nine o' clock, and he was already trashed. I saw the fabulous Jayse Monroe leave our table and saddle up to his cute little boyfriend. Dash nodded to them and mumbled something to Hank. Hank erupted in an angry laughing-at-you-not-with-you cackle. My face burned right along with my insides. I glared at Dash, but it was a pointless exercise. He continued to ignore me.

I really had the overwhelming urge to slap the hell out of him for telling Reg to 'go have a drink.' No matter what Dash thought of him, Reg was the father of my child, and I wanted him to get better. I *needed* him to be well. And it seemed like he really *was* on the mend, which made me proud and made me want to rip my hair out at the same time.

I had to ask myself, why now? Why had he managed to cobble his shit together after all this time? And right when I was fixin' to marry another man! Seriously? What was it about Annie that was so damn special that she was able to pull him back from the precipice when I'd fought tooth and nail to do so and failed so spectacularly? Oh sure, she was pretty, but so the fuck am I, dammit! I suppose the most appropriate question was this: what was it about me that had made it so easy for him to remain punch drunk and absent from my and Maisie's lives for so long?

Every time I tucked my daughter in at night...when I sang her lullabies....whenever I looked at her angelic little face, I encountered Reg's beautiful blue eyes. She was the spitting image of him and looking at her continued to further fracture my battered heart each and every day. I'd resigned myself a long time ago to the fact that I would *never* be over him, but that I would never be able to let him back in.

Never.

So why the hell was it that I could not stop staring at him in that amazing black tuxedo that fit him like a glove? Why did my heart have to race like the Kentucky fucking Derby when his eyes found mine across the crowded dance floor? Why did some primal part of my soul splinter when he'd grabbed Dash for being rough with me? And why on earth was I sitting here wishing it were him at my side instead of my fiancé?

Calm down, Violet. It's just Reg. Remember?

Yes, I *did* remember. I remembered all too well. As if I'd ever be able to forget a single instant since the moment we met. Since that day, every millimeter of him was burned into my memory as if by a scalding brand.

"Violet, this is my brother, Trip." Sam's simple introduction that sunny morning at the sidewalk café was almost an afterthought. Sam had been preoccupied, waving to someone passing on the sidewalk. He hadn't even glanced in my direction as his brother took a seat next to me. But Reg was looking at me. *Into me.* And that's all it took. One look from those crystal blue eyes and I was a goner. Don't get me wrong: Sam was very handsome and amusing as hell, but Reg? His smile was molten sunshine, and when he took my hand to shake it, his touch was like lightning, and I was the rod.

"Trip?" I remember wrinkling my nose at the silly moniker, and his crooked smile in response nearly made me come undone right then and there.

"It's not my given name." He responded, and his smirk immediately drove me crazy. I barely noticed when Sam excused himself to go say hello to an old friend and left us alone. The tension in our silence was raw and wanting. "Trip" put a long black cigarette to his lips, looking a lot like the leading man in some old black and white movie. He flipped open his zippo, and I have to admit I was ready to jump him right then and there.

"Well? What the hell *is* your name?" I asked, waiting for him to finish his drag. He exhaled through his nostrils, immediately seeming even more devilish. He leaned back in his chair and seemed to chew on the inside of his lip as if having an internal debate. I reached out and plucked the cigarette from his fingers, placing it to my mouth. Though I wasn't a smoker, I'd done my time as an angsty teenage girl during my stint in boarding school, so inhaling wasn't much of a problem. I relished the panty-dropping smile that spread across his lips like wildfire. When he sat forward and slipped his arm over the back of my chair, I tried not to sigh out loud.

"Reginald Jefferson Beaumont, the Third." He drawled with fake flourish, and I couldn't contain a giggle at how completely ridiculous his real name was.

"Well *that's* fairly horrific." I recall batting my

eyelashes at him and shamelessly flipping my hair, which I've since chopped off. I crossed my legs and leaned toward him, pretending to survey his features judgmentally. In reality, I just couldn't stop myself from inching as close to him as was publically acceptable. His near black hair and ivory skin contrasted dramatically, giving him an exotic appearance. "You look like a Reg to me. Yep. It suits you."

His eyebrow twitched as my bare legs seemed to momentarily distract him. His eyes, framed with those stunning dark lashes took the scenic route as they trailed slowly all the back up to mine. "All right. Reg it is."

He had me fatally hooked, and I was inexplicably okay with that.

Sam had managed to get over me quickly enough, though a couple of days after the café introduction, the two of them had a terrible row. An actual physical fight…like a couple of hooligans straight out of a Jerry Springer episode. I was so pissed at their brutish bullshit that I nearly walked away from both of them. Oh, who the hell am I kidding? I couldn't have walked away from Reg any more than a moth can stop itself from flying directly into a flamethrower.

So as you might imagine, an evening of watching him lead Annie merrily around the dance floor had been a bit like having bamboo shoved underneath my freshly painted fingernails. And Dashul could evidently sense this because he was doing an Oscar-worthy impression of Nicholas Cage in Leaving Las Vegas.

Or Reginald Jefferson Beaumont III.

Honestly, Dash's behavior tonight had been an anomaly. We'd been seeing each other for almost ten months, and he truly was a good man. He worked hard and laughed easily. He respected his parents and was generous to his church. He treated me very well, and was nothing short of spectacular with Maisie Mae. Frankly, Dash's only real flaw was that he wasn't Reg.

You'd think that would have been a relief, considering the speed with which our short marriage had dissolved from every girl's fairytale into an abysmal nightmare.

We were amazing in the beginning. Since we were both still in school, we had to make do with phone dates and stolen, sheet-tangling weekends. He made me believe in true love. Believe me when I say I *know* how ridiculous that sounds. While my sorority sisters were listening to silly love songs and trying to land a husband, I rolled my eyes at them and plotted to take over the world. But meeting Reg finally enlightened me about what all those starry-eyed songwriters were tapping into.

We'd talk until sunrise about anything and everything. God, I still get butterflies when I hear "At

Last," which was his ringtone in those early days. And anytime anyone mentions Wormsloe Plantation, I break out in a sweat. Reg took me on a picnic there. After a sordid and dirty bit of misbehavior off in the woods (the kind that left me with tree bark burns for days), he took me for a stroll down The Avenue of the Oaks. He explained that he wanted to paint me there, to immortalize the day. Then he pulled out the most beautiful ring I'd ever seen and slid it on my finger. I have to confess, I still keep it in a bedside table. I pull it out and stare at it more often than I care to admit.

Reg always nailed those big moments. The grand gestures, so to speak. I learned way too late that marriage, like ballet, is not 'in position,' it's 'in transition.' It's those little day-in, day-out moments that truly matter the most. They're what build a firm and reliable foundation. I was just too stubborn to throw in the damned towel. And I loved him enough to believe we could glue the broken pieces back together again. Come to think of it, I always questioned what I was taught in dance class, too. I think I was sixteen when I burned my tutu on my instructor's front lawn.

I could've put up with other women making a play for him. It happened with appalling regularity, especially when he was drinking. Everywhere we went, they were all over him. Could you blame them? He had so much money it was criminal, and he was…well…Reg. I'd have been a fool to think he'd ever walk around in public without women making passes at him. Whether or not I was present really didn't seem to factor into that equation. There were countless nights that he never made it home. I tried not to think about it too much.

I was more than capable of dealing with his moody, dark periods when he'd lock himself in his studio for days on end. Not eating, not shower-ing…just drinking bottle after bottle of Johnny Walker and painting insane pictures that scared the hell out of me. It was no picnic calling 911 when he grabbed the wrong glass, guzzling three fingers of paint thinner before realizing his mistake. But after all, I had agreed to 'in sickness and in health.' I sent him to rehab and kept a stiff upper lip like a good wife should.

But I could *not* live with having to protect my child from her own father. I believe with all my heart that Reg would have rather have chopped off his right hand than harm a hair on Maisie's head, but oftentimes Reg wasn't the one flying the plane. More often than not, Johnny Walker had the con-trols, or at least was acting as his co-pilot.

So when Sam hauled him away to rehab for the second time, I contacted my lawyer. Night after night, I cried myself to sleep and every time Maisie asked where her daddy was, I had to have the nanny read her a story while I hid in my room and privately broke down.

So it was fate's cruel joke that he arrived at the gala looking so together and at peace while I clung tenaciously to my dignity. After all, I had divorced him. And with damn good reason. And yet I was miserable on a level that was positively indescribable.

Dash planted a kiss on my cheek that was a little too hard and entirely too wet. "We're gonna go see if Hank won the trip to Bermuda that he bid on."

I simply nodded and produced a polite smile. As I watched them stumble away I scanned the crowd, searching for Sam. I had to talk to someone. Sam would listen, and he would get it. He always did.

I saw no sign of him, but I did see Reg. He had his jacket flung carelessly over his shoulder, and he'd rolled up the sleeves of his black silk shirt. He was devastatingly handsome as always, but it was the sorrow in his eyes that had my undivided attention. I felt my pulse quicken when I watched him stalk diagonally across the ballroom. I couldn't quite tell if he was angry or sad, but his gait was rapid and purposeful.

And he was hurrying in the direction of the bar.

That tiresome slut Marybeth Dutton tried to place herself in his path, but he completely ignored her as if she were some sort of specter. Just three feet short of his destination, he came to an abrupt halt and dramatically spun on his heel. For a full minute he stood in what appeared to be silent contemplation, as if weighing the pros and cons of launching into a stupendous bender.

I fought hard to stay planted in my seat, but I just couldn't resist the pull of him. As I drifted in his direction I felt like my limbs were no longer under my control. In moments I was at his side. I placed my hand on his arm. His skin felt almost feverish, and he jumped at my touch.

"Baby, what's wrong?" As soon as it came out of my mouth I wanted to die.

Baby?

Dammit, Violet. Pull yourself together.

Fortunately, whatever had upset Reg also seemed to have affected his hearing. He said nothing at first, and I watched as he lifted his gaze to the stars shining down on us through the glass ceiling. And when his hand covered mine, I couldn't pull away. I mutely stared at his familiar features and when his gaze shifted to me, I searched his red rimmed eyes. They felt as if they were caressing me.

"I'm sorry, Vi. For all of it. All I ever wanted was to give you the world. And I just kept failing you. I understand that you can't forgive me. I'll never be able to forgive myself. I just needed you to hear me say the words."

I closed my eyes, unable to bear the agony on

his face. I was terrified to the core that he'd see mine reflected back at him and know just how much power he still had over me. My lungs seemed to be failing me, along with my voice. I felt his finger tip trail down the nape of my neck and my eyelids felt weighty as I reluctantly opened them.

"I've made so many stupid mistakes, Violet. But none of 'em as big as lettin' you go."

My lips parted and I finally inhaled as if to speak, but I couldn't find the words. I wanted to hit him, to cry, to throw myself into his arms and kiss him until our lips were bruised. But I just stood there like a damned ice sculpture, unable to move, but slowly melting into nothingness.

Reg nodded as if understanding my silence. With one last resigned look, he touched my cheek and disappeared into the crowd.

CHAPTER FIFTEEN
Sam

As I wandered down River Street in a shocked haze, I was vaguely aware that Annabelle trailed behind me, but it didn't slow me down. I had to put space between myself and my family before I did or said something stupid and made a jacked-up situation worse. And I wanted to get wasted. Not at the first bar I stumbled upon, though. Trip always used to say "never just wander into the first bar you see, Sammie. *Always* hold out for the second one. Trust me; the girls are *always* prettier and the liquor is *always* less watered down." He was the resident expert, so I planned to take his advice. Truth is, I really didn't care where the hell I drank, but I wasn't about to get plowed at the hotel where Mama and her lover toasted Savannah's upper crust. And if anyone deserved to get plowed, it was me.

Annie called my name. I didn't look back at her. Embarrassed and angry, I willed her to just go away. When I didn't respond to her a second time, I heard her swear under her breath. For some reason I welcomed the sound of her heels which clicked rapidly on the aged cobblestones. Moments after I passed the first bar, I heard her exclaim "fuck it," and the sound of the heels disappeared. I assumed she'd abandoned her quest for a front row seat at my breakdown. It turns out I was wrong about that; she'd just given up on her shoes.

Trip's "second bar rule" happened to work out well this time around. As I pushed the door open, the table of hotties right inside all looked up at the sound of the bell jingling. All three smiled at me and whispered fervently amongst themselves. Yep. Black tux— works every time.

Bernie's was a cool little joint housed in a converted warehouse. Darkly lit, the exposed brick walls were peppered with beer signs. There was enough of a clientele that my tux didn't draw too much attention, but not enough that I couldn't find a seat. Perfect. I owed Trip a shot for his expertise. Or not.

I snagged a quiet booth near the back, and in moments a waitress appeared at my side.

"What can I get ya, hon?" Her eyes briefly surveyed my tux with an amused smile that made it pretty clear I'd been pegged as a 'big tipper.' Normally it bugged me when strangers called me by a term of endearment, but tonight it was oddly comforting. It probably helped that she was so easy on the eyes.

"We'll have two pints of Shock Top and two dozen medium wings." Annie interjected as she tossed her shoes and her sparkly purse onto the seat of opposite me. The waitress dropped the grin. She nodded and zipped away before I had a chance to object. Beer wasn't going to be strong enough to dull my racing mind.

"Annie...I think I just need to be alone." I started, but she held up her hand.

"You know what I think?" Her retort was swift and pointed.

I folded my hands on the table in front of me. "No, but I'm sure you're going to tell me."

"I think *you* are a dangerous over-thinker. *I* think you have spent too many years wrapped up in your head. I think what you need is to talk this out with someone who isn't too close to the situation."

I cocked an eyebrow, though I couldn't argue with her forensic assessment of me. "You're dating my brother. You're hardly a neutral party."

"Sam...have you *seriously* not figured out that Trip and I are just friends?" My jaw nearly hit the table at her revelation.

"What?"

"He's crazy in love with Violet. From what I can tell, she loves him, too." She placed her elbows on the table and leaned forward for emphasis. I felt my eyes drawn to her chest-I couldn't help myself.

Her cleavage may as well have had a bull's eye painted on it. "So go ahead and drink up. But I'm not leaving you to drink alone, so you may as well get used to the idea."

My eyebrows shot to my hairline, and I gaped at her. The waitress skidded by and shoved two pints onto our table without coming to a complete stop. "But how are you going to drive if you're drinking too?"

"Please. I could drink you under the table." She set her beer down and reached into her purse for her buzzing phone. "So talk to me."

"I'm not sure what you expect me to say." My palms felt sweaty at the image of laying her back on her bed, and I nearly dropped my beer. I took a long sip of the cold liquid to buy myself time to think. What was there to say? She knew everything about this situation that I did. I had no great insight into the calamity that was my existence, nor was I interested in seeking advice from the amateur Dear Abby across the table. I wasn't in the mood to psychoanalyze my feelings. I wanted nothing more than to just forget.

Her eyes were soft and full of sympathy I didn't want. "I don't expect anything in particular. There are no protocols for this situation, Sam."

I raked a hand through my hair and stared down at the beer. "Now I get why Trip drank so much."

"Oh yeah?" she replied, silencing her buzzing

phone. She tossed it on the table, her attention firmly fastened on me.

I shrugged and barreled onward. "I feel stir crazy. I have the urge to do… *something*. Right now I could jump out of my skin, but the damage is all already done. There's nothing I can do to change the outcome. It's already upon us. I'm literally living proof of it. Maybe keeping a basal rate of alcohol in your system just dulls the feeling of helplessness to a tolerable level."

"That's why we have beer, Sam. Enough kick to take the edge off so that you can process all of this but not hard enough for you to forget."

"It's probably for the best. Alcoholism doesn't just run in my family, it carries the Olympic torch." The moment I'd said it, the fallacy of the statement snapped back and hit me like a rubber band. Did it run in my family? Not on the Moore side. The fact of the matter was that I had no idea what ran in my father's side of the family. I filed that little kernel away to chew on later.

"You've got a lot to take in." She responded levelly. I'd misjudged Annabelle when I made the snap decision that she had no filter. I'd fallaciously believed she always said what was on her mind. Presently, she could have gone head to head with any Harvard-educated arbitrator.

"It explains why Trip can't stand to be around Mama. And it explains why he was always their favorite," I offered as our waitress delivered two baskets of piping hot wings. "Daddy...he must have sensed it...even before..."

I picked up one of the wings and then set it back down on my plate. Then I drank deeply from my pint instead. My stomach already felt like I'd guzzled acid. The trust fund wasn't even mine. It belonged to Trip...or Maisie. I was never destined to be the savior of the Beaumont business legacy; I wasn't even a Beaumont. The mansion I grew up in wasn't half mine; it was one hundred percent Trip's because I was *illegitimate*. A bastard. 'Born on the wrong side of the blanket' as my grandmother used to say. Or was she my grandmother? I felt the blood rush from my face as I continued to fling open closet doors in my mind, and the skeletons just kept coming. I felt tears stinging my eyes, and I held them back.

As if she could read my reeling mind, Annabelle shook her head at me.

"Your father went through a lot of trouble to keep all this from you. To protect you. *Those* are the actions of a dad, Sam. Contributing DNA? That does *not* make someone a parent." She slid out from her side of the booth, and with a flick of her head, motioning for me to scoot over. She joined me, resting her arm on the booth behind me. "That man you call 'Daddy' raised you as his own. He left you your inheritance as if you were his child. Your mother made *her* choices. He made his, too."

A warm feeling covered me like an electric blanket on a cold northern night. I wondered if this was because I actually believed her soothing words or because I'd just polished off my pint. Perhaps it was because she was inches from me, with her satin covered leg touching mine. For a moment, my mind wandered to what she was wearing under her impressive gown. Lace panties or a thong? Stockings and garter belts or bare legs? I was almost positive that she wasn't wearing a bra. Clearing her throat, she turned to her beer and twirled a tendril of hair around her finger. The waitress appeared and swapped my empty pint for a full one. Embarrassed, I realized that I'd been staring at Annie again and looked away wondering if her beauty was to me what booze was to Trip. A distraction. A drug to ease my troubled mind. Maybe that was why I was so fixated on her. I tried to focus hard on what she'd just said.

"You're right. Daddy made a point to take Mama out of his will. It was the perfect time for him to do the same with me, and he didn't. I'm not sure what to do with that. Or Mama. Or Trip…" The thought of Trip carrying this burden around with him for years suddenly gave me a tremendous feeling of shame.

"You press on. We are who we are *because* of *and* in spite of our families. All we can do is learn from their mistakes. Use the strengths you inherited and overcome the weaknesses." She said this all as if she was a boxing coach in my corner between rounds, indelicately and with more than a hint of condescension. She must have noticed my incredulous look, because she put down her beer, her eyes darting back and forth as if she were calculating the risk versus rewards of pressing on.

"Things could be a lot worse, Sam. Everyone *wanted* to claim you. I never knew my father. I don't remember him at all. He paid his child support, but never even tried to see me. My "mother"... well..." she scoffed, and the way her delicate features twisted for a moment chilled my blood. "She's probably the single most selfish human being on the planet. I practically raised my brother and sister all by myself. I could have ended up on a milk carton or knocked up and calling the cops from the trailer park every Saturday night. There were times when I was headed in that direction. But I chose to use my childhood as a template for what *not* to do. As it is, I ditched my sister and brother to save myself."

My stomach fell as I listened to her. More tragic than her country ballad-style childhood was the frank way she laid it all out on the table. Her voice trembled slightly when she brought up leaving her siblings, but otherwise, she held herself proudly and without apology, chin up and shoulders back. I wanted to borrow her strength, her self-assurance. I was envious of these qualities and wished I could tap into them. And more than that, I felt the driving urge to unburden her so she never needed them for herself again.

"You're so courageous, Annabelle."

She sighed and turned back to her beer at my words, but I leaned forward and gently tilted her chin so that we were facing one another again. "It's the truth. Learn to take a compliment."

"I'm not courageous. I did what I had to do to survive." She sounded wispy and a bit breathless. Her skin practically hummed under my fingers and those amazing eyes of hers had a glassy, heavy quality that made me want to pay the check and take her home.

I was unable to stop myself as I stroked her cheek with my thumb. "Is there a difference?"

She turned away, focusing her attention on her food. I nearly cackled out loud when she shoved a napkin in her cleavage as a makeshift bib to protect her gown. Watching her dig enthusiastically into the bar food reignited my appetite. We mowed down on wings for a couple of minutes in complete silence. It was a surprisingly comfortable silence, unlike any experience I'd ever had with another human being. I rarely feel compelled to fill quiet with words, but most people seem to have a compulsion to do so. My motto? Only say something if you have something to add, not just to hear yourself talk. Annie seemed to lean toward my way of thinking.

Eventually, she turned to me again, her brows knitted in contemplation. "Have you ever heard of Maslow's Hierarchy of Needs?"

"Sure. In Sociology and Psych 101. Dealing with base needs like breathing, food, and shelter before you can worry about loftier needs like self-esteem and morality."

"Right. I've spent my whole life trying to get a handle on the lower rungs of the pyramid. Some might call that a disadvantage, but I think it's given me a deeper appreciation for what little I do have because of it."

"I follow you. I have rich white boy problems." I chuckled a bit in a self-depreciating way, and her lips twitched as if concealing amusement. She bit her lip which was wildly arousing and continued.

"I believe that life is one-fourth genetic, one-fourth luck, one-fourth willpower, and one-fourth focus." She stated, her conviction unwavering. "Being out of balance can completely screw up your equilibrium. I guess sometimes you have to over-compensate in the last two categories to keep your life on course while it's careening down the side of the mountain."

I nodded, rolling her philosophy around in my head and trying it on to see how it fit. She pulled the napkin from her cleavage and wiped her hands with it.

"Alright. You've got me sold. I think you missed your calling. You should have gone into business, Annabelle."

"You're an easy sell, Sam," she teased, and I was about to put my arm around her when the front door swung open and no less than twenty people shouted Trip's name in unison. Trip gave the room a halfhearted wave and took a seat at the bar accepting a high five offered by the bartender.

Five months sober or not, Trip still defaulted to his second bar rule. I let out an exasperated sigh. "Fuck."

"Shit." Annie was out of her seat and at his side in a New York minute. I followed and quickly took the stool next to him in time to hear her ask, "What are you doing here, Trip?"

"Hey…" It was evident we were the last people he expected to see. His color was high, and he wouldn't meet my eyes.

"Why don't we find someplace else to be?" Annie suggested. If there were any doubt in my mind that I was smitten with her, she abolished it with this one easy sentence. With the exception of Violet, Annie was the first woman who'd held my interest for more than a couple of hours. One might argue that I'd been hanging around the wrong women and likely be correct. But I was beginning to make peace with the fact that happenstance and fate factor largely in my life. I'm far from religious, but

I couldn't help but feel like I'd been sequestered by forces beyond myself until this moment in order to fully appreciate Annabelle's uniqueness.

"I'm pretty sure I belong right here. I appreciate your concern, Angel." His self-depreciating smile felt hollow.

"Come on, Trip. Tonight isn't worth blowing five months over. Let's get out of here." I rocked my shoulder into his. He glanced at me doubtfully.

"I should have told you right away. That night."

I shook my head at him. My words were firm. "It's done. Let it go."

"Here's your coffee, Trip. Sure you don't want a little Irish in it?" The bartender asked, handing him a to-go cup. Annie's surprised expression mirrored my own.

"I'm sure. Keep the change, Paul," he replied and stood, lifting his cup to his lips.

"Well. I feel like an asshole." Annie put a hand on her hip, and her relieved smile lit up the hazy bar.

"Don't. *I* would have assumed I was ordering a double." Trip replied. "The limo is waiting for me out front. Are you ready to go home or..." Trip's unanswered question hung above the three of us like a cloud. Her eyes flicked to me and back to Trip. He seemed to ask 'are we continuing this charade, or can we call it a day?'

"Sam knows."

Trip nodded. "Good. I've kept enough secrets from him to last a fucking lifetime."

"You go on ahead. I'm gonna drive him home." She made a point of not looking at me when she said this. I exchanged a long pointed look with my brother.

"Alright." Though Trip didn't smile, that one word of his was loaded with amusement.

The bright morning sun seared through my closed lids. When I lifted my head from the pillow, the pain was overwhelming, like someone sticking icepicks into my brain. I rolled over with a groan and covered my head with the other pillow that smelled exactly like Anabelle. I groaned even loader as the details of the night crashed around me like marching band cymbals dropped from the ceiling.

Once we got back to my car, she took my keys and climbed behind the wheel. She informed me we were going to her place. She claimed she'd decided I shouldn't be alone and I wasn't about to argue with her. When we arrived at her apartment, we could hear the familiar sound of Jayse once we entered the building.

"Shit. I thought he was spending the night at the hotel. Maybe we should go to your place." Annabelle frowned as we ascended the stairs.

"Don't be ridiculous. Jayse is cool," I murmured. Frown lines marred her perfectly sculpted face as she unlocked the door, and we stepped into a chorus of male voices shouting "Annie!" Dale and four additional members of Noteable were sitting around the kitchen table doing shots. After no less than six attempts to refuse, I was coerced into drinking two shots of Hot Damn and two shots of Absolut Citron. By the time Annie dragged me away into her bedroom, I was stumbling.

"Unzip me." She demanded and I grinned like a fool as I helped her out of her gown. To my surprise, she *was* wearing a bra underneath, but I couldn't understand what the purpose of it was based on the tiny amount of material it contained. Matching black panties (the kind you could see through, praise God) were the only other things standing between me and her naked body. And for some baffling reason, it freaked me out a little.

Before I knew what was happening, her hands were in my hair, and her lips locked on mine. The ferocity of her kisses left me struggling to breathe. This wasn't at all how I pictured our first kiss, and believe me, I *had* pictured it many times. I wanted to take my time…to savor the taste of her. As it was, her teeth clanked against mine and I thought I tasted my own blood.

She'd pushed me back on the bed and flipped

off the lights. Then she was on me again, straddling me and grinding against me. I pulled away from her lips gasping for breath and her bra hit me in the face. I snatched it off and tossed it aside, and her hands went straight to my fly, tugging on my pants. Seconds later she had the zipper down, and my pants around my ankles. Her aggressiveness was hot, but more than a bit disturbing. The little blood left in my brain sounded warning sirens. Something was off here, and I needed to slam on the brakes.

"Stop, wait…hold up," I murmured, finally fisting her hair to pull my tongue free of her vice-like mouth. By the light of the streetlamp outside her window, I could see concern on her face.

"What's the problem?" Sounding slightly out of breath, her voice was hushed and anxious. "Oh. Don't worry. I've got condoms."

"No. That's not it. I'm…I'm not sure this is a good idea," I stammered, fumbling in my drunken state to articulate my reluctance. "I mean, it's a great fucking idea…but..."

"But what, Sam?" Annie climbed off of me and pulled a pillow to her chest to cover her perfect bare breast. The fifteen year old boy in me was kicking and screaming, but a man had to listen to his instincts. Mine said this was too good to be true. Too much too fast. Tonight was not the night.

"Annabelle…" I slurred, "I like you."

"But…" She drew the word out sarcastically,

and it was obvious she was furious.

"But I would kind of like to slow down a bit, if it's all the same to you." She jumped up off the bed and yanked open the dresser. I pulled myself up on my elbows and watched her toss on a big t-shirt and boxers. Somehow she looked even sexier like that, and I wanted to tell her it was all a joke. The gentleman in me, killjoy that he was, wouldn't allow it.

"I'm sorry." I said lamely, preparing to launch into an explanation that I hadn't even fully thought through.

"I'll sleep on the couch," she snapped and zipped out of the door. I lay awake a while longer, trying to decide if I should go to her and if I did what I would say to her. I tried to work out why I'd back-pedalled, but I was far too drunk and too tired to stay awake long enough for that.

So by the light of day, I wracked my dehydrated brain for something to say to her. Every option sounded lame and decidedly un-masculine. Then the reality of my life-altering discoveries from the night before crept back into the forefront of my mind, and I knew I had other issues that needed my attention.

Finally, I found the constitution to drag myself out of the bed and stumbled into the living room. Jayse and Dale sat on the couch drinking coffee and wearing mud masks that made them look like Jim Carrey. On the television, Faye Dunaway was doing her best Joan Crawford impersonation, shouting at Tina to not use wire hangers. Gaping in greenface, the two men seemed as surprised to see me as I was to see them.

"Morning, Sunshine," Jayse drawled. "I didn't know you were still here."

"Where's Annabelle?" I managed, as my eyes shot around the room.

"It's Sunday. I imagine she's at The Market-place." Jayse replied, standing and flouncing off to the kitchen, his red kimono robe trailing behind him. "Coffee?"

"You're too kind." I replied, following him to the kitchen.

"So…" Jayse began, "How are you feeling? No offense, Sam, but you look a little green."

"That's funny, I was about to say the same about you." I replied and then greedily sipped the searing liquid. It burnt my tongue and the roof of my mouth, but it didn't slow me down.

"Wacka, wacka, wacka." Dale called from the couch, smiling appreciatively. "Speaking of which, it's time to rinse this damned thing off."

As Dale vanished into the hallway, Jayse turned back to me. He managed a serious expression underneath his cracking visage. "Is everything cool? Annie was on the couch when I came out this morning."

"I have no idea. Last night was a clusterfuck of

epic proportions." I replied, collapsing into a kitchen chair. The site of empty shot glasses and half-drunk bottles of schnapps made me instantly regret it.

"Listen…" Jayse began, sounding apprehensive and unsure of himself for the first time since we'd met, "Annie's got more baggage than Virigin Airlines. She requires patience. She's high maintenance and not in a 'buy me that diamond studded nipple clamp' kind of way. If that's biting off more than you can chew, just do the both of you a favor and exit stage left."

Three times I began to reply, and three times I stopped short of speaking. If anyone was worth exploring my limits with, I was certain it was Annabelle. But the hurricane that was my life was trashing its way through Savannah, and there was no need to drag her into my maelstrom. The irony that I, not Trip, was the family fuck-up nearly made me laugh out loud. I did smile in a way that seemed to disturb Jayse.

I quickly wiped said smile from my face. "I have to go."

"Of course you do." He pursed his green lips, unceremoniously dumping my coffee into a travel cup.

CHAPTER SIXTEEN
Annie

"You're a quick study." The pharmacy manager grinned at me over her half-moon glasses, and I couldn't help but smile back. I'd been assigned to a compound pharmacy for my practicals, and though the added pressure initially freaked me out, now that I was here, I was *loving* it. Such an assignment afforded me an opportunity beyond what most pharmacy students would ever get to explore in their careers, let alone while still in school. Most of my classmates would end up working at a chain drug store and maybe compound amoxicillin and add some flavoring. There I was, in the process of customizing fertility drugs. Being third in my class, I was one of three who got to intern at such an establishment.

This type of work had helped keep my anxious brain occupied. I'd always enjoyed the rigidity of chemistry. Basically, it was cooking. Read the recipe from beginning to end, follow it precisely, and you can't go wrong. Common sense stuff, which apparently wasn't so common in the era of Starbucks and Pop Tarts.

But no matter how hard I focused, I couldn't get Sam out of my mind. I wondered if he'd confronted his mom. I wondered if he'd spoken to Mr. Wakefield. I wondered why the hell he hadn't called me or shown up on my doorstep. It's not like his brother didn't have my fucking number, and he sure as hell knew where I lived.

To be fair, I'd ditched him the morning after my botched seduction attempt. I had a standing date with my booth at The Marketplace, so it was a great excuse to flee, but let's face it—I was hiding. I'd wanted so badly to make him feel better and had thrown myself crotch first into the situation accordingly. I couldn't help myself. It was a huge part of my pattern to use sex as an attempt to connect, but for whatever reason, Sam didn't want any part of it. I was glad, though, since the second part of my pattern is to push away those who got close to me, but I was also disappointed. Sam was different. He meant something to me. So logically, I avoided him.

I began calling Trip before our sittings to verify Sam was nowhere near his studio. True to form, Trip didn't press me for an explanation, and I didn't volunteer one.

It had been two weeks since I'd mauled Sam in my bed when Trip turned to me, paint brush in hand, and asked, "You're still coming to Tybee for the birthday party this weekend, aren't you?"

"Ummmm…" I'd blocked out Sam's birthday. Not his minty taste on my tongue, or the warm way his words felt against my throat, but his party at the beach house? Sure.

"Annie, Violet is bringing Maisie for a few hours on Saturday night. This is our last shot." He wore sullen bags under his eyes and I couldn't blame him. Violet's engagement party had gone off without a hitch the weekend before at Black Keys. Martin had begged me to pick up that shift, even offering me a bonus. But I knew my limitations. There was no way I was serving drinks to Dashul Stein and keeping my job. Word in the club was that all went like clockwork, and all the most important people in Savannah showed up, with the exception of Imogen Moore Beaumont. One of the waitresses told me that she walked in on the future bride crying in the ladies room. I'd kept that little nugget to myself, afraid to give Trip any more hope.

He was right, of course. I had to go. Violet needed one final shove in Trip's direction, and it was now or never. "Who's all going?"

Trip spouted off a small guest list, which included a couple of Trip's art world pals, Sam's frat brothers, and Randall and his fiancé. "You're bringing Jayse, right? Because I told Violet he'd be there."

I tried to not show how annoying that was. Jayse was way too fascinated with Violet for my taste. They'd been to lunch twice, and I'd walked in on him making plans to shop with her just before her engagement party. It seemed childish, but it hurt me. Not that I couldn't share a friend, but Jayse seemed incapable of splitting his attention and had a knack for making me feel excluded when it came to Violet. And I didn't seem to be the only one who had a problem with Jayse's behavior. He'd been blowing Dale off a lot lately, and Dale seemed to be getting pretty frustrated about it.

"Yes," I replied, trying to keep all emotion out of my voice.

"Have him bring Dale." Trip called from the other side of the painting.

"Got it." I'm pretty sure he heard the hard edge in my voice anyhow, because he sat down his pallet and walked around the canvas, wiping off his hands on this flannel shirt.

"I don't get it, Angel. You and Sam seemed pretty cozy." He folded his arms and leaned against the wall. His jaw was set, and I knew he wouldn't let up without some sort of explanation.

"Nothing happened. He's overwhelmed with all your family drama and besides, I have finals, and I don't have time for anything anyway." My mind spun as I thought about seeing him again. I had to get a gift for Sam, and I was as clueless about what to buy him now as I was a few weeks before.

"Listen, Annie. Sam has always been a bit of a loner. I'm not saying he doesn't like other people, but he's more at home with a punching bag or a book than in a crowd." Trip tossed me a bottle of water and we both popped the lids off and drank. He peered out the window thoughtfully for a long moment, and then finally looked me in the eye again. "My brother is definitely a solitary man, at least compared to me. I think he's in his element when he's alone. It'll take him some time to get used to a relationship."

I chuckled. "I don't want a relationship, Trip. I have shit to do."

"Even better. Casual is something Sam is very comfortable with. You two should hit it off even better than I thought." His crooked grin dissipated when he saw my surprise.

"But...he said...he said he wanted to 'slow down'. Who does that?"

Trip raised both eyebrows and blinked at me in surprise. He opened his mouth then snapped it shut.

"What?" I demanded. Now I crossed *my* arms over my chest expectantly.

"As far as I know, there's only one other girl he's ever liked for more than one night, Angel. And that was Violet. You must have made a hell of an impression on him."

"You've got to be shitting me!" I blurted, unable to contain myself. Sam and Violet! "Before or after you married her?"

He smiled and shrugged. "Before. Yes, I'm a scoundrel. It was kind of a thing for a while."

"I bet it was," I said, annoyed at the image of Sam and Violet together. It made her invading my territory with Jayse sting even more.

He didn't pause to acknowledge my loaded remark. "My point is, you obviously mean a lot to him. More than he can probably verbalize, knowing Sam. Take my word for it. So if you seriously don't want anything to do with him, you probably shouldn't come to Tybee. But I really wish you would."

I reflected on Trip's words as I ate my lunch at the coffee shop next to the pharmacy. I knew in my heart he was right. Sam wanted more. I also knew I wouldn't be able to stay away from him for much longer. But I was damaged goods, a fucking walking tornado of well-earned issues and insecurities. Sam had his hands full with his own chaos; he didn't need mine to complete the set.

I thought about Sam calling me courageous in the bar. I sure as hell wasn't acting courageous now. Sam's world was upside down. To think that the circumstances of his birth led to his father's suicide and his brother's disintegration was a heavy burden to bear. And instead of being the friend I'd presented myself to be, I'd simply disappeared. The least I could be was a decent listener. At that moment, over homemade chicken noodle soup and a café mocha, I made up my mind to go to the party.

My phone rang. It was a number I didn't recognize, but it was local.

"Hello?"

"May I speak to Annabelle, please?"

"This is Annabelle."

"Well, hello. This is Lola Andresen. I'm the manager at Imogene's Gallery. We've sold out of your tombstone rubbings, and I have your commission check. I don't suppose you have any more inventories you'd like to unload."

I blinked stupidly at my bowl of soup. "I'm sorry? I don't understand."

"Trip Beaumont brought in your rubbings. Thirteen of them. We've sold all of them." The woman replied. "Would you like us to mail you a check?"

"N…No, that's quite alright, I can come pick it up." Trip said nothing about reselling my stuff and I was flattered he thought it would sell in an actual gallery, but I was completely taken aback. The pharmacy wasn't far from Imogene's, and I was curious to see what kind of price they were charging. "Are you sure you want more?"

"Absolutely. They are very popular and easy to move. We'd love to have twenty more if you have them."

My mind and heart both raced. If Lola wanted my inventory on any sort of regular basis, I wouldn't have my Sunday marketplace obligation anymore. That meant a lot more time to study.

And more time for other things.

I told Lola that I'd stop by later that day with more rubbings and to pick up the check. She informed me that they were pricing them for twice the amount I'd been charging and that Imogene's only kept thirty percent of the sale. I could feel my face and chest flushing with excitement. As long as they continued to sell well, with that kind of profit, I'd definitely have my weekends free. Relief rolled over me like the tide. More free time. Time was my most prized possession, and I felt like I'd won the lottery.

After wrapping up my work day, I decided to call Trip to thank him for the vote of confidence. He laughed at me when I started jabbering excited thank-yous about the rubbings.

"Slow down there, Angel. I can't take any of the credit."

"Of course you can. She said you brought them in. It's not like they saw me on the street and begged to showcase my work," I cracked, guiding my car slowly around the square. An old man walking his dog waved to me. I waved back cheerfully.

"It was Sam's idea, Annie. I kept my favorite and he paid me for the rest. He picked one out for himself and told me to deliver them to Lola. He had it all arranged. I'm just the delivery boy. You can tip me if you like." My stomach did a flip as I parked in front of Imogene's. Sam again. My mouth felt dry at the thought that he would do something so thoughtful for me, and I felt my pulse quicken to a dangerous pace.

"I guess I'll thank him at the party," I murmured as I ran my hands over my pencil skirt in a lame attempt to smooth out any wrinkles.

"You do that." Trip's lazy drawl made me smile. I hung up and peeked at my upswept hair to make sure it still looked presentable after my busy day at the pharmacy. Noticing several loose strands, I pulled out a hairbrush and reassembled my up-do and as an afterthought, pulled some deodorant from my purse. If I was going to be doing business with Imogene's, I didn't want to start that relation-ship smelling like armpit.

I pulled out the four framed rubbings I had in the back seat and entered the gallery. I practically went into a diabetic coma from the eye candy that they showcased on every surface, nook, and cranny in the converted warehouse. There was one wall on the end that featured Trip Beaumont's work exclusively. Two dark, haunting paintings hung at the bottom, but the rest of his brilliant work practically jumped off the wall at me from under the crafty lighting. An older couple stood holding hands as they admired one of my favorites, which featured the fountain in Lafayette Square. The colors Trip used reminded me of the chalk drawings in the movie Mary Poppins, which had been one of my favorites as a little girl. His painting style had a way of showcasing the world with childlike optimism and exuberance.

Most of the time.

I wondered if the dark paintings, which were arguably stunning and the kind of art that Jayse would love to buy, were done at the height of his drinking days. Not that they lacked the bold and crisp detail that was signature Trip, but the mood was morose and full of longing and desperation that was absent from the paintings that I skirted through every time I went to his studio.

I saw that there were stairs leading up to another floor and was itching to explore further, but I knew they were closing soon and didn't want to keep them. The frames in my hands were getting heavy, and I hurried to the counter just as a curvy middle-aged woman with striking green eyes came out of a back office. Her name tag said 'Lola.'

"I'm Annabelle Clarke," I offered, sparing her the customer service spiel. She smiled broadly and pulled open a drawer, removing an envelope.

"You've got great technique. And your framing skills are top notch. I have one of your rubbings in my office at home." Lola smiled, and I felt giddy imagining her hanging one of my hobby projects in her home.

I bit my lip. "Really? Which one?"

She raised a dark eyebrow. "Jonathan Kessler. 1897"

"The one I did in terra cotta. I love that one." A genuine smile overtook me. She stared at me with wide eyes.

"You remember mine?"

"I remember all of them."

"How?"

We chatted for a couple more minutes about my photographic memory and a couple of small local cemeteries I had yet to visit. When I turned to leave, I practically smacked face first into Imogene Moore Beaumont herself. Her face contorted in surprise and distaste. I tried to maintain my cool, but I wonder if mine did as well.

"Annie." Her greeting was as crisp as a Minnesota winter morning.

"Mrs. Beaumont." I nodded and made to sidestep her. She planted her statuesque self directly in my path.

"Let's discuss this sordid business like ladies, shall we?" Her penciled eyebrows knitted slightly, as she gave my attire a quick once over.

Baffled, I folded my arms across my chest defensively. I couldn't imagine where she was going with that opening line. "Discuss what?"

'Cosmo,' as Trip and Sam called her, stopped short of rolling her eyes, but she did look toward the ceiling. "Your *relationship* with my son."

"Which one?" It was so worth looking whorish in front of my new pal Lola for the look my comment produced on Imogene's face.

"Why, Trip...of course..." Her pauses were barely perceptible as she worked to maintain her finishing school demeanor.

I inhaled deeply, trying to control my forest fire of a temper. "Trip and I are friends. There's nothing more to say."

"I have it on good authority the two of you were lewd in a dressing room. If you must behave like a porn star, young lady, do it with someone else's son."

I could actually feel my eye twitching, and my cheeks caught on fire. She had a point, but what we'd done or not done was none of her damned business. "Trip's a big boy. He doesn't need a permission slip from you anymore. If I were you, I'd be a bit more focused on your other son about now."

I could see the well-oiled wheels turning behind the grand dame's eyes. She glanced past me, and I could hear Lola scrambling into her office.

"Listen to me carefully, Annabelle," she began through a terrifying smile, "Trip is one thing. He's been flailing for a while, but I have high hopes he's pulling himself together. Samson…is my baby. And *he* has unlimited potential. I won't tolerate some trashy blonde lamprey sucking him dry. He may have lost his compass, but he's exceptionally brilliant and perceptive. He'll find his way back to the path. Be a dear and make sure you're not blocking it."

I emitted an ugly chuckle. "You've obviously lost touch with reality if you think *I'm* Sam's problem. If I were you, I'd stop worrying about other people's kids and have a serious chat with your *own*."

I pushed past her and fled, exiting before my big mouth caused any more issues. Shutting myself in the sanctity of my car, I could feel angry tears threatening to escape me, but I bit them back. I would not let that snooty bitch make me cry. As much as I wanted to wave her infidelity in front of her upturned nose, Sam's battle with his mother was his to fight, and I had no business opening that gangrenous wound.

CHAPTER SEVENTEEN
Sam

"Are you sure we should bring beer to Trip's?" Randall called from the back of the convenience store, holding a case of Dos Equis up over his head.

Loaded down with every kind of chip the place carried, I leaned to the side of the fountain drink display so that he could see me. "He's cool with it. He said it makes him more uncomfortable to not have it around. It makes him feel like a party pooper."

It was December twenty-first, and while some were celebrating Jesus's birthday with their families, my chosen family and I were celebrating mine. Having a birthday so close to Christmas sucked when I was a kid. Most of my friends couldn't come to my parties because we were on holiday break, and Trip got loads of presents twice a year, whereas mine came in one big cluster a few days apart.

Now as an adult, I kind of liked it. My college friends and I always used it as an excuse to party.

Even in law school, when I'd grown more solitary, I could kick back and watch the snow fall with a glass of wine and a great book. It somehow seemed fitting that as the wheel of my life turned, another year was in its death throes.

"I'm pretty sure that being around a bunch of partiers isn't recommended," Patience (Randall's fiancé) informed us, her dark eyes full of doubt. Patience was an elementary school teacher and a kick boxing enthusiast. She and Randall had been engaged for nearly two years, and they hadn't set a date. I guess you could say she was aptly named.

"Trip insisted. He said if he is going to live sober, he wants to live. Not join a monastery in Tibet. Who am I to argue?"

"As long as we aren't shoving him down a flight of twelve steps..." Randall shrugged and proceeded to the cash register. Both Patience and Randall had valid points, but I hadn't asked Trip about liquor; he'd offered this information. "It was a party, after all," he'd said, and he *was* the host. Trip made it clear he wasn't going to provide booze—that would be opening Pandora 's Box with a sledgehammer – but he had absolutely no problem with us bringing our own supply. Considering Annabelle was coming to the party, I figured I'd need some for medicinal purposes.

Taking Jayse's advice, I'd kept my distance. Annabelle was not my idea of a one-nighter, but I was way too fucked up and disorganized to try to give her whatever it was she deserved. I was in no position to try my hand at dating for the first time since Vi. Not that Annabelle probably wanted anything to do with me since I'd turned down sex with her like I had. She probably thought I was a total pussy. I still kicked myself for walking away from *that*.

I was completely blown away when Trip told me she was coming to my party. I assumed since Violet was on the guest list, the motivation was matchmaking, not celebrating the blessed event of my entering the world. Still, seeing her and knowing she would likely ignore me all weekend, I'd need something to dull the ache in both my chest and my groin.

I was still obsessing about Annabelle twenty minutes later when we turned onto Trip's private road. Randall whistled with admiration as he pulled into the driveway of the six bedroom beach house. My brother had bought it as a wedding present for Vi, but during the divorce, she told him to keep it. She already lived in the house they'd bought in Savannah, and I always figured that was reminder enough of the life she'd expected to have.

"Nothin' like a beach party." Patience eyed the house as she pulled her overnight bag from the trunk.

"Well, we won't be skinny dipping, but sixty

degrees is great grilling weather," I replied, feeling a little bit foolish. Most thought it was pointless to go to Tybee when it was too cold for a dip in the ocean, but I loved the salty smell of the Atlantic. Whether it was the river or the sea, water had always been some sort of salve for my soul. I'd never needed the hydrotherapy quite so badly, and I was tempted to ditch my guests, take my bottle of single malt and hit the sand.

My week had been an exhausting one. I'd signed offers on both the riverfront condo and the vacant building my realtor claimed was in the slums. We were all set to close on both Monday morning. As promised, Marybeth had managed to get me the empty building for a song, and true to my word, I'd offered full price for the condo. When I declined her offer to go back to her place and celebrate, she boldly backed me against her office door and placed her hand squarely between my legs.

"Your loss, Sam," she whispered in that raspy voice of hers. Part of me—a very hard, very specific part of me – agreed with her.

In addition to my real estate purchases, I'd hired Trip's P.I. to do a little digging on Sebastian Wakefield. I told him budget wasn't a concern and to spare no expense. He'd reported back to me just yesterday, and his investigation had produced very little that I couldn't have found through business contacts and internet gossip. The P.I. looked particularly embarrassed when he told me he'd been made. Two nights before, Wakefield had strolled up and knocked on his car window. With his goons over each shoulder, he informed the private investigator to tell me he knew "what I was up to." That brought a smile to my face. One of the things I'd counted on was Sebastian's assumption that he was smarter than me. While his smug ass was telling off my P.I., my second investigator – the one he *didn't* know about – proved to be a much better treasure hunter.

While my people had been busy stalking Wakefield, I'd signed the final documents for my trusts and consulted with my brokers to make some portfolio changes. I had liquidated all of my mediocre stock and after paying cash for both my condo and my Savannah building, I set orders in motion to start a foundation in Daddy's name. I also filed paperwork to buy copious shares of stock through several shell companies my grandfather had founded for this type of purpose years before. I called a board meeting at Beaumont Enterprises that was scheduled for two weeks from yesterday. Together, Trip and I owned controlling interest. Though we hadn't discussed it yet, I had no doubt he'd vote whatever way I asked him to. I was about to be a very busy, very wealthy man. Therefore, saying I needed to decompress was like saying you don't want to let Mike Tyson near your ear.

The door swung open, and Jayse Monroe materialized before us. He let out a theatrical cry and using the porch as a stage, began a disturbing impersonation of Marilyn Monroe singing "Happy Birthday." I could feel all the blood in my body rushing to my cheeks, and I would have paid serious money to bottle the look on Randall's face. Patience cackled so uproariously that she nearly fell over. As the three of us applauded our serenader, I realized Annabelle was standing in the open doorway. Her eyes sparkled as she rested against the doorframe. Displaying her typical attitude, she smirked over at Jayse with her arms folded across her chest. Our gazes locked and held just long enough to make me blush a second time. A tiny smile tugged at her lips as she descended the stairs from the porch. It was almost impossible not to stare at her shapely legs so generously revealed by her gauzy pink dress. It made me think of the ballet, which led to a fantasy about a mirrored room and the barre, an interlude that I filed away for later.

"Annie! How's it goin'?" Randall called to her.

"I'm good. Need me to carry something?" She passed within a foot of me and I felt the pull of her so intensely that for a second it was hard to breathe. Randall's eyed me knowingly as he turned to her with several grocery bags full of chips.

"I can carry more than that!" She put her hands on her slim hips and cocked her head sideways at him.

"Be my guest, Honey. I just got my nails done," Patience interjected, displaying her dragon lady talons before her. Jayse's mouth formed in a silent "o," and he claimed one of her hands for inspection, shoving her duffle bag at Annie who took it without a word. Annie blinked at Jayse as if ready to drop-kick him. Randall snatched Patience's bag from Annie's hands and cut his eyes sideways at his fiancée. Patience raised contrite eyebrows at him and then turned to Jayse with a "oh no he didn't" shrug, which Jayse rewarded with a dimply grin.

As we lugged our supplies inside, Trip and Dale waved from the kitchen, where they were prepping enough food for an army.

"Jesus! Did you invite everyone I've ever met?" I asked. Trip laughed and nodded to the adjoining living room. Lounging on the sectional were two of my sorority brothers and their long-time girlfriends. Charles and Michael were the only guys in my frat I really considered friends. Both were in situations not so unlike mine – legacies who had always been interested in blazing trails of their own. Okay…so maybe I couldn't officially call myself a legacy anymore, but old habits and whatnot. Chuck and Mike also stood out from that crowd as a couple of genuine human beings and we'd stayed in touch even after I went off to Harvard. I trusted both of them implicitly.

Leaving the others to mingle, I beckoned them both to help me stock the outdoor bar. As we unpacked my intoxicating bounty, I asked if they'd be interested in exploring a joint business venture. I skimmed over the details and they both nodded in agreement over their ice cold mugs of beer. I felt like I'd maintained my World Championship of Poker face. The intricate orchestrations I'd woven were holding tight. I promised to email them the detailed proposal early next week and insisted that we *not* discuss another word of business for the rest of the weekend.

We were finishing our second beer when Trip, resembling a modern day Bacchus, led the others outdoors in some sort of odd processional of culinary gifts. He'd had the smoker going since yesterday, but proceeded to add what looked like an entire cow's worth of meat to the grill. Both Mike and Charles' girlfriends giggled when my brother muttered some off-the-cuff joke, and I rolled my eyes at Randall. We had long commiserated about my brother's inexplicable panty-dropping skills. Randall tried to bite back a grin. I turned back around to see Annabelle behind the bar with me. She lightly brushed against me as she popped the fridge open, passing drinks to Jayse and Dale.

"Happy Birthday, Sam," she murmured in a very quiet, very unAnnie-like way.

"Thanks." My heart hammered at the shy look

in her eyes and the vivid memory of her straddling me like a cowgirl. Jayse and Dale took one look at us and vanished like an apparition.

"I'm the one who should be thanking *you*. Lola sold all my rubbings and she wants more. I need to reimburse you for what you paid Trip." The sea breeze blew a strand of her golden hair between her lips as she spoke. Without thinking, I reached out and brushed it away, letting my thumb linger on her cheek. She looked up at me from under those impossibly long lashes, and I realized that we'd crossed a line in her bedroom that we'd never be able to come back from. And I had no regrets, a fact which seemed like the most astounding of all my recent revelations.

"Don't be ridiculous," I whispered, "I own a quarter of that gallery. Just consider it test product. I'm really glad it worked out. I imagine you can think of better ways to spend your Sundays."

The glorious shade of pink that appeared on her cheeks at my innuendo made me smile.

"Daddy!" I turned away from Annie at the ear-splitting squeal just in time to witness a blonde head streak past the bar and slam full force into Trip's legs. Unmistakable glee radiated from Maisie as Trip swung her in a circle, instantly transforming our casual gathering into a party. She clung to Trip as if she were afraid he'd cease to exist if she let go. I approached them slowly, wondering if my niece would recognize me after a whole year.

Her oversized blue eyes widened when she looked over Trip's shoulder in my direction. "Uncle Sam! It's your birthday! We brought you a cake! Mama said red velvet was your favorite!"

Unable to contain my joy, I knelt and opened my arms and she flung herself at me with such energy, I nearly fell onto my back on the concrete. "Maisie! You're a monster! How did you grow so big?"

"I eat broccoli," she replied, as if mine was the stupidest question in the history of the world.

"Well, that explains everything," I replied dryly, and she nodded in agreement. I heard Annie giggle and couldn't help giving her a sideways glance. I noticed that Jayse was holding the door open for Violet. She was carrying an obnoxiously large cake box that dwarfed her tiny frame. Annie began clearing empties from the closest end of the bar to make room for Violet's contribution. Trip stepped forward and effortlessly relieved Violet of her cargo. The silent exchange that passed between them was loaded, but not with their usual post- break-up ugliness. Annie and I looked at each other simultaneously. Yep, I wasn't imagining things.

"There's the birthday boy. Ready for your spankin'?" Vi gave me a quick side hug. Her nearly platinum short hair popped against her red blouse. She'd clearly dressed to impress, and my brother couldn't take his eyes off her. To me, it seemed like that was what she was going for, based on the various not-so-secretive glances in Trip's direction.

"Promises, promises," I quipped in return. "Glad you could make it."

"Barely. I wasn't sure the big man was gonna let me out of the kitchen once he heard whose party it was." She frowned, taking Maisie by the hand. Her voice had more than a little bite to it, and I had no doubt that there was trouble in paradise.

"Hey there, Hot Stuff. Love the kicks." Jayse pulled Violet away and I saw Annie peer unhappily at them as they bantered. I watched her slink away and busy herself behind the bar. Randall called her over to the far end of the bar and whispered something to her. Annabelle nodded emphatically in response. As Trip's friends arrived, I mingled with my guests and made small talk with my frat bros and their ladies. The entire time, I kept tabs on Annabelle, who carried on a long conversation with both Randall and Patience. Their body language made it seem like they'd known each other for ages, and I was oddly pleased that my best friend hit it off so well with her.

Later, after we'd all gorged ourselves on low country fixings, Annabelle pulled open the cake box and started in with that wonderful laugh of hers. I whipped my head in Violet's direction and saw her lips curled in a devilish smirk.

"What?" I approached the cake box like it might contain explosives or a cobra. As I drew near, I saw a white cake which a first glance seemed fairly unremarkable. It had a black punching bag with red boxing gloves on each side near the bottom. The positioning of the gloves gave it the distinct resemblance of male genitalia. Worse was the message Violet had the baker put on the cake. In red flourishy letters it read, "Keep beating your bag, Sam." I shook my head. Soon everyone was gathered around the box laughing and posting pictures to Facebook via their phones.

"What's so funny, Uncle Sam?"Maisie asked, genuinely perplexed.

"You Mama's naughty, Mae," I replied, biting back a smile.

"Yeah, she is," she agreed and ran off toward Trip who was busy lighting twenty-five candles with his Scream Zippo. After the particularly showy 'Happy Birthday' greeting from Jayse, the group's encore performance seemed to lack je ne c'est quoi. A bit overwhelmed by all the attention, I slipped away while Jayse and Maisie argued over who got the first piece and made my way up several flights of stairs to the fourth floor cupola. Sipping chardonnay, I gazed out at the South Channel and the impressive ocean view. An unexpected feeling of contentment consumed me, and for the first time since leaving Harvard, I was truly glad I'd come home. I heard someone on the stairs. Glancing over from my chair by the window, I noticed Annabelle approaching me with two bowls of cake and ice cream.

"Hey," she greeted me, pausing at the top of the stairs as if asking if it was cool that she joined me. I patted the seat next to me and she plopped down on the sofa, handing me some napkins and a heaping bowl of sugary goodness. Seeing she'd presented me the piece with the words "your bag" on it, I rolled my eyes with a reluctant smile. She grinned in that saucy way she always did. After a few seconds of heated eye contact, we both lost our amused expressions. I realized in that instant that there was nothing funny about the way I felt about her. It seemed like the feeling might be mutual.

"So about the other night..." I began, but she adamantly shook her head, her thick mane spilling in sexy waves around her shoulders.

"That was obnoxious. I'm so embarrassed." She blew out a loud breath and turned appalled eyes on me. "I have the shittiest timing. I'm so sorry."

"Don't be. I'm not." I set my untouched bowl on the end table and turned sideways to face her. I saw a tiny bit of frosting on the corner of her lips, and I wanted to taste it. I scooted closer to her and dabbed that delicious mouth with a napkin. "Someone had to break the ice. But please understand-I was way too wasted to express myself coherently.

That night was so messed up…no matter how you look at it. You and I…it was just too much too soon."

She seemed to concentrate on the ocean, but I suspected she didn't really see it. Her voice sounded distant when she finally spoke. "It's probably for the best. There's a lot about me you don't know. When you said I had daddy issues, you were right. I have problems, Sam. I…"

"Can you just forget I ever said that? Please?" I sighed, running a hand over my hair. I hated that I'd shot my mouth off to her because I was a jealous little bitch.

"Only if you can forget I jumped you like a cat in heat," she retorted, fervently studying her shoes.

"Well then…don't forget it, 'cause I sure as *hell* am not giving that memory up," I shot back, causing her to meet my eyes again. To my surprise, she slowly unveiled a dazzling smile.

"I want a do-over. What do you say we just give this a try? Are you done pretending to be my brother's girl yet? 'Cause I may just have to out the two of you." I reached out and entwined my calloused fingers with her perfect ones. She didn't pull away; she just stared curiously down at our unified hands.

"I'd really like to, but have so much going on. School and…I have a fucked-up family," she whispered. I noticed her hand tremble slightly under mine and squeezed it.

"Who doesn't?" I put my arm around her and pulled her closer to me. If she was going to shoot me down, I wanted to feel her against me one more time.

She leaned her head on my shoulder, and the sensation of her warmth against me was so perfect that I had to close my eyes and savor it. "Point taken."

"My life's far from perfect, Annabelle. I'm pretty sure that won't change anytime soon. And you should know right now that I'm bad at this. I've got almost no experience with relationships. But I'm willing to try." She lifted her head off of my shoulder, and I saw her eyes were shiny and filled with fear.

"Your mother? She hates me." She blinked at me with childlike innocence.

"That hardly makes you unusual." I cracked a lopsided grin. Her lips twitched, and she chewed on her lip in a nervous manner.

"This whole thing scares me," she admitted. I brushed her hair out of her eyes and leaned in for a soft kiss. Her soft lips were inviting…welcoming. She moaned quietly and melted into me. The feel of her body against mine was addictive. I pulled away before I got myself into serious trouble.

"Me, too." My lips grazed her forehead.

"Hey, Sam! Quit making out with Annabelle

and get your ass back down here! You have presents to open!" I heard Randall yell. Laughter drifted up the stairs to us, and with matching eye rolls,
we pulled away from each other. Standing, I pulled
her into my arms again. Her hands wrapped around
my neck, and she pulled my mouth down to meet
hers once more. Our tongues touched delicately as
we explored each other with caution and fascination. I was in no hurry to go downstairs; it was going to be impossible for anyone to compete with the
gifts she was already giving me.

CHAPTER EIGHTEEN
Annie

After several more wet kisses, Sam groaned regretfully and held me at arm's length. I wanted to whine and tell him to forget about his party, but instead, I let him lead me by the hand down the stairs. Everyone else had assembled in the living room, and a tide of knowing eyes washed over us. I felt Sam's grip on my hand tighten. My eyes were drawn to his pitiful knuckles, which were beaten to shit. I squeezed back gently, and he didn't flinch. I guess the abuse from pummeling other men in the face had conditioned them to handle worse. He pulled me toward a love seat which was conspicuously empty. In front of us, the coffee table contained a mountain of gifts. Maisie hovered near the presents as if she were about to dive in and rip each one open herself.

With enthusiasm that rivaled his niece's, Sam proceeded to tear each gift free from its wrapper. Seeing him interact with Maisie was a heart squeeze. He was so good with her, acting as if he wasn't strong enough to rip the wrapping paper and gushing about her muscles when she could. This sweet side of him was an unexpected surprise, and my face hurt from smiling.

There was no mistaking Sam's love for the cuff links Trip bought, or the first edition of *The Sun Also Rises* that Violet had found for him. As the treasures began to pile up beside him, I got more and more nervous about my gift. After stopping by the gym to see Randall and pick his brain, I was pretty sure he'd like it, but most of Sam's friends operated on a different playing field than I did.

Jayse and Dale, who'd been fighting about anything and everything for days, both seemed pleased with Sam's reaction to their rare vinyl copy of a Frank Sinatra album they'd given him. They'd wanted to give him something musical, and Trip had recommended anything by the Rat Pack. As Sam or each gift-giver explained to the group what had prompted each selection, it was a bit of a crash course on the man I was so enamored with. He apparently had a love of old music, preferably on vinyl ('nothing sounds quite like it'); fitness gear, like the wrist monitor Randall gave him to track his progress; books, especially classic novels; and ties. Now *that* was an intriguing bit of information...

We didn't have everything in common, a state of affairs which was, in my opinion, ideal. It guaranteed we'd teach each other stuff...expose each other to new and interesting things. Startled, I realized I felt all of those "new crush" tingles, but an odd sense of peace accompanied them that I'd never experienced before. My nerves kicked in, and I realized I was building sandcastles in the clouds. I'd inserted Sam into the role of knight on a big white steed who'd ride in and save me from my ghettofabulous tower. I wouldn't say I slammed on the imaginary brakes, but I was definitely pumping them. Sam seemed to smell the fresh doubt on me like I exuded it from my pores. Every time I started to fidget, whether he was looking at me at the moment or not, he reached out and touched me. He'd hold my hand or stroke my hair as if silently telling me to not think so much. I did my best to comply.

At one point, I noticed Violet eyeing me curiously. It made me curious about her past with Sam, but there was nothing possessive or territorial about her demeanor. She seemed pleased when he put his arm on the back of the couch behind me. In return, I was delighted that she was sitting next to Trip on the sofa. Maisie now settled on Trip's other side, and they looked like a picture-perfect happy family. The only thing that marred the Norman Rockwell moment was the garish diamond on her left hand that was from another man.

As coincidence would have it, Sam's last unopened package was from me. His almond shaped eyes found mine as he picked up the large, thin, rectangular present and his eyebrows knit curiously. Embarrassed, I fought hard not to show it in front of the room full of people watching our relationship sprout fresh from the soil. He slid his fingers along the seam, ripping open the shiny lavender paper that reminded me so much of the color of his eyes.

His mouth fell open slightly as he held up the framed fight poster signed by Joe Frazier and Muhammad Ali in 1971. Randall jumped up and ran around the back of the loveseat, so he could admire it over his shoulder.

"This is...wow." Sam's remark oozed the type of reverence one might expect for someone viewing the crown jewels.

"Madison Square Gardens. How many times did my dad tell us about this fight?" Randall gushed, slapping Sam on the back like only someone in the throes of a bromance can. I watched them with fascination, like an anthropologist studying a long-lost tribe on a previously undiscovered island. I got that the poster was from a landmark fight in boxing history, and Randall had made it clear when we talked at Hard Knocks that Sam worshipped Ali. Internet searching had led me to this poster, and thanks to Trip's check for my modeling work and Imogene's Gallery, I could afford the splurge.

"She's a keeper, Sammy." Randall mumbled and before I had a chance feel too humiliated by his assessment, the doorbell rang and several people used the opportunity to refill empty plates or glasses. Jayse challenged Maisie to a game of foosball, and half the guests vanished toward the rec room.

Sam ignored them all. He leaned in as if he were whispering in my ear and kissed the spot directly behind it on my neck. It tickled, and I fought off the urge to laugh. His warm breath had every hair on my body standing on end.

"How can I properly thank you for such a generous gift?" His husky voice was thick with testosterone and adrenaline.

"I'm sure we can think of something," I whispered back, sounding more than a little breathless. Raised voices snapped us both out of the moment. Trip's hostility emanated from the front door, and I immediately looked around for Maisie. It seemed she was still with Jayse. Randall and Sam hurried toward the altercation. Violet disappeared in that direction as well, and I cautiously trailed after them.

I turned the corner in time to see Sam dart out the front door. Whatever was going on had apparently spilled outside onto the porch, so I followed Randall and Violet outside.

I stopped in my tracks when I saw Trip on the lawn. He was waving his finger in his mother's face. She stood at the bottom of the stairs with Sebastian Wakefield.

"Don't be ridiculous, Trip," I heard her say

through gritted teeth, "Sam is my son, and I'll bring whoever the hell I wish to his party."

She seemed to spot Sam descending the stairs and smiled up at him. "Sam! There you are. Tell your brother to stop acting crazy. You haven't been giving him scotch, have you?"

Sam stopped one step from the bottom. "Trip hasn't been drinking, Mama. But I think you'd better leave. Your guests aren't welcome here."

I glanced toward the car and saw both of Wakefield's body guards moving toward the stairs. Cosmo looked at Sam as if he'd just hacked a loogey in her general direction.

"How dare you speak to me that way? I didn't raise the both of you to carry on in public."

"You didn't raise us at all. Athena did," Trip snapped and by the look their mother gave Sam, I could tell his expression concurred. I stepped closer, wanting to see Sam's face. I wanted to try to read how this unexpected confrontation was affecting him. The planks creaked beneath me, and Cosmo looked up and saw me. She gave me a poisonous once-over, an unmistakable look of abject disapproval etched in every age line on her face.

"Oh, I see. I guess I shouldn't be surprised. You've both become clones of your father. Not a lick of ambition between the two of you. Spending your days running around with common whores." Her voice dropped nearly an octave as she glowered first at Sam, then at Trip. Wakefield watched the entire exchange with what looked like polite amusement. Trip fumed.

"Mama," Sam snapped, his tone dark and impatient.

"Don't ever speak to us about Daddy. And *how dare you* bring this man to my house?" In his rage, Trip seemed to misjudge the distance between himself and Wakefield, and slammed his pointer finger into Wakefield's sternum. His bodyguards sprang at Trip, and the smaller of the two punched him in the jaw. Trip took it like a champ and swung on the guy, missing him entirely. Sam leapt forward, knocking the smaller bodyguard to the ground. Everything seemed to happen at once. There was some general shoving, and Sam grabbed the larger of the two bodyguards by the hair and raised his right fist. Randall hopped down the last half of the flight of stairs and flung himself into the fray. He pushed Sam back before he could land a punch and put himself between the two warring factions. Sam and the larger bodyguard were still practically eye to eye. For a moment, I was sure the larger bodyguard was going to hit Sam.

"Unless you plan to pull that piece you're wearing under your coat, I suggest you step off of my boy." Randall's non-negotiable tone brimmed with promise. Wakefield seemed to decide now was the time to speak up.

"Everyone, relax." His clipped voice and enigmatic presence drew everyone's attention. Everyone seemed to focus on him instantly. I was aware of someone next to me and turned to see Violet. Her green eyes surveyed the scene below as if it were a booby trap that might ensnare her if she wasn't cautious. "Coming here was a mistake, Geenie. Let's go back to the car."

"No." Imogene seemed immune to Wakefield's spell, her eyes never leaving Trip's. "I think I'd like to hear why my son seems so hell bent on hating you...and me."

"This really isn't the time or the place for this conversation, is it?" Wakefield tried to take her arm but Imogene whipped it away without so much as a glance in his direction.

"I'm being turned away from my son's birthday party. I think this seems like exactly the time for this conversation," she snipped, her eyes shifting slowly from Trip to Sam and back again.

"I'm inclined to agree with Mr. Wakefield. This is Trip's house. He can decline anyone he wishes to. We *were* raised better, Mama. Let's not make more of a scene." Sam's level reasoning seemed to give her pause. She turned her blue eyes on him again, and her shoulders relaxed as she shrugged back into her public persona as if it were a custom mink coat.

"Fine. But I have something for you, Samson."

Sam could have been in P.R., he handled her so skillfully. "Thank you, Mama. I'm sure I'll love whatever it is."

"We'll do brunch next week?" She asked, firmly ignoring every other person present. It seemed as if she were trying to reconstruct the encounter. I wasn't sure if all that effort was for her benefit or ours. Whichever, it was the creepiest metamorphosis I'd ever seen.

"Shall we?" She turned to Sebastian as if they were at a garden party with the mayor instead of just moments post fisticuffs on the front lawn.

He nodded. They took two steps toward the car, but he stopped and turned back. He looked apologetic, like a politician who'd been caught in the midst of a sex scandal. "Happy birthday, Sam."

Sam had his back to me, but I saw him nod once. This seemed to appease both of his parents, because they climbed into Wakefield's swanky car and once the bodyguards lumbered back in, they drove away.

"What the fuck was that all about?" Violet asked, slanting her eyes in my direction.

"Ask Trip." Slapping at a mosquito resting on my forearm, I turned and walked back into the house.

CHAPTER NINETEEN
Sam

An hour after the encounter, Trip was still livid. His jaw was bruised, and Violet kept trying to force a bag of frozen peas against it, but his gestures were so animated as he vented that she could barely maintain contact. I told him to let it go, that I'd handle it, that I had a plan. Violet finally pulled him away from the rest of the party when Maisie resurfaced and started asking questions. They retired to the wrap-around porch off the second floor. On the way out the door Trip gave me a questioning look. I nodded at him. It was long past time for him to tell Violet everything.

Jayse apparently had hit it off with Patience much in the same manner he had Violet at the gala. Dale fussed with the food, but it was clear to me he and Jayse were on the outs by the way he kept himself busy and Jayse occupied his time with everyone and anyone else at the party. The overall tension was palpable to everyone present, and Trip's friends and Mike and Charles (who had thankfully missed the entire event outside) soon packed up their dates and left.

Annabelle helped Dale in the kitchen, putting leftovers away and wiping down counters. I walked up behind her and wrapped my arms around her. I wanted to reassure her that I in no way condoned my mother implying that Annabelle was somehow a second class citizen. But that wasn't all; like some sort of vampire, I needed to feed off the way she made me feel. When I focused on her, I felt unstoppable.

She turned to me and gave me a pouty look. "I'm sorry they wrecked your party."

I tilted her chin up toward me. "Nothing could ruin today. Let me help you with the rest of this stuff. I want to take you for a walk on the beach."

Annabelle's color was high as we raced to finish cleaning up. We were about to go out of the back door when Violet and Trip reappeared. Violet looked even paler than usual, and her frown was full of complexity. Trip looked blotchy, and I imagined their conversation had been pretty emotional. He was holding a dripping bag of peas to his face and called to us in a muffled voice.

"You two might want some bug spray. Those mosquitos out there are ravenous." Annie dropped my hand and took off for the stairs. She returned a moment later, offering the half empty aerosol can to me.

I held up a hand. "Thanks, I'm good."

"Suit yourself." She set it down on the nearest end table and off we went. We were halfway down the wooden walkway over the marshy dunes when she took my hand.

"Are you sure you're okay?" she asked. I stretched my neck from side to side and realized how much tension I'd been holding.

"I was afraid Randall was going to get himself shot." I pulled my hand from hers and slipped my arm around her shoulders. She responded by wrapping her arms around my waist. As I leaned in to kiss her temple, I inhaled the intoxicating scent of her hair. My chest felt tight as I clung to her more tightly. Somehow Annabelle had become my security blanket. In my spiraling life, she was a talisman against all the gathering insanity. I needed to touch her and be touched by her to remind myself there was tangible good amongst all this ugliness.

"Me too" Her voice was thin, like a hesitant child. It was wild to see her this way. Vulnerable…frightened. It made me want to curb stomp someone.

"And Trip?"

I moved on to what had really been eating at me. The truth spilled out of me now, and rather than be embarrassed by it, all I felt was relief. "If he vented this much way back when, we'd have all been way better off. I guess we have his therapist to thank for him *finding his voice*."

She stopped walking and turned to face me. Her eyes were weary, but welcoming. "We all screw up, Sam. If I had a Mulligan for my life, I can't count how many times I would have zigged instead of zagged."

"I know. I just wish…fuck! I just wish he would have told me. I wish we could have dealt with it together. Daddy might still be alive, and maybe Trip wouldn't have felt the need to carry the entire world on his shoulders."

"Then again, maybe not. It's hard to know how one decision might change things. Where does your mom factor into that scenario? Maybe your mom would be the one who killed herself if you all ganged up on her."

I chuckled a bit. "Not Cosmo. She's way too vain to consider self-harm."

Annie didn't laugh. "What about you, Sam? Were you more – or less – vulnerable back then?"

The smile I wore melted away. She'd made an excellent point. I'd just lost my girlfriend to my brother and the icing on the cake had been their engagement. That had actually been the beginning of my estrangement with Trip, not his drinking. Watching him take Violet down with him was merely another platinum nail in the designer coffin of our relationship.

"No, I was pretty fucked up back then." We stepped down onto the alabaster sand, and I silently took in the endless blue expanse of the Atlantic. I already felt small, but seeing its magnitude made me feel less than microbial. The sun hid behind suspiciously dingy clouds, and I had a feeling we were going to get wet before the night was over.

Annie raised her eyes to the water and practically gasped and then wore a sheepish expression. "Sorry…I just never get used to that sight."

"I can't even imagine not being near the ocean," I replied as we strolled in the direction of the North Beach Bar and Grill. Doubt tripped some of my inner alarms. Would Annabelle leave Georgia after school was over? I knew so little about her that it was beginning to feel obnoxious. It was time to turn the tables on little miss 'tell me about your problems and dreams.'

"Are you planning on going back to the Midwest? After graduation?" I kept it causal. I had the distinct impression Annabelle wasn't the type of girl who tolerated an interrogation well.

"I don't think so." Her answer was swift and her expression firm. I got the distinct vibe she was closing that conversation, like locking a metal security gate on a store front.

"So what do you do in your free time? When you have some, that is?" I switched directions, like changing tactics on the chessboard. I'm no chauvinist – at least I've never considered myself to be one – but this woman operated on a different playing field than the other women with whom I'd surrounded myself, and my tried and true strategies were useless.

"I read…constantly. I only average about three books a week when school's in session. And I like to wander around aimlessly. I go out for a bike ride around the block and end up ten miles from home." She flipped her hair over her shoulder, and my gaze was drawn to her dewy collarbone. I had to battle the compulsion to plant my lips on it.

"I wander, too. I do it on foot. I almost always end up at the river," I confessed.

"I usually end up in a cemetery. I have one of those old lady bikes with the baskets on it. I always have some rubbing supplies with me," she huffed out in amusement. "Bonaventure is amazing. By far my favorite. It's no wonder it's world famous. So peaceful. What a great place to spend eternity."

"I suppose it is kind of pretty. I'd never been until Daddy's funeral. He's buried there." I thought about the big Beaumont Mausoleum and the large draping trees around it. How weird was it that I didn't really belong there?

She frowned and seemed a bit embarrassed. "I'm sorry; I should have realized…"

I waved it off. "Don't be." She tucked her hair behind her ears.

"My dream trip is to go to that cemetery in Paris."

"Père Lachaise. Where Jim Morrison's buried?" Mystified that she seemed sincere, I tried not to sound surprised. She nodded.

"And the Catacombs. I get goose bumps just thinking about it." She stole a glance at me and chuckled. "I sound like Wednesday Adams, don't I?"

"A little. Most women I know gush over the Eiffel Tower. Or the shopping," I admitted.

She shrugged, unabashed. "Not me. I'm a cheap date."

I let out a shocked laugh, and she smirked, then continued: "Shopping always *sounds* like a good idea. Kind of like Monopoly. About an hour in, and I'm bored and ready to be done."

"No doubt. I'd much rather crawl around in caves filled with thousands of skulls than be dragged into a single boutique." I twitched an eyebrow at her and met her ensuing smile with my own.

"So how long have you been boxing, and when do I get to see you fight?" She was staring at my swollen knuckles as she spoke.

"Well, you've almost seen me fight twice now," I joked, thinking it wasn't a coincidence that she'd been present during both of my near violent outbursts. Since she'd turned up in my life, everything seemed more intense. Like an exposed nerve. It was as if I'd been snoring at the wheel, and she'd come along and woken me up. "That's not how I typ-ically conduct myself, by the way. I'm no cowboy or street thug. But nobody screws with my brother but me."

"Yeah, I get it. I shot someone in the face with a BB gun once for screwing with my sister." Before I could demand details, she shifted the conversation back to boxing. "Seriously. How did you get into it? Is it popular at the Yacht Club?"

I scoffed. "Not so much. My family thought I was nuts. When word got out at school, I got called all sorts of names."

"Why?" She looked genuinely confused.

I looked away, my mood clouding over at the memory of Hank's angry laughter when he'd called me a 'Nigger Lover.' He wasn't laughing a minute later when I knocked out his incisor. "I got the dis-tinct impression they felt it was a 'dark' sport."

She shot me a look of understanding. "How very progressive."

"The attitude at the gym wasn't much different. I was the token white boy they mostly tolerated. And they didn't let me forget it. I was there for two years before the majority of the guys would even say 'hello' to me. I guess at that point they figured I wasn't going anywhere."

"Holy shit." She murmured.

"Racism in Savannah is about as common as draping moss." I shrugged, remembering how casually my great aunt referred to Athena as 'your colored Mama.'

"So what about that sport in particular made you want it badly enough to stick it out?" She continued.

"Boxing is about speed. And strategy. It reminds me a lot of chess, but a hell of a lot more gratifying. Have you ever been tempted to punch someone in the face when they are talking to you?"

"All the time." She elbowed me conspiratorially. "I *might* have the urge right now."

She laughed at her own joke, and if there was a shred of doubt that we were compatible, she'd just erased it. "Yeah, me too. Boxing is major therapy. When I first walked into the gym, Randall was squaring off with some dude a foot taller than he was. He dismantled the guy. I wanted to know how he did it so badly that I could taste it. Here I was, on the debate team and constantly surrounded by people who rarely said what they meant. After that, I planned to go to business school and law school. Ugh. Just all so nauseating. The duplicity of society has always exhausted me. It was…freeing to climb into the ring. Slap gloves with someone and know their only agenda was to knock me the fuck out."

We flanked an outcropping of rocks, and the restaurant came into view in the distance. The outlandish color combinations of the mostly open-air eatery always made me smile, but the menu was astonishingly epicurean.

"Oooh..." Annie's tone was drier than Death Valley. "Are you taking me on a date?"

"Nah." I replied, "I thought I'd just get you liquored up and take advantage of you."

The complex expression she wore was impossible to read, and that drove me absolutely insane.

"I like margaritas. On the rocks, with salt."

CHAPTER TWENTY
Annie

Sam and I were on our second fishbowl margarita when we decided it might be a good idea to eat something. He'd shrugged off his jacket, and I nearly choked on my sour drink as I got a good look at his rippling muscles. Apparently his work in the gym was paying off big time.

More importantly, hanging out with him was effortless. Our silences weren't awkward at all. I found him remarkably easy to talk to before the tequila, and after it, I had to bite back several remarks. I'd been completely wrong in my initial assessment of Sam Beaumont; he was just about the least judgmental person I'd ever met.

He was full of questions about my choice of grad school, my undergrad degree, and my past. Most of it I discussed openly. I explained that I'd gone to Mankato State for undergrad. I told him about working at Hooters which made him laugh for a couple of minutes straight.

"How many customers did you bitchslap?" he managed.

"Only two." I replied, fascinated by how ravenous his laugh made me. I never realized how sexy laughter could be. Maybe because I knew he was laughing with me, unlike virtually all of my past experiences.

I went on to explain that I'd spent several years living with my grandparents, and since grandma couldn't see well and grandpa was forgetful, I got involved in helping them organize their medications. Old people love to talk, and it wasn't long before I was helping their neighbors, and after a few conversations with pharmacies, I started to consider it as a career option. From the awestruck look he gave me, Sam seemed to think this made me some sort of saint. Having met his mother, I shouldn't have been surprised.

After I dodged the subject of my family for the third time, he finally called me out.

"I don't get it, Annabelle. You *know* my family's certifiable. Why won't you tell me about yours?"

" 'Cause I really don't like to think about them." He sat back in his chair and angled his head disapprovingly. I cocked an eyebrow back at him and he folded his hands and didn't flinch. I abandoned the staring contest, stirring my drink with my straw. "What do you want me to say? My mother's got a major gambling problem that controls her life. On top of that, she was a slut. She chose more than one boyfriend over us kids. One time she went out and didn't come back for three weeks. Left me with an eight year old and a four year old. I was only *fifteen,* Sam. She'd drag us all over the state from one shitty rental to another every time we got evicted. She'd drag Dylan and me to the food bank and make us carry out boxes of food so she didn't have to spend our child support on groceries. We wanted to die we were so embarrassed. And my *Dad*? Well...he sent me birthday cards...when he remembered. I haven't seen him since the day he didn't arrive to pick me up at preschool. That's my story. That's *my* mommy and daddy."

I could see him processing each sentence. Anger and indignation rippled under his placid features. "What about your siblings? Did you say you have a brother and a sister? Are they still with your mom?"

"Kind of. She has visitation, but my grandparents have custody. Dylan turns eighteen this year, so he'll be free soon. Becca...well...I'm pretty sure she doesn't stand a chance at any kind of regular life."

I bit my lip, wishing I could take back my last comment. I could tell he wanted to press me on it, but he kept his mouth shut. He seemed naturally intuitive about me, which was a very attractive quality.

"See? That wasn't so hard, was it?" he quipped, and I smiled at the subtext in his boyish eyes. We'd both coated our fragile centers with a twisted sense of humor and no small amount of flirty innuendo. But my truth still lurked beneath, like some sinister stranger watching through the window. I knew I needed to say "I haven't even begun to talk about how hard it was." I should have said "Just wait till the first time you touch me the wrong way or say the wrong thing while we're making out." I should have told him right then about my hypnotherapy and that thanks to fucking Travis the Pedophile, I hadn't been close to anyone except Nick. Nick, who'd knocked me up and dumped me the second that I'd miscarried. Leveling with Sam about my suicide attempt might also have been the polite and ethical thing to do.

But I didn't say a word. I was fucking falling for him, and I wasn't ready to kick him to the curb, even though he deserved a head-start toward the exit. Because I *wanted* to believe. I wanted to pretend, for at least a little while, that we were heading off on a romantic sunset voyage instead of hauling ass straight for an iceberg.

What came out of my mouth instead wasn't incredibly productive. "I can't believe how good this food is! I expected fried shrimp and French fries."

Though the food really was impressive, we

both gave up halfway through our heaping plates. They were blaring a Jimmy Buffet tune and we were about to bail on the remnants of our oversized drinks when Jayse, Dale, Randall, and Patience sniffed us out.

"Hey! Look who it is!" Randall feigned surprise as he approached our table. "Where's my drink?"

"You can have the rest of ours," I replied, trying to hide my relief. Sam's serious face had resurfaced right before Randall announced their arrival, and I was done discussing the past.

"Since when can't *you* get through a margarita?"Jayse chided me. I tried to choke back my annoyance with him. He'd been ditching me for "better people" a lot lately. I knew I was his best friend – we had matching little black heart tattoos for the love of God – but Jayse had a very hard time discussing his problems. Instead, he tended to tamp them down with careless sex and strong cocktails. More frustrating than the way he'd been treating me was that he'd pulled some fickle crap on Dale. He'd been chatting online with other guys, and his over the top flirting with every man he met was pissing me off. Dale was great for Jayse, and like me, he didn't know what to do with *great*.

"These are our second fishbowls," Sam announced and Jayse did a double take.

"Two whole drinks! Annie Clarke! Look at you

having a good time! Someone call a press conference because they must be having a snow day in hell!" Sam flashed a white smile at him. Sam had no idea how tense things were between us, and Tipsy Jayse was even more abrasive than regular Jayse. I was relieved when Patience led him off toward the open-air bar. Randall and Dale took seats across from us. A band began to tune for some live music, and the scene was morphing from bar and grill to just plain old bar.

"How's it going?" I called to Dale over a musician droning 'check...test one two' repeatedly into the microphone.

"Oh, I'm about done with *his* bullshit." Dale's freckled face twisted in distaste that wasn't aimed in my direction. We both looked over at Jayse, who was already chatting up a male bartender. Jayse flipped his curls out of his eyes, his dimples on full display. As his BFF, it was my job to save Jayse from himself, so I stood and leaned down to Sam.

"I'll be right back," I said near his ear. His hand was on the nape of my neck in an instant.

His eyes danced when they met mine, and his full lips curved playfully. "You'd better."

His aggression took me by surprise. That voice of his was so deep...so...hot. He released his hold on me, and I was caught off guard at how aroused I was. I'd been up close and personal with Sam that night in my room and knew just what I could expect wrapped up in those boxers of his. Feeling warmer by the second, I wanted to ditch everyone and drag him off into the dark. With a last lingering look at his broad shoulders and bulging denim, I thrust myself toward the bar. I planned to school Jayse about his behavior as quickly as I could and get on to something *a lot* more gratifying. I walked up in time to see Jayse playing with a cell phone that wasn't his.

"Dammit, Monroe, this better be Patience's phone." I snatched the cell from his hand, and my shoulders fell when I saw Jayse had taken a picture of his designer jean-clad ass and had been plugging his digits into the bartender's phone. "What the hell are you doing? Are you fucking mental?"

"Would you relax, warden?" Jayse drawled, plucking the phone from my hand and sliding it across the bar.

"Are you *trying* to get yourself dumped?" I scowled at him, and he plopped down on the bar stool like an angst-ridden teen. His petulant expression fanned my temper. "Be a man and break up with Dale if you wanna be a manwhore."

"You know what I don't need?" Jayse had his flip switched to the ultra-bitch setting. "I don't need sex advice from *you*. When was the last time you got some, Annie?"

"Screw you," I shot at him, stunned by how much his words hurt me. He knew my past; it wasn't that different from his own. Jayse's dad died when he was little, and his family had been homeless for three years after that. Though he'd never shared the gory details, he'd strongly implied more than once that he'd been abused as well. Since the moment we'd met, he and I had clicked. We looked out for one another. We called each other on our bullshit and kept each other in line.

"No, screw you," he shot back and then erupted in a catty chuckle. "Oh...that's right; you don't screw anyone, do you sweetie?"

I slapped him across the face so hard my hand stung. I spun away and walked off, but not before glimpsing his dark eyes spark with anger and surprise. I nearly plowed into Patience, who had to have witnessed the whole incident, as I strutted back to the table where Randall, Dale, and Sam were all having what seemed like a carefree conversation.

"We should go." Something in my voice caused Sam's head to snap in my direction. He stood and snatched up his jacket.

"Is everything all right?" Randall's enforcer voice he'd used with the bodyguards was back full force. He was reading my face. Dale paled with concern.

"I'm great." My sharp comment caused Dale's eyes to narrow, and he stood. Unable to watch the fallout, I walked off into the dark, and soon Sam was at my side. The feel of his strong hand on the small of my back allowed me to take a much needed deep breath.

He gave me time to walk off some of the adrenaline coursing through my system, and we were all the way back to the planked walkway when he finally spoke. "Wanna talk about it?"

"I'm done talking." I pushed him against the guardrail and pulled his mouth down to mine. He recovered quickly from his initial surprise, and his hands were in my hair seconds later as our tongues touched. His salty, tart taste made me lightheaded, and I pressed the full length of myself against him.

He pulled his mouth away as his hand slipped inside the low neckline of my dress. His calloused thumb caressed my nipple, and the slightly scratchy sensation made me tingle low in my belly. I sighed as his wet kisses trailed from my jaw to my collar-bone. His hands gripped my ass, and he picked me up, my legs squeezing around him before I was consciously aware I was doing it. With one arm I clung to his muscular shoulders while the other tugged at his thick hair. He swung around and set me on the guardrail, pushing his groin between my legs. One hand was still on my ass and the other down my top and I knew if I didn't stop him, our first time would be right here out in the open. Our friends at the restaurant could come back any time, and the thought of Violet or Trip bringing Maisie down to the ocean sobered me up instantly.

"Sam. Stop," I whispered, and he pulled away with curious, glassy eyes. "Let's get to the house. I don't want the others to walk up and see this."

I thought he might get pissed, but he laughed. "Good. We can take a shower together. No offense, but you taste like bug spray."

I laughed at his frankness, and he helped me down from the guardrail. Every cell of my body felt ripe and engorged, and I think he felt the same since we practically power-walked back to the house. As we opened the sliding glass door, he turned to me.

"Which room are you in?"

"The second floor. First door on the right." I replied.

"I'm just across the hall," he replied with a smirk. "Trip's got a twisted sense of humor."

We climbed the stairs to the second floor. He opened his door first and then mine. His had a king sized bed, but mine had an en suite bath.

"We have a winner." He gestured to my room like a game show host, and I shushed him. That's when we heard the strangest thing. We paused, both listening intently. The all-too familiar sound of mattress springs squeaking rhythmically drifted from the room at the end of the hall. The master bedroom. Our eyes met...then widened.

"Oh my fucking God," he whispered as we both realized it had to be Trip and Violet.

"Well, that was easy," I whispered back as he practically shoved me across the threshold into my room. "Where's Maisie?"

"She has a fairy princess room that takes up half the third floor." He closed the door behind him, and when we could still hear the mattress spring symphony, he switched on the radio on the bedside table. I snorted appreciatively, but my smile evaporated as Sam began to unbutton his shirt. Unlike last time, the lamp was on, so I got to fully appreciate the impressive view as he reached over his head and tugged his undershirt off. The definition of his body impressed me enough that the first thought I had was to snap some pics with my cell.

Remembering I wasn't just a spectator, I kicked off my sandals and unzipped the side panel of my dress. His eyes never left me as he unbuttoned his jeans and kicked them off. The thin fabric of his boxers could barely contain how ready he was, and like a kid on Christmas, I was anxious to see what was in that stocking.

I was in only panties now, and I suddenly felt the urge to cover my breasts with my hands. It was the way his eyes seemed to see all of me at one. No…into me. The connection we shared was powerful and very overwhelming.

He stepped forward and pulled me to him, his eyes ensnaring mine. I started to say something— I'm not even sure what-- but he covered my mouth with his. He lips were full, soft, and perfectly matched with mine. The sandalwood scent of him filled my nostrils, and when he pulled his lips away, his stubble made me shiver as it scratched the sensitive skin of my neck and chest. When his tongue darted over my nipple, I stumbled back toward the bathroom with him still attached to my breast. My breath came out in small gasps as he switched to my other breast, sucking it hungrily, as if attuned to every sound that escaped me. His mouth returned to mine, and his kisses grew more and more urgent. As I ran my hand across the smooth skin of his rock-hard chest, I could feel his heart thudding under my palm.

He put a hand on the bathroom door behind me, and when we tumbled through, we were greeted with no shower, but an oversized claw foot tub. Instantly, I recalled my bathtub dream and though I didn't think it were possible, I felt even wetter.

"So much for a shower." Sam's words were practically a growl, as he swept me into his arms and carried me back to the bed. He lowered me onto the comforter, and his show of strength was so hot that I tugged at the waist of his boxers, desperate to have him inside me. His hand slid up my thigh and under the fragile material of my panties, and the moment I felt his finger slide into me, it was as if I'd plunged headfirst into an icy pond.

I froze, every muscle in my body suddenly rigid and tense. My mouth went dry, and I felt my heart leap into my throat. I wanted to beg him to stop, but my words were caught. I stared trembling. I felt my arms go numb and dropped them to my sides. Sam pulled his mouth from mine and leaned over the edge of the bed.

He pulled a condom from his jeans pocket, but when he turned back to look at me, the smiled left his face, and the condom fell from his hands and floated like a feather onto the bedspread.

"What's wrong?" He collapsed onto the mattress, his eyes narrowing as he propped himself up on one elbow. "Did I hurt you?"

I tried again to speak, but a sob came out instead. I felt like I was trapped inside a soundproof prison, but the cage was my own traitorous body. I really wanted to be with Sam. *I needed* him to touch me, to hold me and *connect* with me. But the muscle memory my monster left behind overruled all my wants and wishes. I raised my shaky hands to my face and hid behind them. Something sprung free inside me, and I erupted in tears as I felt all the wheels fly off at the same time. My emotions were overpowering…crippling. Along with my innocence, *he'd* stolen this from me, too. That bastard had taken my ability to enjoy Sam and to allow him to enjoy me. I couldn't contain the feral moan that escaped my lips. I'm not sure how long this went on because when the patchwork fabric of your soul is it torn in two, it seems to happen in slow motion.

I was sure by the time I pulled myself together enough to remove my hands from my tear-stung eyes Sam would be gone. Instead, I felt a comforter placed on me and his arms around me. He kissed my hair and stroked it, and I felt my entire being unclench in that second. I felt like a pile of jelly as I collapsed into him. As my breathing began to steady, I had the chance to mentally scold myself for being such a hot mess.

Wow, Annie. That was sexy.

CHAPTER TWENTY-ONE
Violet

The sherbet hues of dawn shifted the color of the sky, and as the last bit of the blissful insensibility that is sleep slipped from my weary mind, I bolted up in bed. The sheet fell from my bare body, and I snatched it up, twisting it in a knot between my naked breasts. Reluctantly, I turned my head to the right and saw that Reg was awake. He sat on the edge of the bed with his back to me. Though he'd never once smoked in the house even on his drunkest day, he held a lit cigarette in his right hand.

Seeing his scars from the fire for the first time, my breath caught painfully. I found myself ambushed by their beauty; only Reg could manage to perfectly burn himself. The remnants of his excruciating debacle matched his tattoos with astounding accuracy. A Monarch-worthy result that, as with all things regarding my ex-husband, mesmerized me. I nearly succumbed to temptation and reached out to touch his damaged flesh. I hated that I wasn't there to nurse him and shower him with all the love and energy he deserved. But I'd been all tapped out by then and working through the final stages of my grief. Losing Reg to alcohol was like losing a limb. No matter how clean the cut and how long I was without him, his phantom pain would always haunt me.

Still sore from hours of raw animalistic sex, I crawled gingerly across the mattress until I could kneel behind him and wrap my arms around him. I pressed my cheek to his grafted skin and my naked chest to his back. I breathed slow deep breaths, matching my rhythm with his. Reg was my missing other half, and the only time I was at perfect peace was when we were intertwined. Sadly, it was also when I waged my bloodiest wars.

His hand rested on top of mine and the wings of my heart flapped as if preparing to soar. Alarmed, I sat back and severed the connection. I was afraid of him and also tempted to slip my hands around his throat. The story of our engagement party and Sam's real father was a tragic one, but it hadn't needed to be. I'd been his fiancé and his wife not much after that. Had he taken his vows to *me* as seriously as the promises to his father, we'd probably be fighting about names for our third baby. Instead we sat here naked, clinging to the tattered shreds of our dignity after stupidly tumbling into bed together.

At first, the night before had all the trappings of closure. After the others decided to track down the birthday boy, Maisie claimed to be hungry again. The three of us pulled out leftovers and had what resembled a family dinner around the dining room table of what should have been our weekend getaway home. The bittersweet moment was punctuated when my cranky daughter decided to throw a tantrum about wanting a second helping of cake and ice cream. Trip handled her expertly, with the same casual grace he used to use on me, and talked her into a story instead. She begged him to read her favorite book to her in her canopy bed, and two and a half storybooks later, she was out like a light.

We tiptoed downstairs and went onto the wrap around porch for round two of confessions and apologies. Reg laughed as he confessed his and Annie's plan for him to get me back and explained how Sam overheard his fight with Wakefield outside the gala. He said when I saw him struggling by the bar afterward…that *that* was the most tempted he'd ever been to have a drink. And he'd found the inner strength to walk away dry. He finally felt like he'd turned a corner; sobriety would be his lifestyle, not a passing fad. And I believed him. Because *he* believed it, and I knew that had been the missing link all the times before.

"I'm glad, Reg." I'd told him, and though my smile felt real, it also felt *really* dismal. "I wish…"

I trailed off, knowing we shouldn't go down that road. Our marriage had been a series of tragic mistakes. Looking back, our entire relationship had been insanity blended with carnal sex and topped off with brandy infused whipped topping.

"What?" Those sad bedroom eyes implored me to open up to him. I had to break eye contact, but my aching heart muscles were too weak for the task.

"I wish you'd believed more in us." Saying it out loud made my throat tense painfully. Discussing "us" was a lot like talking about a dead friend. I sipped my warm tea in an attempt to thaw the frost settling over me. Fixated on the steam rising from my mug, I didn't see him move until he was right in front of me. He took the cup from my hand and set it on the windowsill beside me. My pulse quickened at the layers of emotion in his eyes, and I felt my body respond to him. His hand was on the windowsill above me, and I took a half step back against the glass. I felt the pull of his magnetism and braced myself as if perched at the top of the first drop of a roller coaster. He inched forward, his eyes searching mine for a white flag of surrender, and the heat that flared between us could have burned the place to the ground.

"I always believed." His nose brushed mine, and he pulled back an inch at the electric sensation that passed through us both. I was a prisoner to his imploring determination and unwilling to escape my bonds.

From the moment Reg's lips had brushed against mine to my third orgasm, Dashul hadn't even crossed my mind. Now, as I sat in the dawning light waiting for Reg to turn my way, he crept into my consciousness like a cat burglar. Regret wafted up as the dust of my actions settled around me. My breathing became more labored as I willed Reg to look at me, to at least acknowledge that I wasn't alone with my guilt. He moved suddenly, stamping out his cigarette in one swift violent motion.

"I shouldn't have kissed you, Vi. I'm a wrecking ball. I'm sorry." He was on his feet, and I watched him rake his hands through his tousled hair and recalled with painful clarity doing the same to his hair when his head was between my legs the night before. His movements were jerky as he pulled on his jeans. I felt the blood rush from my face as I slowly rose to my feet.

"You're sorry? No, Reg. *I'm* sorry. I've had enough of your apologies to last me three fucking lifetimes. Why the hell do I keep doing this to myself?" With the frantic speed of a child at an Easter egg hunt, I flitted around the room searching for my discarded clothing. Shame avalanched over me as I stepped into my panties and hurriedly hooked my bra.

"I ruin everything," he sighed, crossing toward me, but I held up a hand, clutching my clothes to me with the other. His hurt was obvious, and for a moment I felt victorious. Petty as it was, it felt nice to inflict pain on my torturer for a change.

"Don't you touch me," I seethed. "Watching you with your mother yesterday, you'd think you had some fight in you somewhere. But I guess Maisie and I aren't worth the effort."

You'd have thought I'd stabbed him in the chest. He looked crestfallen. "I love you *and* Maisie. With all my heart. The two of you are all that's kept me alive."

His tardy words were another assault on my barricade, but I was having no more of it. I tossed my shirt on over my head and tried to breathe through my narrowing windpipe. My face was so hot, it felt branded as I hopped a leg into my pants. I choked out my words. "If you *loved* us, Reg…really loved us-you'd go away and never come back."

The wounded look on his face clawed at me. I couldn't help but hurt when he ached. No legal piece of paper could undo our "for better or worse" clause. Fucking soul mates.

I picked up my shoes and flung open the bedroom door. Annie and Sam were in the hall with their bags, and startled, they both spun in my direction. I barely paused as I traipsed past them and up the stairs to rouse my daughter. When Maisie's bed was empty, I realized that last night's indiscretion was likely the talk of the house. I took a moment to gather my scattered dignity and covered my face with my hands. I was painfully aware of my frigid platinum engagement ring against my brow, and I dropped my hands to my sides with a dramatic exhale. I was humiliated that I'd defiled my prospective happily-ever-after for one blissful night of what could've been. I cursed the day Reg had sauntered into my life with his sleepy eyes and sexy voice. I remembered the final card that I held, and in my fury I raced down the stairs to deal it.

I stormed toward his room through the now empty hallway and flung his door open. He'd just pulled a shirt on over his head and looked astonished that I was back. I crossed to him, not only so no one else would hear me, but so I could watch every muscle in his face as I tossed my Molotov cocktail into his trenches.

"A month after you wrecked our car with *my* baby girl in the backseat? I went and had an abortion. It was the best decision I ever made."

His outright disbelief was my only reward. A second later, he looked at me as if he'd never seen me before. For some stupid reason, I hadn't expected the backsplash of pain his reaction caused me, and I shrunk back like he'd slapped me.

"Why?" That one quiet syllable from him spoke volumes. Without taking my eyes from him, I backed toward the door. Having just thrown my worst mistake in Reg's face was like tossing him a hand grenade without pulling the pin. I had no choice but to retreat. He took a step toward me, and I lifted my chin with all the courage I could muster.

"You know exactly why." I fled down the stairs and tried not to show how embarrassed I was when I saw Dale, Annabelle, and Sam eating cereal at the table with Maisie. They looked like a pack of deer in headlights, and Annabelle actually dropped her spoon when she looked up at my face.

"We gotta go, Baby Girl." I scooped Maisie out of her chair and shot toward the door.

"But Mama, I'm not done with my Crunchberries!" she wailed as I raced for the car. I heard Reg call my name, but it only made me move faster. "You forgot my shoes, Mama! I want to give Daddy a bye-bye kiss!"

My hands shook so badly that I struggled to buckle her car seat. Somehow I prevailed, and I scrambled into the car and locked the doors when I saw Reg running toward me across the lawn.

It didn't take a lip reader to see he was shouting my name, but my soundproof car spared us having to hear it. His anguished face made my heart hurt regardless, and as I backed out of the driveway, he threw himself onto the hood.

"Vi!" His muffled voice seemed to reach down inside me and get tangled in my heart strings. I slammed on my brakes and helplessly watched the tears stream down his cheeks. Maisie barked frantic demands at me from the back seat, and I realized that I was crying too. Unable to take back what I'd said, I resorted to hiding behind my anger. I stared him down and blared on the horn. Slowly and without taking his eyes from mine, he pushed off of the car and backed away. I managed to get about a mile down the highway before I had to pull over.

I beat on the steering wheel like a child in the midst of a temper tantrum. After several minutes, my hands throbbed but nowhere near as badly as the gaping hole in my chest did. As my breathing began to steady, I nervously glanced at my child with eyes like her father in the rearview mirror, wondering exactly how many years of therapy I was going to have to pay for. She undid her seatbelt (a move I'd often scolded her for) and reached out for me. Swinging her over the seat, I clung to her as if her life depended on it. She kissed me loudly on the cheek and chirped. "It's alright, Mama. It'll be alright."

I tightened my grip on her and closed my eyes tightly. In the back of my mind, a haunting voice called out a rebuttal.

Oh no it's not, Dahlin'. And you're downright mad if you believe it ever will be.

CHAPTER TWENTY-TWO
Sam

I strolled out of the conference room, letting the door behind me swing with flourish. The mur-murs of the board members followed me out into the corridor, and hearing Trip's footfalls behind me made me grin. We were halfway down the hallway when he finally caught up, matching my stride.

"Sammy." Daddy used to call me 'Sammy' and with a smile leaking into his voice, Trip sounded just like him. "You are a *total* dick."

"Yeah, well...I learned it by watching you," I quipped. At the first board meeting two weeks before, the board had made a united effort to treat us like upstarts, practically patting us on our heads. Unfortunately for them, I wasn't quite the doe-eyed virgin they took me for. All attempts to interrupt me during my presentation were met with smooth ad-monishment and swift, unarguable facts. When a condescending senior board member tried to snap me back by the leash, I replied that we'd gladly sell off our stock, since neither Trip nor I were interested in keeping our considerable wealth tied up in a company with no agility. Two weeks later, they were falling over themselves to accommodate us. Hardly a shocker, since the two of us owned nearly sixty-five percent of Beaumont Enterprises. It appeared that, blood relative or not, I possessed the razor sharp teeth of a Great White Beaumont.

"Well now that you've proven you have the biggest set of balls in Chatham County, do you want to celebrate? I have to deliver the last of my paintings, but after that I'm free." A disappointed frown escaped me when he mentioned the art. Since his blow up with Violet, Trip had been focused on accepting the responsibility that was his to own. Though his first instinct was to move to The Keys and give her the space she asked for, visions of Dashul raising his daughter quickly squelched it. His sponsor Vanessa told him to 'quit being a pussy' and in more diplomatic terms, his psychiatrist agreed. So when Vi refused take his calls, he'd written her a long email, explaining that he would never lay another amorous hand on her again, but that his daughter needed her father. Since Violet and Maisie were supposed to move to Charleston after her Valentine's Day wedding, Trip made plans to leave Savannah. Though I knew it was killing him, he slapped on a smile and claimed the city held far too many painful memories for him anyway. He needed a 'fresh start.' Imogene's was hosting a show to liquidate his inventory. Moving all of those paintings would be ridiculous, he explained. Frankly, I think they held far too many memories, too.

Trip had been to Charleston to house hunt a couple of times, and the week before Annie and I had joined him. Charleston was a charming city, but I had a very hard time imagining Savannah without my brother. When I pictured him elsewhere, I was taken off guard at how emotional it made me. It totally sucked that I was laying roots just as he was replanting. Now that he and I could speak to each other unfiltered, I discovered that I was going to miss the hell out of him. Though his relocation made me blue, I got it. I worried about his being without a support system. I openly questioned the strategic intelligence of it, but as he pointed out, I wasn't faced with losing precious formative years with my child. What he failed to mention was that he'd continuously face the loss of his true love to his own past transgressions.

The abortion bombshell was devastating for him. He'd heaped the blame on himself in typical Trip fashion. Annie had proceeded to chew him out for that, telling him Violet was a grown-ass woman and that what she decided to do with her body was *her* call. Then she ordered Jayse, Dale, Randall and Patience to remove all the booze from the beach house. They did as she asked, each one of them looking relieved to have an excuse to blow the emotionally charged scene. Then my girl demanded his phone from him and proceeded to call Trip's sponsor herself. I'm not sure exactly what Annabelle said to her, but twenty minutes later a busty, foulmouthed blonde showed up on the porch. Pushing up her glasses anxiously, she introduced herself as Vanessa M. I was about to invite her in, but Trip met us at the door, and the two of them commenced a chain smoking marathon that I'm certain continued long after we left. With Vanessa M's company, Trip seemed a hell of a lot more stable and he had insisted we go. At some point I had to trust him with himself, but Annabelle seemed as leery about going as I did.

By that time, we were both fried. We'd been up talking most of the night after she'd had her breakdown. Crushed that I'd hurt or upset her, I begged her to tell me what I'd done. She just kept telling me to go, but I refused to leave her. Once she'd finally cried herself out, she caved and confessed about the abuse. I tried not to combust as I held her while her sweet voice described horrors that I don't dare dwell on. The calm way she recalled the atrocities and the unforgiveable way her mother ignored them threatened to unhinge me.

She told me about the miscarriage when she was a girl and that she'd felt so low she'd nearly overdosed after. Though she'd had years of therapy, she said sex was predictably complicated for her. To use her words, "My extenuating circumstances have extenuating circumstances." She'd had plentiful meaningless sex, and for a short time it gave her an odd sense of control. But there was no bond involved with any of the men, no connection. She said it was like having an out-of-body experience at the absolute worst time to be outside of one's body. This sounded to me like some coping mechanism, like she'd learned to detach herself from the act to preserve her sanity. We were still spooning on the bed when she added that she'd never had an orgasm. She sounded embarrassed as she confessed that, at its best, sex felt about as pleasurable as a back rub.

Finally, she rolled over and looked at me in the dark. Though it was hard to see by the light of the moon, her expression appeared resigned. "I just wanted you to know that it's not you, Sam. You did nothing wrong. I'm really attracted to you and I *really* want to be with you. I won't blame you if you go."

"I'm not going anywhere." I stroked her cheek with my knuckles and dared to kiss her forehead. The trust she'd shown me was humbling and my instinctive need to protect her, ferocious. Frowning, she glanced sideways up at me. Her doubtful eyes immediately spiked my adrenaline. I'd seen similar transformations before; like a fighter between rounds, she'd put her mouth guard back in and was leaving her corner.

"Don't feel obligated. I can deal if you go, but I can't handle you staying because you feel sorry for me." She tried to turn away, but I flipped her back in my direction, caging her with my arms. I doubted myself immediately...nervous about being physically assertive with her after all she'd been through. But she only seemed curious, not afraid.

"I need you to listen to me. Don't ever put words into my mouth." My voice was firmer than I intended, but I was still humming with barely contained rage at those who'd wronged her. The best I could do was hope she could feel that my words came from the right place. "You should know by now that I never do *anything* that I don't want to do. Just accept that what I say to you is true. You don't live inside my head, alright?"

After a long pause, she nodded. It may have been a trick of the moonlight but I thought I saw tears standing in her eyes.

"But what if I...what if this happens again? Sam, I don't...I just don't know what to do. All the times before, I've always had to be in control. But it's always been about the power; the other person was a tool. When I'm in the act, that's all it feels like...*an act*. With you...I don't understand it, but I feel differently about you." She reached out and stroked my facial hair, and I turned my head to kiss her palm. I felt differently about her, too. I remembered Jayse's warnings and her sexual aggression that night in her bedroom, and it all seemed to click into place like a tumbler on a combination lock.

We finally agreed that when it came to intimacy, she'd have to take the lead—at least for the time being. She told me she'd recently found a therapist and intended to make it a priority to schedule an appointment with her. Now, a full month since my birthday, there had been some heavy moments, but we always stopped before things got too crazy. Though I'll admit that I was frustrated, I felt like things were going really well. We spent time together each and every day. I'd been swamped with moving, overseeing construction on the building I bought and all my Beaumont Corporation deals, and Annabelle's scheduled made me look retired. Her class and studying schedule were brutal, not to mention her job at the piano bar and her pharmacy externship. We made it a priority to get together every night. I'd "help" her study, which usually digressed since I made her take a piece of clothing off every time she missed an answer. Lord, she was gorgeous. I could kiss that girl for hours and never tire of it.

I even made a habit out of stalking her while she worked at Black Keys, but she didn't seem to mind my being there. She said she enjoyed the place, and Martin, her boss, had absolutely no problem taking my money for cocktails. I didn't miss the fact that she got hit on a lot, but she didn't seem to take any shit and assured me she could handle herself. I really wanted her to quit that job, but when I suggested it, she narrowed her eyes at me. She confessed that she'd been happy that I'd meddled with the tombstone rubbing business, but I think she saw my comment about Black Keys as crossing a line. Perhaps she saw it as some attempt by me to 'keep her.' Pride was deeply ingrained in Annabelle. I'd learned not to push it when she gave me *the look.*

Spending my evenings with her made avoiding Cosmo a snap. Mama and I'd had our brunch, and she behaved like the altercation at Tybee never happened. I expected as much; Mama practically had an honorary doctorate in revisionist history. Annabelle wasn't comfortable staying at the carriage house or even coming to the estate, so I usually slept at her apartment.

At her place, tension reigned. Things between Annie and Jayse continued to be uncomfortably quiet. About two weeks after my birthday, Annie and I were making out on the couch when Jayse stumbled into the apartment drunk off his ass. We shot apart like two junior high kids. Jayse mumbled something about Dale dumping him before puking his guts out in the kitchen sink. I helped Jayse into his room where he made a halfhearted attempt to hit on me while Annie cleaned up after him. When I returned to the living room she was dialing Dale's number. After a lengthy one-sided conversation, Annie said Dale confirmed the relationship was over.

"Sam?" Trip snapped his fingers in front of my face. "You really ought to get some rest, bro. You've been burning the candle at both ends. Or doing *something* with both ends. Either way, you look like you need some sleep."

"Sorry." I put a hand over my eyes. "I was up late unpacking the last two nights. What were we talking about?"

"Celebrating," Trip replied as we walked out into the cool January breeze. "I thought we could do it, Daddy-style."

"The club?" I smiled at the idea. The notion had a bit of poetic justice. "Sounds perfect. I'll call Annabelle. She's got a big test coming up, but she could probably use a break." As I climbed in the car, I pulled out the phone and dialed her number.

"Hey." Her alto voice sounded huskier than usual, and I could tell she was happy to hear from me. Jayse was obviously home, judging by the thumping of the dance-mix in the background.

"Hey." I glanced over at my brother. Trip's expression taunted me; I could tell it was obvious how ridiculously in love with her I was. I didn't want to spook her by saying the words just yet, but keeping my poker face when I talked to her or about her was practically impossible these days. I'd even gone out and bought a bike so I could ride with her on her marathon cemetery excursions. Every facet of her fascinated me, and I found watching her process for making rubbings intriguing. Honestly, she seemed to have no method to her madness, and when I questioned why she chose one headstone over another she'd just get this thoughtful look on her face and claim it just "felt right." That was Annabelle. She always went with her gut. This attitude seemed to be rubbing off on *me*, much like the charcoal handprints all over my ass when I'd whisk her off into the trees. Since I'm a person typically driven by logic, it both worried and exhilarated me that when it came to her, I went with my heart over my brain at every crossroads.

"Still cramming?" I tried hard to focus on my reason for calling and not the memory of our groping sessions in the woods near the cemetery.

"Yes…" she moaned in a way that made me think all manner of filthy thoughts.

"She's a whiny little beoch because she got an Asian A!" Jayse's voice blared through her phone at me as if he were in the backseat. I held the phone back from my ear six inches, and Trip chuckled.

"A "B"? Annabelle…" I mocked horror, knowing she'd go through the roof.

"A "B plus." Assholes," she cracked, and I smiled. The material had been hellish, but she was such a perfectionist when it came to her grades that

I knew she'd be kicking herself for days.

"So dinner's out?" I pretty much knew the answer, but it was worth a shot. She signed regretfully.

"I wish I could. I want to get a head start on the next unit. And since we're going to be unpacking this weekend, I'd rather make that sacrifice now." I couldn't argue with her reasoning. I was itching to wake up next to her in my new bedroom that overlooked the Savannah River. She'd texted me that she hoped Friday would be 'the night.' I'll admit the thought had me drooling.

"Alright. Trip and I are going to the club. I'll see you after."

"You'd better." It was our running joke, and her bossiness made me laugh. I hung up right as we pulled into The Chatham Club.

While we waited for our private dining room, I spotted one of Wakefield's bodyguards leave the main dining room. Trip and I exchanged a glance. I asked a silent question with my eyes, and he responded with a smirk and a nod. His message was clear.

Now is as good a time as any.

As we crossed to his table, my brother waved to several ladies along the way. I was too distracted by the sight of Mama canoodling with Wakefield to even notice who else was in the room. Approaching them was awkward, but when she looked up and saw Trip and me, her initial reaction was priceless. It was short-lived. Embarrassment quickly transformed to enthusiasm.

"Well if it isn't *both* of my boys. Join us!" She sounded a bit like Henry the VIII at an orgy. Trip and I exchanged a micro-glance and took the empty seats across from them.

"What brings the Beaumont brothers to The Chatham Club this fine evening?" Wakefield asked, and the way he emphasized the last name Beaumont made me want to rip out his throat, literally and metaphorically.

"The Oglethorpe Club was closed for a private party." It was a test jab, just an acknowledgement that in my investigation I'd discovered he wasn't invited to join the Oglethorpe Club, which prided itself on being the most exclusive club in town. Batting his taunt back at him, I effectively called him *nouveau riche*. His frown dialed down a notch.

"We're here to celebrate." Trip's delivery was congenial, and I was impressed with his composure.

"Well, that sounds fun!" Wakefield's sinister grey eyes sparkled as he flagged down a passing waiter. "Two bottles of Dom Perignon. Oh, I'm sorry, Trip! It slipped my mind. Ah well…we need a bottle of sparkling cider, too."

Mama surveyed the exchange suspiciously, and I observed Wakefield without emotion. I was jazzed, but I didn't want him to see my cards so I simply blinked slowly. His pomposity was going to make this *way* too fun. I turned slowly to Trip with feigned disappointment. To his credit, Trip seemed bored, raising his eyebrows at Sebastian in polite surprise.

"It's really too bad you can't have a drink, Trip. If ever there was a grand occasion..." I trailed off, waiting for them to take the bait.

Trip's smile lit up the dim room. "Oh, hell no. I want to be crystal clear for this."

"I'm surprised you're in a celebratory mood, Trip," Mama remarked, her demeanor shifting to concern. "Moving to Charleston, of all the God-forsaken places. And all so you can be an every-other-weekend dad?"

It took a lot of willpower for me not to fly off the handle at her. It was one thing for Wakefield to cut Trip down, but Cosmo? The way she'd treated him since my birthday brought a lot of buried memories to the surface. She's had the same approach with me when I wasn't her favorite. Back then, every move I made was greeted with a 'why can't you be more like your brother.' I assumed she no longer trusted Trip's enthusiasm after he'd been popped in the face by her boyfriend's thugs. Mama could be a perceptive one when she wasn't staring admirably at her own reflection.

"No, Mama. Beaumont Enterprises just made a major acquisition." I smiled like I was saying 'cheese' for the cover of *The Wall Street Journal*. "Please forgive us; we're just a bit heady. It's kind of a big deal."

"Really?" Mama practically purred, dollar signs dancing in her eyes.

"Oh yeah." Trip looked pensive, but I knew it was a sham. "What was that term you used, Sam?"

"A hostile takeover." I said it quickly, my delivery flat and crisp.

Trip snapped his fingers. "That's right. How could I forget? Ah well. You know me. I'm a lover, not a fighter."

"Well…it really doesn't fit that definition, Trip. In a hostile takeover, the management of the target company fights the takeover by the acquirer and the shareholders usually overrule them."

"It's all so confusing. I guess I killed too many of my brain cells drinking." Trip shrugged casually.

Wakefield seemed to sit forward in his chair. I folded my hands.

"That's why you keep me around. No, it seems someone let it slip that their Chief Operating Officer has some questionable ethics. A very public inquiry would've annihilated their stock price, so they were more than willing for us to take them over. Investigations by the trade commission and the IRS weren't on their to-do list."

Trip turned his eyes on Wakefield whose necktie looked to be a bit tight on his neck all of a sudden. "That still sounds pretty hostile to me."

I uttered a mock sigh as Mama's eyes locked on Sebastian. She was pulling at her pearl necklace so aggressively that I was sure she'd spill them into her crab bisque. "My God, Trip. You really didn't inherit the Beaumont nose for business, did you now?"

"Nope. But neither did you," Trip cracked, and I snorted a genuine laugh. God, I was going to miss him. I took my champagne flute in hand and clinked glasses with him.

"Touché. I may be a bastard, but shady behavior definitely runs in my family." Mama nearly choked on her champagne at that one.

"I'm no scientist, but I suspect it's the dominant gene on *both* sides." Trip didn't miss a beat. Impressed, I poured him a second glass of sparkling grape juice.

"Oh, Mama. In all this excitement, it nearly slipped my mind. We have a belated Christmas present for you." Trip turned to her, and I swear she practically cringed. "Sam and I have deeded you the den of lies you call a home. Consider it a farewell present from me." The maître d' appeared at my side as if he were a walk-on extra for the scene we were performing.

"Your table's ready." He smiled, oblivious to the ambush he'd just interrupted.

"Oh, wonderful. We've gotta jet." I stood, but

held up a finger to Trip as I downed the champagne. With a satisfied lip smack, I poured myself another glass and delivered the coup de grâce. "Mom, Dad. Thanks for the drink."

"You certainly are a chip off the old block." Somehow, in the face of utter ruin, Sebastian actually managed to look proud. If he was half as sly as I suspected him to be, he had contingency plans. Until that moment I hadn't felt the least bit bad about my actions. Right then, I wished I thought of something much worse to do to him.

"I'm my Mother's son, alright." I agreed, and both my parents blanched. Trip was still laughing when our dessert arrived.

A few hours later, I was knocking on Annie's door. She flung it open, and my eyes wandered over her body in admiration. Her hair was down and wild, and she wore a tank top and boxers, my favorite look on her, which she well knew. I cocked an eyebrow, and she yanked me in the door by my collar.

After several kisses to remind me how much she'd missed me, she broke free.

"Where's Jayse?" I asked. The resonating silence made it clear he wasn't home.

"Out. As always," she sniped, but she pulled me by the hand to the couch. We sat, and I pulled her legs onto my lap. Her legs were amazing, and worshiping them was one of my favorite pastimes.

"How was dinner?"

Her facial expressions as I told her about the events of the day were out of this world. When I got to the part about dinner, she actually picked up a throw pillow and slugged me with it. "I cannot believe you didn't *make* me come! What the hell, Samson?"

Ignoring her new penchant for calling me that atrocity, I chuckled and lifted her onto my lap. "We had no idea they'd be at the club. Believe me: had I known, you'd have had VIP seats."

"So how do you feel? Satisfied?" She asked, looking down from her perch on top of my tortured lap.

"Not entirely." If I lied to her now, I'd undo what we were building. She deserved better, and so did I.

She moved in for a long and tantalizing kiss. "Let's see what we can do about that."

And there, on her couch, with her straddling me and in complete control, we made love for the first time. It started slowly, with me apprehensive as hell to touch her. Guiding my hands, she allowed me to slowly survey every inch of her with my fingertips. Piece by piece, she lost each item of clothing. Soon I was naked too, and she slowly pulled me inside her. Slow and torturous at first, our rhythm soon built to a feverish pace. We were both so worked up that when she came, she clawed my shoulders bloody. Pain or no pain, it didn't take me long to follow her lead.

Afterward, we lay naked and silent on the couch. Exhausted and euphoric, I kissed the hollow of her neck, inhaling her sumptuous scent. I wasn't sure where we'd be the morning after, but luck definitely seemed to be on my side that night. I decided to seize the moment.

I cleared my throat. "Annabelle."

Her voice was barely a whisper, but not without a bit of Annie-tude. "Yes, Samson?"

"I love you." I held my breath. I had no idea what to expect.

"You'd better." Her melodious laugh rang out in the dark, and I silenced it with a kiss.

CHAPTER TWENTY-THREE
Jayse

February proved to be a banner month for our entourage of misfits and troublemakers. The winds of change blew their skanky-ass breath at us, and they blew hard and used *way* too much teeth. As Violet's wedding lumbered our way like a drunk, plus-sized queen, Homegirl called me more and more often to commiserate. Vi didn't just have cold feet; that girl's nipples could have cut glass. It was no secret to those who'd stayed at Trip's palace by the sea what'd gone down between those two. Patience and I wagered on how long it'd be before Trip found the nearest liquor store. She said one day, and I said three. We both lost. Who'd have thunk it?

Weeks later, Violet *still* continued to vamp for best actress in a telenovela. It was getting rather old, and I was tempted to open-hand slap her like Cher in Moonstruck. But...I wasn't completely unsympathetic. I could tell she was beating herself up for blabbing about the abortion, but she didn't trust herself to be anywhere near Trip. Based on the sounds coming out of that bedroom, I couldn't blame her. Silly breeders. Can't live with 'em...

So when Miss Thang called me and asked if I could do a girl's night out, I was like 'duh.' Since Dale had decided I was far too much man for him, and Frostycrotch had grown a libido and decided to let Sam love her, things had been *boring*. Annie and I hadn't really talked since she pulled a C. Brown and bitchslapped me at the bar for everyone's viewing pleasure. Still, I was happy for the little shit and for Sam, even though they're cutesy bullshit nauseated me. They suited one another. No. They *grounded* each other. And it was long past fucking time they realized it. Hey-zeus, it's tiresome being the only one who can read the skywriting in the great blue yonder. Ah well. Let's fade to black on that made-for-Lifetime movie for a bit. More about *me*.

Annie was spending nearly every night at Sam's new pad, so I figured I'd get out the door without another third degree about where I was going and who I was going with. I already had one shitty mother, and I most certainly didn't need another. So imagine my disappointment when She-Who-Shan't-Be-Named emerged from her room and scared the living hell out of me. We got into it almost immediately.

"How do I look?" She turned around, looking all plucked and luffa'd up.

"Bless your heart, you even shaved! What's the occasion?"

She seemed surprised, but not the slightest bit offended. "I'm going to Trip's show at Imogene's, remember? Aren't you coming?"

I paused for a moment. I'd been out every night for over a week, and the gallery show had totally slipped my mind. "I've got stuff. And I'd change the skirt. You look like a Japanese crack-whore."

She shot me *the look*. "Takes one to know one."

"My, my. All work and no play makes Annie a dull hag." I rolled up the cuffs of my sleeves and turned my head from side to side, assessing my new haircut. That bitch had taken too much off the top. I was glad I hadn't tipped her.

"You need to check yourself, J. You've been spiraling the toilet ever since Dale dumped your ass." She turned away from me and reached over to pick up her jacket. I was tempted to kick her in the ass.

"I'm doing just fine, dahlin'." I folded my arms and waited to hear what other shit she'd sling my way.

"I suppose if you call hooking up with every bear and twink-boy in Eastern Georgia 'doin' fine'..."

"Jealous much?"

"Yeah. Jayse. You found me out." She scoffed at me. "Maybe you should quit climbing the STD tree before you slip and hit every branch on your way down."

"And maybe you should quit being such a judgmental fuckerbitch."

I'm sorry to report that it was all downhill after that. I'd cut and run when she started swearing every other word. I didn't want to be late for my dinner plans with a couple of the guys from Noteable. I was distracted by Annie's accusations throughout the entire meal. Thirsty for a mojito, I made my excuses and took off early for the club. I texted Violet to let her know I'd be early.

Vi looked amazeballs when she pulled up in her red hard-topped convertible. She was wearing this silvery-blue silky blouse, and I heard some old queen gasp on our way in the door that he wanted to steal her Louis Vuitton bag. I love being seen with Vi; she's one classy tramp.

She was acting kind of nervous as we walked through the club, and after skulking around a while, she picked a booth all the way in the back. The Countess, a six foot tall drag queen with breast implants and a bad attitude, came up to greet us. I complimented her on her new wig, which was fiery red and clearly high-end. She forced a smile back at me. She was the headliner and my sometime nemesis. Divas rarely can occupy the same place and time without paradox.

After a quick hello, Vi scurried to sit with her back to the wall, so I had to sit with *my* back to everyone but her. Re-Goddamn-diculous! I asked her what the hell was going on, and she said she'd had a big fight with Dashul that morning. Naturally, I pressed for details. She confided that Maisie had been eating Crunchberries for breakfast when Dash arrived. He said 'I haven't had Crunchberries in years.' Then Maisie said 'I haven't had them since we stayed at Daddy's beach house.' I laughed so hard I nearly peed in my pants. From the look she wore, I thought Violet was going to pick up her keys and stab me. Once I settled down, she went on to explain that Dash gave her a suspicious glance and said "Oh?" Then little Maisie turned to Vi and said "you know, when daddy jumped on the car!" She held her head like she had a migraine. She claimed Dashul was still in Savannah and that he might be following her. I told her she was being paranoid, but her expression wasn't one of the convinced.

"Well, isn't that healthy? Tell me why you're marrying this throwback again." I pouted. No one was going to see my carefully constructed look, and it made me moody. Vi looked about as unhappy as I felt as she aggressively stirred her Princess Martini.

She looked sheepish. "It's a good match."

"Like hell." After fighting with Annie, I was too pissy to blow smoke up her skirt. "You'll have a lifetime prescription for Prozac *and* Xanax before you leave for the honeymoon."

"Oh hell, Jayse. I *already* have them." She replied with a nod at her purse. Then she got the strangest look on her face as she peered over my shoulder. Feeling like I was in a horror movie, I stole a nervous glance in that direction. I'll be damned if Dale wasn't walking hand in hand into the club with some hot bit of eye candy in an expensive suit. Dale looked amazing, but I whipped back around before he could see me. I was suddenly glad that Vi had picked the seating arrangements.

As if shining a spotlight on us, a couple of the regular barflies staggered up and proceeded to gush about my amazing karaoke skills. I wanted to crawl underneath the booth and chew open my own wrists, but I smiled and nodded and acted gracious. Being a local celebrity could be so draining. I refused to look back over my shoulder, but I swear on a stack of bibles I could *feel* Dale staring at me. I'd always loved the intensity of his eyes—they drew me to him the moment we first met. Now, when he turned them my way I felt as uncomfortable as a chubby girl when her Spanx are too tight. He was probably telling that white-collar Casanova of his all about how selfish I was and how when he counted the condoms in my drawer, he came up three short.

I felt like the walls were shrinking in. My leg bounced like I'd just chugged thirteen Red Bulls, and I felt all glisteny and moist. I'd had seafood chowder earlier, and I wondered if I was developing an allergy. Unable to bear the tension for one more second, I managed to hold my shit together while Androgeno and Wondermut gushed about Violet's Jimmy Choo's, said their goodbyes, and wandered away.

Violet frowned when she turned back to me. "Jayse, honey, are you okay? You don't look so good."

Well, you can bet I gasped at that bullshit. "What the fuck are you talking about? I look *great*!" She was about to reply when she did the spooky over-the- shoulder stare again. "Shit. They're coming over here aren't they? Quick! Act like I just said something hilarious, and we're having the best time!"

I turned sideways in the booth so that I could get a good look at Dale's approach. Instead, I saw Dashul at the door. He scanned the room and then stalked up to Dale, seething. Damn, that guy talks with his hands! He was waving around some piece of paper, and Dale's new beau shrank back in his seat as if trying to act like he didn't know him. Dale stole a glance in our direction, but quickly looked away. It was obvious to me that he wasn't going to point us out. Dash's voice carried, and people were starting to turn and stare. With a bone- shuddering sigh, I jumped up and marched toward the unfolding drama. Dashul Stein had a foot of height and seventy pounds on Dale, and I'm a sucker for an underdog.

"Hey!" I shouted as Dash backed Dale into the bar. I took long strides to close the distance. When he ignored me, I grabbed Dash by the shoulder and yanked him around. "Pipe down and back off of him."

"Where's Violet?" His spittle hit my face, and he's lucky I didn't whip his ass for *that* infraction. I blinked rapidly and wiped it off with the back of my hand.

"She's trying to have a drink with a friend. Why are you here?" I raised my eyebrow as Dash's eyes shifted around at the swelling crowd. "Or do you always troll gay bars when you're in town?"

I know he really wanted to punch me, but he took a long, slow breath instead. "I was driving by and saw her car."

"I'm right here." She stepped out from between two blonde drag queens. I was struck by how much she looked like the one dressed up as Marilyn. She could have been her 'Mini Me.'

"We need to talk." He took her by the arm and pulled her toward the side room we called 'the ball room' because it was where all the lesbians gathered to play pool. I tailed them; he gave me a bad vibe, and I'd never been wrong about that kind of thing. He looked over his shoulder and frowned when he saw me. "I'd like some time alone with my fiancée."

"I would, too. And since she came here with me, I think I'll stay."

"This won't take long." His gritted teeth didn't reassure me. Violet nodded at me in reassurance, but something about the way he clutched that piece of paper made me dubious. I pretended to watch two diesel dykes racking their balls as I eavesdropped.

"Explain this." He practically slapped her in the face with the piece of paper. Vi flinched away, but snatched it from him. I watched the color drain from her face.

"You read my email?" The level tone of her voice spelled trouble for tall, dark, and furious, but he seemed too wrapped up in his own indignation to notice hers.

"'...I won't lay *another* amorous hand on you...?'"

"Dashul..." she started. Her voice was firm and unafraid.

"What happened on Tybee? Did he kiss you?"

She gripped her hair with both hands. "Do you really want to hear this?

"That fucking little prick. You won't have to

worry about him touching you again. I'll break every one of his fingers, and he'll never paint again." He stormed toward the door, and Violet chased after him as if she weren't wearing peep-toe stilettos. I was sure she'd twist her ankle, but Sistah must have been born and bred in those mothers because she caught up to him at the door.

"Stop, Dash!" She grabbed his arm, and he shrugged her off, heading outside into the night air. Violet shot me a desperate glance, and we both followed.

All the smokers were outside huddled together for a breath of 'fresh air,' and their collective heads snapped up in unison as I shouted.

"Dude! Orange is *so* not your color." It was my attempt to be supportive. He glared at me as if I'd just pissed in his mint julep and continued toward his Hummer.

Violet called after him, "Dash! Come back here and talk to me!"

He spun on her. "No. Enough is enough, Violet. I have put up with an intolerable amount of shit with regards to your ex-husband, and now he's following us to Charleston. It's about time he learned his place. I will not tolerate his laying hands on you."

He opened the door to his vehicle and was about to climb in when Violet shouted "I kissed him!"

The collective gasp from the crowd was sheer brilliance. I nearly shouted 'ta da!' Dashul's square jaw clenched as he slammed the door and came around the car toward her. Without a moment's hesitation, I shoved her behind me.

"You did what?" His voice was quiet and low. She pushed past me, though I tried to pull her back by her sleeve.

"I kissed him. It just kind of happened." Her cheeks bloomed red, and Dash's eyes flashed murderously. I saw him pull back. Ohmygod, that oaf was going to backhand her! My hand shot out, and I grabbed his thumb, pulling back on it with force. I don't really know what happened next, but my head throbbed and I found myself lying on the concrete, blinking at the stars. Violet cried out and slapped him hard on the cheek.

"You asshole! I can't believe I was going to settle for a piece of trash like you," she hissed going in for a second slap. Her diamond ring scratched him when she made contact. He snagged her hand, and his hand came up as if to hit her. That's when Miss Gay Savannah, Countess Chardonnay, stepped between them, towering over Dash. Her voice dropped an octave.

"Oh, no, you didn't."

Finding the strength, I forced myself up onto my elbows in time to see the grand dame haul back and slug Dash so hard he spun around and fell back against his overpriced gas guzzler. He slid down the side of the passenger door, glassy- eyed. Violet yanked off her diamond and chucked it at him, nailing him on the forehead and leaving an impressive gouge. A standing ovation erupted amongst the smokers. Violet knelt beside me, dabbing at my lip.

Flicking her still lit cigarette at his crotch, the Countessa had the last word. "Nobody lays a finger on Jayse Monroe at my club!"

CHAPTER TWENTY-FOUR
Annie

Just before my smack down with Jayse, I'd spent some of my therapy session discussing him. The self-destructive turn he'd taken was eating at me like an aggressive form of cancer. He and I had bonded instantly when I answered an ad on the Craig's List for a roommate. We both had the same snarky humor. I was self-depreciating, and he was a narcissist; it was a match made in hell. I'd voiced my concerns to him, and he'd shit all over me. He was fronting, and I was so over it, I could scream. Jayse was like family, the kind you want to have, not the one forced upon you. Fighting with him made me feel isolated. Though I tried hard to act like it didn't bother me, I felt like he had cast me aside.

My shrink, Dr. Wilson, seemed to find my relationship with Jayse mere entertainment. The Doc was a mind-blowing contradiction. She was a tiny slip of a woman with a sweet sounding voice, but she was rough as sandpaper. Not one for those touchy-feely methods, she was a straight shooter, perhaps too much so. It wasn't uncommon for her to flat-out roll her dark eyes while I was talking, and I often wondered where the hell she got her medical license. She had been especially short-fused with me today.

"Alright, alright. Let's skip the thirty minute conversation about Jayse's problems. He doesn't pay my bill. Let's talk about you, Annie."

I shrugged. "School's good. Work's okay."

She went for the jugular. "How are things with Sam?"

I uttered a surprised laugh. Then I took a huge breath. "He asked me to move in."

Her eyes widened. "What did you say?"

"I told him I'd think about it." She looked at me like she wanted to smother me with a couch cushion. My meetings with her often had this after-taste. It was a bit like having a friend who had no choice but to listen to me…and who got paid to re-mind me of it.

"Do you love him?" She folded her arms and dared me to lie to her.

I huffed. "Of course. I told you so."

"Well then, what's the problem? What are you afraid of?" she snapped impatiently. Normally I would have chewed her out and called her an unpro-fessional bitch, but I was feeling a bit fragile. My brother had texted me. He said my mom had borrowed Gram and Gramp's silver bullet camper and didn't bring it back last weekend as promised. I wondered if she was in Reno yet.

"I…I'm not sure. I guess I'm afraid that these feelings I have for him will fade. That the more he gets to know me, the less he'll like me." My voice cracked a little on the last word. Dr. Wilson exhaled with obvious exasperation and ran her hands through her short dark hair as if she were trying to keep her brain from exploding.

I thought back to the week after I told my grandparents about Travis touching me. My mom showed up at my school and told me that she loved Travis too much to make him leave. She couldn't let me come home again. I cried all day thinking I was being kicked out on the streets…wondering if my grandparents would take me in. Wondering if I'd have to leave my school and my friends and move to live with them.

Later that afternoon, Mom came back and said that Travis told her to 'keep her fucking princess.' He left her. Consumed with relief, I remember thinking my terror was over, and I was overjoyed that I got to stay. Looking back, it might have been a blessing if I hadn't. Instead, it was another two years before I ended up with my grandparents, and I'd spent a lot of that time raising Becca and Dylan. But the fact that Mom's go-to place was to kick me to the curb followed me like a shadow. Jesus! I was her baby. She carried me *inside* her, and she just used me like a bargaining chip against my dad and then tossed me aside like a used tampon.

"Maybe I'm afraid I'm unlovable." I added, forcing myself to meet her eyes. The look on her face when I said it told me I'd struck a chord.

"You are far from unlovable, Annabelle. But I want to answer your other concerns: yes, these feelings will fade and yes, the more he gets to know you, the more he'll get tired of your shit. That's the natu-ral progression out of the honeymoon phase. But that's normal and healthy, believe it or not."

Our time was up right after that. I can't say I felt any more at ease after than I had walking into her office. I went home and got ready for the gallery opening and ran into Jayse on my way out. I tried to keep it casual, but it blew up in my face almost immediately.

All the way to Sam's, I rewound and replayed my fight with Jayse, fighting the menace of threatening tears. It wasn't the first time we'd resorted to name calling in the past few weeks, and most likely wouldn't be the last. Sure, he'd pissed me off and hurt me, but I refused to mess up my make-up because of that little shit.

I parked my car across from the Lowden Building. Sam's new place was impressive in every way. With over twelve hundred square feet of renovated space, his condo was nearly as big as any house I'd lived in. Blonde wood floors, white painted brick walls, and corrugated metal ceilings made it the kind of place I had always dreamed of owning, but never really believed I'd set foot in. I nodded at the doorman and climbed on the elevator. By the time I set foot inside his building, I was jonesing like an addict for the kind of therapy only Sam Beaumont could give me.

He lit up when he opened the door, welcoming me with a knee knocking kiss. As he pulled me against his chest, I instantly felt like a million bucks. "Hey, baby. You look mighty fine tonight."

It was hard not to immediately argue with him. I suppose years of being called an "ugly mutt" couldn't be erased by a few weeks of being treasured by a good man. Make that a *phenomenal* man.

"Hungry?" He led me into kitchen and poured me a glass of wine. My continuous obsession about when the other shoe would drop had caused more insomnia than usual, so I was hyped up on energy drinks and horny.

"Not for food," I spat out, and he shot me a sly smile. He looked completely at home surrounded by the custom cabinets, granite countertops, and stainless appliances. I tried not to obsess about Sam's natural air-brushed perfection. When I did, I ended up twisting my hand behind my back like a child who's just done something naughty. Even if I'd spent a month with a fairy godmother in a room full of wands, I couldn't have come up with a blue print for a guy more perfect for me. These too-good-to-be-true moments put me on edge.

"I want you to eat something. It'll help you get more rest if you fuel your body," he insisted, lifting a plate of fruit and cheese from the counter. It was a sweet gesture, though I knew he hadn't been the one who prepared it. He'd been way too busy with his mystery project to do anything domestic.

Sam led me into the open living area, and the open shutters pulled my eye to the windows and the inky view of the night sky over the river. He had one of my rubbings hanging near the fireplace, and I tried not the cringe every time I saw it. It wasn't one of my favorites, and I planned to make him a new one; but I wasn't sure how that'd go over.

We cozied up on the sofa, which was fast becoming a routine for us. I'd been spending a lot of nights here since he moved in. We drank our morning coffee on the balcony overlooking River Street. It was an incredible spot for people watching or viewing the boats and huge container ships as they passed by on the Savannah River. It's where I first told him I loved him.

"Are you ready to see your picture?" Sam drew my attention back to the present when he picked up the plate and held it in front of me. I took two pieces of cheese and choked them down. Seeing a life sized painting of myself was the last thing I needed tonight. His worried frown illustrated for me just how well he'd grown to know my tells. "What's going on?"

"I'm just really worn out. Ready for spring break. Just you, me, the sand and the sun." I rested my head on his shoulder, and he pulled me tighter to him.

"Actually...I thought we might go somewhere else for the week." I looked up at him as if the answer would be written in that blue gaze. "Do you have a passport?"

"No..."I sat up and stared at him. "I don't even know how to get one. Why?"

"I want to take you to Paris." Stunned, I must have gaped at him long enough to make him uncomfortable. His smile faded, and he looked nervous.

"No." I shook my head, but I didn't back away from him. "It's too much, Sam."

He beamed at that and set his wine glass down. He intertwined his finger with mine and pulled my hand to his lips.

"It's not too much. It's just right. A day of travel there and back. We'll have a whole week for you to commune with the dead." Flustered, I opened my mouth to explain myself, and he moved in for an argument abolishing kiss. Touched by the idea that he wanted to fulfill my fantasy, I placed a hand on either side of his face, and seconds later, my body responded full force. My hands wandered, and he broke off the kiss.

"Shit. We have to go soon. Give me five minutes." He stood, regret oozing from him.

"You can't take a cold shower in five minutes." I joked, trying not to stare at the bulge in his trousers. Inside I was relieved. The dismissive way he blew off my objection had me deep in thought. I should have been backing him into the bedroom for a quickie, but instead I was awash with relief.

Sam vanished into his room, and I wandered through the condo, sipping my wine. I paused to look out of the window at Talmudge Bridge which was majestically lit. Then I went into the kitchen to pour a second glass of wine. Sam claimed to understand why I needed time to decide, which I found impressive since I certainly didn't understand it. On paper it was simple; I loved him and he loved me. My priorities had done an about-face. I'd started blowing off my study group, so I could watch him spar at the gym. In my defense, he and Randall were a hell of a lot more fun to look at all bulging and sweaty than my spindly study-group boys.

I spent every night in his bed or he in mine. He tagged along on my rubbing excursions and made clumsy attempts to be helpful. He was adorable, and sometime I even imagined what forever would be like with him.

My phone buzzed. I reached for it and saw it was Dale.

Dale: Jayse is here at The Hookup. He's with Violet.

My fingers flew over the screen.

Me: Thanks. This sux.

Dale: :(

I shoved the phone back in my pocket. I realized that part of my anger at Jayse was that he'd taken Dale from me. He'd been a really decent friend, stable and logical. He was the polar opposite of Jayse, but they complimented each other so well. I poked my head into Sam's office to see if he'd organized it yet. It looked incredible, like a mix of a home library and a workspace. I made my way to the desk to take in the full effect. As I rounded the desk, I noticed a folder open on top of it. I couldn't help but notice eight by ten pictures, and my heart hit the floor with a nearly audible thud.

The pictures were of me.

I reached out for the file with a trembling hand. I flipped to the beginning. It was my birth certificate, high school and undergrad transcripts and pictures of me working at Black Keys, leaving the pharmacy, sitting in class. I'd just gotten to my mother's arrest records when Sam opened the office door. When he saw me holding the folder, his eyes grew wide and very child-like.

"What the hell is this?" I thought I sounded

fairly reasonable, considering.

"It isn't what it looks like, Annabelle." He put a defensive hand out in front of him. I couldn't begin to imagine what *he thought* I thought it looked like.

"Explain." It was all I could choke out. I could feel my tension rising and I could hear my pulse in my ears.

He advanced closer to me and I backed away from him, still clutching the folder and its contents. His concern grew at that. "I was looking into your past."

"Obviously." It was a terse reply, but it needed to be said. "Making sure I'm not a gold digger like your mother said?"

"No... Annabelle..." He came around the desk to me, but I was still backing away. I was terrified that he would touch me. He looked wounded at my retreat, and that stung. "This was to track down the asshole who abused you." He blushed, and my body was overcome with that pins and needles sensation one gets when a foot falls asleep. I felt like I was going to be sick.

"Why the hell would you want to do that?" My own voice sounded distant. I couldn't take my eyes from his. His face transformed, and his wide, concerned eyes narrowed just slightly. "What do you plan to do when you find him?"

"I haven't decided yet." I could tell he wasn't lying, but the look in his eyes bordered on deadly. I wasn't thrilled with the answer. I slowly sat the folder down.

"Leave it alone, Sam." I sounded like an order. It probably was. I'd tried so hard to put what Travis had done to me behind me, and here Sam was shaking the bushes to draw him out. Maybe we weren't as in tune with each other as my sex drive told me we were.

"I don't think I could if I wanted to." His chest rose and fell more rapidly, and his color was off. In any other circumstance I would have taken him in my arms and stroked his hair. But physical contact was a bad idea. I didn't want my response to him clouding my judgment. "I don't want this guy hurting someone else. My conscience won't allow it."

I trembled as angry tears spilled out my eyes. I clenched my jaw, trying to swallow. My world had just spun on its axis, and the laws of physics no longer seemed to apply. Grief and anger pulled at me from opposing sides, and it was all I could do to hold myself upright.

"Gee thanks, Sam." My voice was still quiet, but I looked at him utterly aghast. "Until now, I just felt like a used tissue. Now I get to feel *responsible* for it."

I turned and rushed toward the kitchen to grab my purse. I needed to go. To get in my car and just drive. I needed literal distance between us so I could think…so I could breathe. I slung my purse over my shoulder, and I felt his hand close over it.

"Annabelle," he said, his delivery firm, worn around the edges by a generous layer of pleading. I slipped from beneath his grasp and made for the door. He got there at the same time I did, and as my hand gripped the knob, his pressed against the door itself. "Please don't go. Let's figure this out."

Tears stood in his disbelieving eyes. I could have easily crumbled; my defenses when it came to Sam were weak on a good day. But I turned the handle and pulled on the door. He leaned on it, his eyes begging me to change my mind.

"Don't do this. I didn't…"

I yanked on the door and shrugged him off when he tried to reach for me. "Annie!"

I made it to the elevator before the tears started to fall. I got as far as the car before I was sobbing out loud. I wasn't even angry at Sam. I hated myself. He was right. Humiliated or not, I should have told everyone what happened to me. Though I wanted to ignore my suspicions, I was pretty sure Travis had done to Becca what he'd done to me. I threw open my door and vomited wine and cheese all over the pavement.

My phone buzzed. I didn't have to look to know it was Sam. I ignored it. Driving home on autopilot, my thoughts were honed in on my younger sister. If the cold sores in her mouth when she was twelve were more than stress related. If she'd ever be able to trust a man enough to fall in love and have a family. My stomach tried to eat itself as I worried whether Travis had desecrated his own biological daughter or if he reserved such fun for other people's children. So I didn't notice the silver bullet camper parked in my spot until I was pulling up behind it.

I didn't cut the engine. I simply sat there, gripping the steering wheel like a drag racer, my mascara creating onyx trails down my cheeks that I'd have to scrape off later. Finally, I blew my nose on some napkins from a discarded fast food bag and tried to tell myself that my mother's timely appearance wasn't an omen.

I approached the building, hugging myself like some children suck their thumb. There she sat, all splayed out, blocking the stairs like she owned the place. She smiled up at me over her Camel nonfilter.

"There's my girl!" Harlow drawled. Mom had lived in the Midwest my entire life, and she still had an accent as Kentucky as Derby Pie.

"Hi, Mom." When I spoke, I sounded congested. My sinuses were still jacked up from my crying jag. She sat up, concern wrinkling her brow. I looked a lot like my mom, though she had a wide upturned nose that I was thrilled I hadn't inherited.

"What's the matter, Annie-bell?" The combination of her pet name and my fights with Sam and

Jayse corroded my armor just enough to let her slip inside. My eyes burned again, but I'm pretty sure I was out of tears.

We went inside and she offered up her story over frozen thin mints and butterscotch schnapps, the only alcohol in the house that Jayse hadn't polished off. She was on her way to see a sick friend in Jacksonville and looked me up. While she spewed her lies, I pretended to check my phone, googling casinos in Florida. As expected, the dog tracks and poker rooms in Jacksonville were plentiful. I saw unread texts from Sam and Dale, but Harlow wasn't the kind of guest you took your eyes off for long, so I ignored them.

"It's a man, isn't it?" she asked, as I looked up from my phone. Her brown eyes searched me for clues. Under the harsh fluorescents, I could just make out an almost healed bruise on her left cheekbone. I didn't ask about it. She'd only lie to me more.

"What do you mean?" When I remembered who I was bluffing for, I nearly giggled.

"The tears. Boyfriend troubles, baby girl? Becca told me you're seeing someone."

"I don't really want to talk about my sex life with you, Mom. No offense."

She studied her scuffed cowboy boots, and I considered it a small victory.

"Why are you really here, Mom?" Now that we

were done with the social niceties segment of her visit (where I pretend to believe her motives and she pretended we had a relationship), it was time to deal with whatever trouble she'd dragged along with her. Hopefully my apartment wouldn't be raided by the cops before she hit the road.

"Why do I have to want anything to see my daughter?" She actually had the cajones to look offended.

"Because past trends indicate that you want money. I'm a student. I don't have any money."

"When was the last time I asked you for money? It's been years. When are you gonna let it go? I just wanted to stop by and talk. Is it so terrible that I want to see my child?"

"It's too late, Mom." I shook my head. "Some things you just can't undo."

"Talk to me…"She tried to reach out for my hand, and I shrank from her.

"I wanted to talk about it then, Mom! I wanted you to put a stop to it! You were supposed to take my side!"

"I know." She started to tear up, but even her tears-- especially her tears—couldn't be trusted.

"You know what happened the one time I told Travis 'no'? He came to my room an hour later and did it anyway. He put his fucking hand over my mouth to keep me quiet, and he said he wouldn't have to 'do it' to me if my mother would just put out." I spat this bitter truth at her as if it could transfer the diseased part of my psyche. But there was no getting rid of what he'd done. No cure. I had an epiphany then. I had to heal myself. I would never be good as new, but I could stitch the jagged bits of my heart together, and it would beat again. And I was capable of love.

My phone rang, and when I scooped it up a second time, I saw it was Dale. I stood up to take the call. I walked into the living room and answered. "What's up?"

"Thank God you picked up!" Dale replied. "Jayse is in the E.R. I'm a block away. Can I pick you up?"

"Yes!" I sputtered. "What the hell happened?"

"I don't know. I've heard a bunch of rumors. It's like a game of Queer Eye Telephone."

"I'll be out front." I hit end call and turned to Harlow, who was pouring more schnapps into a plastic cup. "I have to go. My roommate's in the E.R. You can stay here tonight, but then I want you gone in the morning. I'm trying to make something of myself, and I don't have time to participate in whatever game you're playing."

She opened her mouth, but I was out of the door before she had a chance to tell anymore tall-tales. Dale pulled up like a Hollywood stunt driver, and I jumped in beside him. It'd still be hours before I realized my mistake. I'd left my purse behind.

CHAPTER TWENTY-FIVE
Sam

I downed my second glass of champagne as I looked up at the grandiose painting of Annie which dominated the gallery's mezzanine. Art critics and collectors swarmed all around me for a look at all of Trip's latest creations, but most were stunned silent at the sight of *Angel*, which is what my brother chose to name the portrait. He'd had many offers, but he'd declined each one. That painting was already spoken for.

I'd kept my problems to myself, not wishing to distract Trip from his admiring public. Reeling from Annabelle's reaction to my investigation, I didn't want to put on a false smile. I'd convinced myself that what I was doing was from an altruistic place...taking a pedophile off the streets. In truth, I'd done it for revenge. I was a decade too late to save Annie, and feeling helpless, I'd reverted to vengeance. If I stayed this course, I would undoubtedly turn into my father.

"She's a beauty." My mother's voice pulled me away from my obsession.

I nodded mutely.

"Samson, I loved your father."

"Mama…I don't want to talk about Sebastian Wakefield."

"I was talking about Reginald. Sebastian isn't your father." Perhaps it was one too many blows in such a short period, but I was stunned silent. She turned a discerning eye on *Angel,* tilting her head to the side.

I finally recovered. "But…he…I don't understand."

"I had a moment of weakness once and told him in a letter once that my son was his. Sebastian assumed it was you."

"Trip's his son?" I glanced hurriedly around to make sure no one had heard me.

She nodded. "They're both better off not knowing that, wouldn't you agree?"

That was the moment I fully appreciated Trip's situation. When a lie of omission seemed like the best possible decision. And I couldn't fault Cosmo's logic, not even a little.

"I did love Reginald. He was a wonderful person. A darling man with the sweetest heart. He would have done anything I asked. But Sebastian was…dangerous. Exhilarating. And I found that irresistible. I made a bad choice that lasted for years.

What he said to Reg…" She shook her head with an ugly frown. "It's unforgiveable. That man was always jealous of your father. If I'd known…I don't know, maybe it would have been worse had I known. But your father loved both of you boys. As do I."

I heard genuine emotion in my mother's voice and regretted not confronting her privately. My ego and temper had gone on a massive bender. My hangover was sure to be an epic one.

"There you are." Trip looked freaked out and out of breath as he skidded to a stop beside us. "Look at this. Annabelle just forwarded it to me."

I took his phone from him and played the video. Some amateur footage of Dashul Stein started to play. Violet, Jayse, and Savannah's most buxom drag queen all played a role. I felt Mama watching over my shoulder. When it ended, her eyes sparkled with excitement.

"Looks like you won't have to move to Charleston after all," she mused, as I passed his phone back to him. Trip actually managed a smile. He turned to me.

"They're at St. Joseph's/Cadler. Annie says Vi's there and they're still waiting for information. I'm heading over there."

"You two go on. I'll stay and handle all of this." Mama offered.

I followed Trip through the crowd in a daze. It

took a while; since he was the guest of honor, even sneaking out the back entrance wasn't easy. All the while, my mind sifted through the new information sluggishly, as if I were snowshoeing through wet sand. My first instinct was to call Annabelle. But I'd demolished us just as swiftly as we'd gotten together.

We cut out the fire escape exit like a couple of criminals and scaled down the back side of the warehouse into the alley. Moments later we were in the Mercedes and zipping toward the interstate.

"I sure hope you're okay to drive. We'll be fucked if you get a DWI," Trip admonished as I cut between two cars.

"I'm fine," I snapped. I planned to beg Annie for forgiveness. Sex wasn't the only part of our relationship she ought to have control of. Her trauma was hers to handle. She'd been strong for years before I came along, and I needed to shut up and remember to have her back. My desire to be her champion made me overzealous, and if this resulted in my losing her, it'd be the end of me.

When we finally walked through the entrance, Dale, Violet and Annie were all curled up in chairs. Violet jumped to her feet and threw herself at Trip. They kissed like he was going off to war, oblivious to the rest of our collective existence. Dale and I exchanged awkward waves, and the moment was even more awkward due to Annabelle's inability or unwillingness to look at me.

"Have you heard anything?" I asked, directing the question to Dale, as he was the least likely to claw my eyes out.

"They took him in for a head CT. He was hit in the face, and when he fell, his head ricocheted off the sidewalk. He never lost consciousness, so it's just a precaution," Dale explained.

Taking a chance, I took the seat next to Annabelle. She looked pale, and her makeup had been washed away.

"I'm hoping it knocked some sense into him," she mumbled. Dale nodded, but I saw fear on both of their faces.

"The silver lining to the black cloud." I took her speech as a good sign and hoped to keep her talking.

The physician approached before anyone else had a chance to speak. Jayse had a concussion and needed to stay overnight. He was doped up on morphine and singing show tunes. In other words, his outlook was promising, and he was expected to make a swift and full recovery.

On our way out of the hospital, I stopped Annabelle on her way to Dale's car.

"Can I give you a ride home?" I asked. She looked up at me and nodded reluctantly. We drove in silence for several minutes as I thought of ways to open a dialogue. Finally, I decided the best way to tell her how I felt was to show her. I turned right instead of left, and she shot me a glance.

"My apartment's that way." Her words had a soft lilt.

"I need you to see something." I glanced at her to read her face.

She sighed. "I'm tired, Sam."

"It'll take ten minutes," I promised and drove through the back streets until we pulled up in front of The Beaumont Building. It was the length of a city block. Though it was originally constructed in 1910, I'd gutted it, and construction was finally finished. Some of the lights were on.

"I don't understand." She frowned at the sign with my last name on it. I took her by the hand, and we walked through the front door. There was a brand-new, full-court gymnasium on the right just visible by the security lights, and to the left was a full blown gym. Randall was fiddling with the speed bags when we walked in.

"Look who decided to come into work today." He called from across the large room. Annabelle waved to him, but she wore a look of unmistakable shock.

"What is this, Sam?" She met my eyes. She no longer looked the least bit sleepy.

"My passion. You challenged me to do something with my money to change the world. I started a foundation. This youth center is a part of it. When

I needed a place to be, to focus and stay out of trouble, Hard Knocks was what worked for me. I wanted to give that back to the community." I led her back out and up the stairs to the second floor dance studio and showed her the computer lab. When we got to the meeting rooms, I flipped the lights on.

"Trip suggested a place for support groups. As he pointed out, it's not just the kids who need to stay out of trouble."

"Sam...I don't know what to say."

"You don't have to say anything, Dahlin'. Just listen." I leaned against the desk and wrapped my arms around her waist, pulling her close. She didn't protest; she just watched me shyly from under her lashes. "You're the one. You push me. You said life was a pie with four quarters. You have heaping helpings of the direction and ambition, and I lucked out and inherited the genes and the money. Together we're unstoppable."

A tear slipped out of her eyes and raced down her cheek. I took her face in my hands and locked eyes with her for emphasis.

"Sam...I'm afraid." She admitted.

"Me too. Annie, I know I fucked up. All I can say is how sorry I am. And I'm sure I'll screw up again and again. But I can't let fear stop me before I've even begun. And neither should you. The day we met, you said something about my lack of ambition. That it wasn't a disease. I agree, but I think it can be crippling just the same. You're my light, Annabelle. You led me off of a dark path, and I'm asking you to continue the journey with me."

She searched me with those gold flecked eyes of hers, and just when I was sure she'd pull away, she rose onto her tiptoes and captured my lips with hers. Her hands gripped my hair, and I felt my chest swell so much it hurt. When she finally pulled away, her cheeks were flushed pink, and she was glowing.

"I'm all in." She panted, happiness shining in her eyes. "Let's do this."

As we descended the stairs, we stopped dead in out tracks when we heard Randall singing along with a Pitbull song. After falling into fits of laughter and throwing a few insults his way, we stumbled out into the night. I stopped her right outside the front door.

"So can I take you to Paris?" I whispered in her ear as I nuzzled her neck

The corner of her lip curled in a fiendish manner. "You'd better!"

EPILOGUE
Sam

I bailed Annie's mom out the following morning. While she and I were busy making out at the Beaumont Building, Harlow had been trying to break into the pharmacy using Annabelle's keys. She got caught just minutes after we discovered Annabelle's purse was missing. Harlow may play a mean black jack, but that woman is no master thief.

With Trip and his sponsor's assistance, we found her a good rehab program and an even better lawyer. She agreed to go to treatment in lieu of jail time; Harlow was many unspeakable things, but she was no fool. Annie told her to keep her distance and lose her address. She was finally *done*, and Dr. Wilson wholeheartedly supported this course of action.

Annie's grandparents already had custody of Dylan and Becca, and their mother's absence didn't seem to be a new phenomenon. Annie called them regularly to keep up to speed on their lives. Dylan would graduate soon and was considering coming to Georgia for school. Annie cried when she heard both the kids were in therapy, but she assured me the tears were happy ones.

Paris was an amazing time. We ate baguettes at street cafes, made fun of snooty Parisian assholes, and left flowers at Jim Morison's grave. The Catacombs were beyond amazing. We wandered around wearing out our cameras, and I honestly think I was more impressed with them than she was.

On our third day in Paris, I dragged her shopping and insisted she buy a cocktail dress. Then I took her to 58 Tour Eiffel, the restaurant at the Eiffel Tower. In an admittedly douchey move that I was *sure* she'd hate, I'd slipped an engagement ring into her glass of champagne. To my surprise, she burst into tears and pummeled my chest with her fists. Then she squealed "Yes! Yes! Yes!" just like a normal girl. She never ceases to amaze. Evidently, even the French applaud when a girl accepts a proposal in such a manner.

Trip and Violet quietly started seeing one another again. Maisie began telling everyone her parents were getting remarried and she was going to be their flower girl. Trip and Vi just laughed at her and gently chided her to slow it down. They assured anyone who would listen that they were in no rush to the altar. Violet told Annie they wanted to take their time this go-round and really savor one another.

Patience got all huffy at Black Keys during our

engagement party. We were too wrapped up in each other to notice a thing, but you can bet Jayse was right in the thick of things. Pending nuptials were explod-ing all around Patience—two of her co-workers were also getting married—and she was sick and tired of being a bridesmaid. She gave Randall an ultimatum, and he finally caved and set a date. They're getting hitched in June, and we're walking down the aisle in October.

Annabelle plans to start a program at the foun-dation when she finishes school. She sees a com-munity need for medication deliveries and pill box assistance for the elderly. The pharmacy school seemed excited for their students to intern in the program. Her professors have been generous with advice in starting such an ambitious program. It's uplifting to know that I have the tools to help so many people touch so many lives. I think if Daddy's looking down at us, he's smilin'.

All lollipops and glitter aside, things aren't al-ways perfect. I wouldn't say we've found ourselves engulfed in a fairy tale. Sometimes I catch Annie staring at her ring when she doesn't know I'm watching. She'll be sunning herself on the balcony or lying in bed with a book, and I'll watch those stunning eyes of hers reflecting on the sparkling rock. Sometimes, she's smiling. Other, more fright-ening times, she wears the blankest look I've ever seen.

Will we make it? I don't have any idea. Are we happy? I think that we are, more than most. We know we're lucky to have found each other, and we aren't likely to let each other forget it anytime soon. I like to think we both saved each other from a life of just going through the motions. I plan to spend every day of my life showing her what she means to me. Will I be successful? Who the hell knows? I want to be. All I know is what my heart tells me. And my heart speaks clearly. It tells me in no uncertain terms that Annabelle Clarke is my Angel.

ACKNOWLEDGMENTS

Without a doubt, this is the hardest project I've ever undertaken. It's a fiction/fact fusion, though which is which, I'll never tell. Laughs were had, flesh was inked, books were burned, tears were shed, and some cocktails may have been harmed in the making of this book. A few folks need to be acknowledged for playing their roles.

Les Pace–my oldest critique partner and long suffering spouse. Oh, how none of this would have been possible without all you do every day. You are my rock and though it isn't at all fair, it doesn't make me any less grateful. I love you beyond description, wordsmith or not.

Robin Harper–who has been with this project since it was nothing more than a title and a cover. You gave a stunning face to my story. Your patience and talent take my breath away-designing and redesigning covers and memes and making every attempt to make me look like a much bigger deal than I am. You are too good to me and worth a hell of a lot more than you charge. Wicked by Design, people. She really knows her shit.

Jay McAtee –One of my oldest and dearest friends. Our adventures together date back to before I was of legal drinking age, and are the stuff of legend. Greek tragedies, mostly. You are the keeper of all of my secrets. I hope you smile when you read this book. Thanks for reading and re-reading and helping me breathe life into one of my all-time favorite characters.

Heather Halloran–What can I possibly say? You know you're my girl, right? We've been through so much in a short period that it seems like I've known you as long as I've known Jay. Every day I wish we lived in the same city, hell…the same state would be nice. Thank you *and* fuck you for planting more than a few of the seeds that ended up growing into this book.

Laura Wilson–The one person in the universe that doesn't make me feel like the reincarnation of Sylvia Plath. No matter what shit I spewed at you, you could always one- up me. Thanks for commiserating via p.m. and text and for telling me to STFU every time I started skipping down Whiny Bitch Lane.

Erin Roth–Dude. I'm so happy you were here in the beginning to point out that the youngest Mr. Beaumont may have sounded a bit too much like his mother. God forbid! Thanks for checking out the mood and visiting with me about these characters in their early stages.

Charles Miles–My southern gentleman consultant! Your contributions in the early days and your defense of the secret language of Savannahians meant the world to me. Cheers!

Andrea Randall–My writing *soul* mate. We both merged onto this road at the same time and continue to take turns helping the other fix a flat. Thanks as always for talking me off the ledge for an entirely new set of reasons.

Tamron Davis–my very own cowgirl-chic cheering section. Thank Jesus you were around this time. I owe you and Stacy Darnell my sanity for a large portion of this endeavor and Rage. Thanks for being the pragmatist and for your "respectful disagreements".

Stacy Darnell–My favorite Georgia Peach. You are the yin to Laura Wilson's yang. I wouldn't have completed this project if it weren't for your presence in my life. Why? Because I would have fucking bailed. Period.

Karen Zippe–Your love for Sam Beaumont encouraged me to press on when I was afraid he was too "Holden Caulfield" for the gentle modern romance reader. Hats off to you.

Sarah Griffin and Tamara O'Dell–Thanks for swooping in at the end to emergency-beta. Having fresh eyes that weren't worn from my constantly morphing story was invaluable.

Self-Publishing Editing Service and Formatting– You came highly recommended by my usual for-matter. It was pure luck and my crappy timing that brought us together. You guys rocked and were the best fusion of professional and approachable. Thanks for your flexibility!

Carmen Comeaux–Another top notch job. I'm so blessed that you and I met. Though this wasn't our first go-round, I am glad you were here to oversee the language of this novel. Thanks for all your bril-liant suggestions. Sorry I'm a bit too "punk rock" to take all of them. If there are errors in this book I can assure you that they are *mine* and mine alone.

Kara King–my avid real-time reader. Thanks for always being enthusiastic and sunny. You pushed me to provide pages when I was too damn lazy and thought I was too tired. I wish you hadn't been in a hospital bed for most of it.

Vanessa Proehl–If it weren't for you, I wouldn't know most of the people in the acknowledgements.

Not only am I continuously thankful you brought me into this little corner of the indie world, I'm overjoyed to have you as a constant discerning ARC reader. Thanks for driving me to drink in the eleventh hour. I really needed it. You keep me grounded and never let me forget where I came from.

ABOUT THE AUTHOR

Michelle Pace resides in north Texas with her husband, Les. She is the mother of two lovely daughters, Holly and Bridgette, and one uber-charismatic son, Kai. A former singer and actress, Michelle has always enjoyed entertaining people and is excited to continue to do so as a writer.

http://www.michellepaceauthor.com/

https://www.facebook.com/MichelleKisnerPace

34645239R00219

Made in the USA
Lexington, KY
13 August 2014